I0706448

Forgotten Rebellion

Also By AJ Park

Seven Rivers Series

Forgotten Rebellion

River in the Sand

Guardians of the Horsemen Series

Silver Song

War's Ending

The Exiled Horseman

Sea and Iron

Stand Alone Novels

The Ring Keeper

Poisoned Splinter

Forgotten Rebellion

by

AJ Park

StarTree Press

Forgotten Rebellion – Seven Rivers Book One

Copyright ©2023 AJ Park and StarTree Press

Cover Design by StarTree Press

All rights reserved. No part of this book may be used or reproduced by any means, graphic, electronic or mechanical, including photocopying, recording, taping or by any information storage retrieval system, without the written permission of the publisher except in the case of brief quotations embodied in critical articles and reviews.

ISBN: 9781962564014 (trade paperback) 9781962564007(epub)

StarTree Press 1706 N 1200 W, Unit #2012, Layton, UT 84041

THE
SEVEN RIVERS

Chapter 1

Andevaar

Bright tongues of flame from burning buildings lit the evening with an orange glow. From his position outside the village, Andevaar waited. Dark shapes of people ran between the houses and shops, screaming in terror. Andevaar remained, watching. The raid was going exactly as planned. Other horsemen gathered around him, gripping their swords, their eyes locked on the clustered buildings.

"Go?" the stocky man at his shoulder asked.

Andevaar shook his head. "Not yet." They had to be patient. He needed to allow the people enough time to become desperate for help. Soon.

The man wiped a bead of sweat from his brow with the back of his hand.

For several more moments, Andevaar observed, anticipation growing inside him with each flame that burned. Then he gripped his sword and met his companion's eyes. "Ready?" He looked back at the group behind him. They nodded. "You know what to do," he told them.

With a shout, he urged his horse forward, his sword held high. The others followed, yelling and raising their weapons. Picking up speed as they approached, they charged into the village. Farmers and tradespeople, confused and poorly armed, jumped out of their way.

As Andevaar and his men entered the fray, the robbers, faces masked in black, abandoned their looting to do battle with them. Many smaller fights raged, but the thieves, most of them on foot, retreated before the onslaught of the band of mounted men. The riders swept through the area, driving the outlaws before them until only a single man on a black horse remained.

He faced Andevaar in the open space of the village square, his sword raised in defiance. The image of a silver hawk emblazoned on his tunic was the only color he wore. His face was masked in black cloth.

Andevaar charged toward him, his own blade ready to crash against his opponent's. The staged battle was effortless. They had sparred together for years, and they knew each other's every move. They fought, striking and parrying, their skills evenly matched. With equal strength and speed, every blow flowed perfectly into the next, and the crowd watched in fascination.

Andevaar's men returned to the square from their sweep through the village. They joined the crowd at the edges of the open space and watched the fight. The remaining outlaws were gone, already out of sight.

The man on the black horse fought hard. He wouldn't give an inch, until eventually, he pulled back, looking around to assess the crowd of enemies. With a shout of defiance, he wheeled his horse and charged toward the street leading out of the square. He aimed a blow at the horseman blocking his path, and the man parried but retreated, allowing the black horse to gallop away.

A moment of stunned silence fell, then suddenly, the people cheered and gathered around Andevaar. Every eye was on him. Every voice shouted his praise. Their adoration washed over him, and he sat a little taller in the saddle, drawing in a long, satisfied breath. Success. He raised his blade in the air and yelled in triumph. The crowd cheered again.

"Thank you!" a man cried, approaching Andevaar as the noise subsided. He wore a fine tunic, cloak, and a gold magistrate's medallion. "You saved us from the attack."

"My friends and I are happy to have been of service." His men raised their blades, and the people cheered and applauded them eagerly. They had done enough here for one night. None of these villagers would ever forget what had happened. It was time to leave. Andevaar turned to the town leader. "We must go, Magistrate. The criminals who attacked you are escaping, and we will pursue."

"Yes, yes, of course!" the magistrate agreed. "You have saved lives and property tonight. Might we have the name of our hero?"

Bowing his head in acknowledgement, he said, "I am Andevaar."

By the time all the horses were stabled and the men were resting, it was nearly midnight. Andevaar rode out alone through the darkness. The land was silent and sleeping around him, the stars sparkling in the dark sky above. He turned off on a slender side road and drew up in front of a tiny cottage. No lights showed as he dismounted, looped the reins over a fencepost, and went to the door, opening it without knocking. Inside, a small flame burst into life in the fireplace. The black figure of a man crouched, using a long wood shaving to light a candle.

The flickering glow illuminated the silver hawk on the front of his tunic. Andevaar smiled as Drake stood to face him. "It went just as well as the others." Drake laughed, and Andevaar slapped his friend on the shoulder. "Even now, they have no idea!" Drake folded his arms across his chest, a sarcastic smirk on his face.

"Were any of your men hurt?" Andevaar asked.

Drake shook his head. "Nothing more serious than scrapes and bruises."

"And the villagers?"

"Some of them put up a fight. We took several prisoners, but none of them were seriously injured. My men are keeping them secure until we can take them back to Sathar."

Andevaar nodded. "Make sure they're treated well. Some of the men you hired are savages. Don't let them attack your captives."

Drake's mouth set in a firm line. "I can handle them."

Andevaar knew this. Drake had lived in a world of violence all his life. He knew how to maintain order by force over men who understood nothing else. "Good. We have the schedule and the locations for the next raids. After these last two smaller communities, we will hit Edrithil. When we take the city, we'll have all of Edri on our side, and I'll be ready to meet the arrogant Princess Tahlea."

Drake lifted one corner of his mouth. "I'm sure you will impress her."

"If the gratitude of those villagers is any sign, she'll *have* to be impressed." Andevaar raised his chin. "By the time we're finished, the people will beg me to take the throne, so they won't have to endure the royal family's tyranny anymore."

Grinning, Drake put his hand over his heart. "And I will remain your most loyal friend and business partner throughout it all. When we're done, we'll rule this land, and everyone will be treated fairly."

Andevaar nodded. He rubbed his chin, contemplating their plans. "When we're finished in Edri, go to the palace in Namradan. The Stone Ceremony is in a week. They'll let anyone inside for the event. See if there is someone there, a young lady, maybe, who is close to the royal family, that you might become friends with." He stared at Drake appraisingly. "I'm sure you can find some charm as well as brute force. Use it."

Drake bowed with a flourish. "As you command, Lord Andevaar."

Chapter 2

Crown Princess Tahlea

Within the ancient palace at Namradan, the guards opened the door of the king's chambers for Tally. Inside, it was entirely quiet. Her slippers made no sound on the marble floor as she crossed the comfortably furnished sitting room into her father's bedchamber. While the room held a large comfortable bed, the focus was on an alcove at one end, which contained a carved wooden chest, its lid open. King Allenthal stood before it, his hand grasping the stone inside. Unearthly blue light spilled out from the box, lending a strange color to his familiar features.

Tally stood still for a long moment with no response from him. Even though he had sent for her, maybe this wasn't a good time? A whisper of unease brushed along the back of her neck. Tally cleared her throat. "Father?"

King Allenthal removed his hand from the chest, closed the lid, and turned to face her. In the natural light from the tall windows, his face became warm and familiar again. He smiled, his brown eyes full of affection, but his brow creased with worry. "Tally, I'm afraid there's not much time left."

Tally's hands tightened into fists. She had known this day would come eventually, and she thought she'd been prepared for it, but it had come much sooner than she expected. "What else would you have me do in your absence?"

His gaze turned back toward the chest. "You must guard Namradill well. During the stonesleep, I'll be under Her power, but I cannot survive it without close contact. If anything happens to the stone, I couldn't live for longer than a few weeks, a month perhaps."

Tally's eyes flew to the chest where the light had come from. His life would be in her hands, and the responsibility felt heavy. "I will guard Her," she promised.

"You'll be in charge of holding the Stone Ceremony every season. It's important that the people see you with Namradill."

Tally nodded. He had never shirked his responsibility, and neither would she. The event was scheduled for the next day.

"But you'll still be here to host it tomorrow, won't you?" She didn't feel ready to commune with the stone in front of everyone. The bond her bloodline maintained with Sacred Namradill was the ancient root of their right to rule the Seven Rivers. If her father made the required connection with Namradill tomorrow, Tally would have another season to prepare herself. But if she wasn't ready after eighteen years, would another season really help?

Tally took a step toward him, and he crossed the space between them to put his arms around her. "My beautiful Tally," he murmured, kissing the top of her head, "you will be an excellent ruler for the Seven Rivers. I've done everything I can to prepare you. I couldn't be leaving our kingdom in better hands."

Did he mean he wouldn't be there tomorrow? Her skin prickled with worry, and she pulled him close. His embrace represented comfort and safety, and he'd always been there for her. The two of them were a small but tightly knit family. "I'm not ready."

His chuckle rumbled in his chest as he held her. "I remember that feeling, though I was a little older than eighteen when I had to rule alone for the first time. The only way to be ready is to do it. Just remember to do what's best for your people, always. I know you will."

Doubt twisted inside her. What if he was mistaken? Many decisions would be hers to make. What if she made the wrong ones? What if people came to harm because she wasn't strong enough, or she didn't know what to do?

"Kylith will be here to help you," her father said. "He's led our army for many years, and I trust him completely. You can also go to the Mystic Thorvan for guidance if you need it. He's a very old friend."

Nervousness twisted in her belly. "What do you think is going to happen that I might need a mystic?"

King Allenthal smiled and stepped back. He gripped her shoulders with his large hands and met her eyes. "Everything is going to be fine. No matter what happens, I trust you to deal with it. Now, come and sit. Kylith will be here in a moment with his report."

A knock at the outer door interrupted them before she could answer.

The guard called, "The general is here, Your Majesty."

"Thank you. Send him in," King Allenthal replied. He offered his arm to Tally, and she took it, leaving the alcove behind to return to the outer chamber.

General Kylith stood in the middle of the room. He was an intimidating figure, nearly as tall as her father but broader. Tally had rarely seen him dressed in anything other than the dark blue army tunic over chain mail, which he wore now. His hair was gray, his stern features serious. A long scar marked the side of his face from his forehead down to his jaw. As a child, looking at his face had frightened Tally until her father had told her the story. Kylith had been injured in a battle where he'd been fighting at Allenthal's side. The king had been wounded, and if not for Kylith's bravery, he would have been killed. After that, Tally felt only gratitude and respect when she saw it.

Kylith placed his hand over his heart and bowed respectfully as they entered. "Your Majesty. Crown Princess."

King Allenthal nodded in return. "Thank you for bringing your report here, General. I don't know how much time I have left. Please, sit down."

They took chairs that had been placed near each other. Tally saw concern in Kylith's gray eyes. She brushed her damp palms against the smooth fabric of her dress. He probably hadn't brought them good news.

"Did you speak with Governor Folcan's messenger?" King Allenthal asked.

Kylith nodded. "Several more villages along the river Edri have been attacked. The reports match the earlier stories of bandits with their faces covered, looting and burning. A few people were killed, and more have simply disappeared. Their leader rides a black horse and wears the emblem of a hawk on his tunic."

"Who is he?" King Allenthal demanded.

Kylith shook his head. "No one has determined that yet, my king. He keeps his face concealed during the attacks. The people call him Hawk. By now, the entire province of Edri lives in terror of him."

Her father tapped a finger against the short beard on his chin as he thought. "We have to find him. We'll send our army to Edrithil to restore order."

"Agreed," the general replied in his gravelly voice. "So far, these criminals have proved very skilled at hiding. No one has been able to find them, and only one man has been there to fight them.

People in all the damaged villages reported that a man named Andevaar protected them from the outlaws."

Allenthal's eyebrows raised in surprise.

The same person happened to be on hand for attacks on several villages? "How was he in the right place every time?" Tally asked. That couldn't be a simple coincidence.

"How indeed?" Her father looked thoughtful. He nodded toward her. "Tally is right. It's very unlikely that one person would be at hand every time the outlaws attacked. Unless..."

"Unless he knew they would be there." Tally said, finishing her father's thought.

Kylith shifted in his seat. "Whether or not that's true, the entire province of Edri adores Andevaar, including Governor Folcan. They can't speak highly enough of him." Kylith's gaze sharpened on King Allenthal. "Are you all right, my king?"

Allenthal's face had lost all color, and droplets of sweat stood out on his forehead. Tally jumped from her chair and rushed to his side, taking his hand. "Father!"

He patted her hand. "I'm all right, my dear. Fine. Just a little tir–" He collapsed, falling forward in his seat.

With a cry of alarm Tally caught him. Kylith was beside her in a moment, helping her support him. Though her father had told her what was going to happen to him, seeing it was something else entirely. She wasn't ready. Not now, not yet. She shook him. "Father! Wake up!"

Kylith rested a heavy hand on her shoulder. "It's his time, Princess. He will not wake until his sleep is finished."

Tally straightened and blinked back the moisture in her eyes. This was not the time to fall apart. She drew in a deep breath.

Kylith stood behind the king's chair, gripping the unconscious monarch under the arms. "Will you help me move him?" he asked as he slid the king from the chair.

She nodded and picked up her father's feet as they made their way into the next room. Kylith heaved the upper half of Allenthal onto the bed and then assisted Tally with his legs.

Bending over her father, she wiped the remaining beads of perspiration from his forehead. His skin remained pale, but he breathed steadily. "Are you all right?" Tally asked, knowing he would not respond, but still hoping. Why did he have to choose now to fall into stonesleep? If this trouble in Edri spread to the other provinces, the fighting could tear their kingdom apart.

"I will bring the physician," Kylith said, starting for the door. "It would be wise to have him examine the king."

"Yes, of course," Tally said, without taking her eyes off her father's face. How was she going to rule this kingdom without him? She drew a chair close to his bedside and sat down, his hand limp in hers. She'd never seen him like this. For as long as she could remember, he'd been tall and strong, constantly in control. He always knew what to do. He'd been the center of her life. Now she was alone.

Tally hadn't moved from the bedside when the physician entered the room, followed by his assistant. The old man had served the royal family since long before her birth.

He came to the king's side and laid a wrinkled hand across Allenthal's forehead. His assistant, a young woman with dark hair, stood at his elbow, holding a bag of supplies. "Is it the stonesleep, Crown Princess?" the physician asked.

Tally tightened her grip on her father's hand and nodded. "For several days, he's been saying that it would soon be time. A little while ago, he just... collapsed."

The elderly physician didn't appear disturbed by this news. "I was here when the old king entered the stonesleep. Don't worry too much. This has been the way of your family for a thousand years. We'll take care of him while he rests, but just like each of your ancestors, he'll wake again when his time is over."

The words offered a little comfort; Tally still had to move forward without her father. She observed in silence as the physician examined him. When the old man finished, he turned back to her. "His condition appears to be the same as your grandfather's during his time. He has entered his journey in good health. He'll be all right. I will organize a schedule for his staff to watch him closely." He smiled gently at Tally and patted her hand. "They will send word immediately to me and to you if anything changes."

"Very well. Thank you for your service," Tally said.

With a nod, the old man shuffled toward the door, his assistant beside him.

The sound of heavy boots crossing the sitting room announced Kylith's return. He entered the room and came to stand next to Tally's chair, resting a hand on her shoulder. "Any change?"

She shook her head. His presence was comforting, and she felt grateful for his solid strength. Whatever happened, he would help her through this.

"He'll be all right," Kylith said.

A flash of fear swept through her, and her stomach tightened. Throughout her life, she'd heard stories of various family members who had survived the stonesleep. Historically, it lasted one season for each of the seven rivers, totaling nearly two years. It felt different now when it was her father lying unconscious. What if he didn't wake up? She turned to Kylith. "Are you sure?"

"Your grandfather was."

Her eyes flew back to her father's still form. That didn't seem to prove anything in this moment, with him unresponsive.

Kylith cleared his throat. "If you're worried, you could ask Her."

Tally looked up at him and saw his eyes on the alcove.

"It's your place to communicate with Her now," he pointed out.

Tally took in a long breath and loosened her tight fists, spreading her fingers out on her lap. She hadn't touched Sacred Namradill since she was a baby. And she remembered nothing about the experience. No one but the ruler of Seven Rivers was allowed to touch the stone. Her stomach twisted with nerves. She was ruler now–at least for a time.

She would have to do it sooner or later. It would be better to speak with Her here for the first time than tomorrow at the ceremony, in front of a crowd. Her studies had taught her that her father should be touching the stone as he slept. Getting to her feet, she placed her father's hand over his chest.

Tally's steps felt heavy as she walked slowly toward the alcove. The ancient chest lay before her. She took a deep breath, willing her fingers not to tremble as she undid the clasp and opened the lid. Blue light glowed from inside. It was time.

She lowered her hand into the chest and touched the stone.

Tahlea, daughter of Allenthal, I know you.

With a gasp, Tally withdrew her hand, staring at the stone. The voice had been penetrating but gentle, much kinder than she expected. All her life she'd been taught that the Goddess Namradill loved her land and people. Namradill was to be revered and respected but not feared.

Tally reached back into the chest and took the rock in her hand. It was large enough that her fingers couldn't quite close around it, but it was not as heavy as she expected.

Are you well, Tahlea?

"Yes, Divine Namradill." She spoke aloud, wondering if Namradill could hear her thoughts while she held the stone just as she had heard those of the goddess.

Of course, I can. The voice contained a hint of amusement.

I'm worried about my father, Tally thought.

Allenthal is with me. He is safe. I shall return him to you at the appointed time.

Tally nodded, her mind filling with gratitude. She carried the stone to rest on her father's chest, arranging his hands around it.

We shall speak again soon, Tahlea.

That night, Tally lay for hours trying to sleep. Somehow unable to find a comfortable position anywhere on her soft bed, she eventually rose and walked across the room, her bare feet cool against the sleek marble floor. Opening the double doors, she went out onto the balcony. The stars glittered above her in a vast dome edged by white mountain peaks. A whisper of mist caressed her cheek, and she heard the rush of the river and the distant roar of the waterfalls.

Worries and fears crowded her mind. She'd known all her life that she would eventually rule this land, but she'd never expected it to be so soon. Her father had left her with a nation on the brink of war. How could one person prevent the conflict from coming? She needed to find the bandits and stop them.

The chill of early spring drove her inside after a while, and she lay down again, finally falling into a restless slumber.

By the time she woke at dawn, her resolve had hardened. She was Crown Princess of the Seven Rivers. Though she would have to function without her father beside her, she would take care of her people. If battle with the outlaws came, she would fight it. King

Allenthal expected nothing less of her. It was her responsibility to rule her nation.

Tally dressed in a simple tunic and close-fitting leggings, adding a layer of leather armor for additional protection. Today, there was no one else to lead her land. She was in charge, and if that included fighting, a little practice would be good.

She opened her door and spoke to the guards stationed outside. "I'm going to the training field," she said. "Please send Gerran to join me."

"Yes, Princess," one of them responded, disappearing down the hall. The other followed her as she descended the stairs. She made her way to the armory, to the space where she stored her own weapons.

As she picked up her sword, she missed her father more than ever. He'd given her the blade two years ago, and they'd spent many hours training together. "Rest well, Father," she murmured, buckling on her sword belt and going to the door.

Outside, the morning was crisp and cool, and the damp scent of the waterfalls wafted through the courtyard. A wide dirt field provided space for all the men-at-arms to practice. Tally had spent many hours here, sometimes with her father or General Kylith. Since her father had turned her training over to Gerran, she had come here countless times with him. Everyone expected the ruler of the Seven Rivers to be a military leader. Her father had always reminded her it was important for her to be able to defend herself.

As Tally grew up, it never seemed to bother the king that few other girls had any interest in swordplay. If Tally's mother had been alive, she might have insisted on emphasizing more feminine skills, but the queen had died of an illness when Tally was only three.

Taking in a deep breath, Tally stretched, loosening her muscles. Her leggings provided freedom of movement. Drawing her sword, she swung it a few times, warming up. At the slight sound of a step behind her, she smiled. "You're late."

"You couldn't let an old man sleep in?" Gerran's deep voice sounded regretful. "I didn't think you'd still find the time to train this morning."

They had met on this field nearly every day for six years. Tally turned to face him. "You heard about my father?"

He nodded. "The rumors are flying faster than wild geese this morning."

Tally sighed. "I had hoped to have more time."

"Don't worry." Gerran grinned. "You've been training for this all these years. You can do it. I thought you were only worried about performing the Stone Ceremony with a black eye or a split lip."

Tally narrowed her eyes. "It's been a long time since I let you hit my face."

He raised his heavy eyebrows and placed his hand on his sword hilt. "Maybe I've been holding back."

Rising to the challenge, Tally picked up her own weapon and walked out into the bare dirt of the field.

CHAPTER 3

CROWN PRINCESS TAHLEA

TALLY DIDN'T STAND ON the practice field waiting for Gerran to attack but sent a quick blow toward his left side. Effortlessly, he blocked, and their blades rang together. They sparred for several moments. Tally had the advantage of speed, and she needed it to compete with Gerran's greater strength. Though barely taller than her, he was considerably bulkier. His long years of service to the kingdom had taught him skills and tricks that gave him an advantage. Every time she thought she'd learned them all, he presented her with a new one.

Today was no exception. Tally failed to anticipate the quick twist that sent her blade flying from her hand. Disarmed, she dove to the ground, reaching for the hilt of her sword. Gerran's boot pinned her to the ground, and her fingers dug into the dirt, still unable to reach her weapon. She twisted away from his hold, but his foot pinned her again, this time on her back, looking up at the sword point aimed at her throat.

He held it there for only a moment before pulling back and offering her his hand. Glaring at him, she ignored the hand and got back to her feet. "That was pretty good for an old man. Again!"

As they sparred, the sun grew high and bright, burning off the mist shrouding the city. It promised to be a beautiful day, with an assortment of white, fluffy clouds. Despite the long list of commitments awaiting her, Tally wasn't willing to end their session until she beat Gerran. Over months and years of practice, she had defeated him more regularly. It took all her effort to accomplish it, and she savored every victory.

Today it took several attempts. She was breathing hard, and her muscles burned. Finally, she knocked him down. Grinning with deep satisfaction, she surveyed him lying in the dirt. This time, she offered her hand to help him up.

He took the defeat in stride. "Well done, Princess." He allowed her to pull him to his feet.

"You too." She clapped him on the shoulder.

"I know," he shook his head. "Pretty good for an old man." He grinned back at her.

During their years of training together, they'd become good friends, and his support was very welcome today. Gerran's sense of humor added an element of fun to their training sessions. Perhaps her father hadn't thought of that when he chose the best swordsman in Namradill to train her. Maybe he had.

Gathering their gear, they returned to the palace. Tally stowed her sword in its place in one corner of the armory. Gerran took his weapon with him. He'd wear it on duty as a guard.

"Good luck today," he wished her, gripping her shoulder for a moment.

His support felt good. "Thanks."

They were just on their way to the stairs when a sternly disapproving voice called out, "Your Highness!"

Gerran winked at her, made a quick bow, and an even quicker departure. Abandoned, Tally turned around, concealing a heavy sigh. "Good morning, Mistress Eltha."

Eltha was a slight woman, barely tall enough to reach Tally's chin. She wore her gray hair drawn tightly back into a knot. "Princess, today is an important occasion, and your role will be vital. Your appearance will reflect on our entire kingdom. *What have you been doing?*" Her sharp eyes examined Tally's face, streaked with dirt and sweat.

"Just a little exercise, Mistress." Tally squared her shoulders and met the old woman's eyes directly.

"But there's dirt in your hair. Hurry upstairs or there won't be time to get it washed and dried!" Eltha looked her up and down, her expression filled with censure. "You do realize that the ceremony is only a few hours away?"

"Yes, Mistress, I was just on my way now."

"Hurry! The bathwater will get cold." Eltha motioned toward the stairs.

That threat motivated Tally to climb two flights of stairs at a run. It was much easier to move quickly in boots and pants. No sane person attempted to run up the stairs in a floor-length gown. Ease of mobility was a foundational reason that, appropriate or not, Tally preferred her leggings.

Back in her rooms, she found a large silver bath with a stack of soft towels and an array of sweetly scented soaps beside it. She pulled off her muddy boots and armor and slipped into the tub. Copious amounts of hot water and soap were required to remove the grit. When she finally finished and dried off, she seated herself at her dressing table to allow her maid, Nita, to comb through her hair.

Though the sensation of slipping into a hot bath was one of her favorites, Tally strongly preferred any other activity over the prolonged grooming required by formal occasions. Shirking her duty today was not an option. The Stone Ceremony was the most important occasion hosted by the royal family.

Quivers of nervousness ran through her as she anticipated the event. Every other time, her father had been there to take charge and be the center of attention. Now, he couldn't help her. She would have to do this on her own. Looking like a princess was the first step.

She applied cream smelling of flowers to her skin. A chemise and drawers of fine silk went on under layers of petticoats. Nita laced her into a gown of heavy, deep blue brocade trimmed with satin.

A light knock on the door interrupted their preparations. Nita opened it to reveal Tally's closest friend. "Come in, Mariella," Tally invited.

Mariella rushed to Tally's side and hugged her. She pulled back to meet Tally's eyes. "Your father... I heard. Is he all right?"

"As far as I know, he is," Tally said.

"And you?" Mariella's blue eyes were soft with empathy. "I know this is hard." She hugged Tally again.

Her genuine concern warmed Tally. Mariella lived in the rooms next to Tally's. It had been that way for years, since Mariella's father had died, leaving her an orphan. They'd already been friends, even then, and Tally had been delighted to have Mariella make her home in the palace.

Now, Tally appreciated her even more, needing someone to confide in. Being a member of the royal family demanded a certain isolation, and it was difficult to know who to trust.

Tally took a deep breath and tried to smile. "I'd be lying if I told you I wasn't afraid," she admitted, "but no one else can know that."

Mariella placed a hand over her heart. "I'd never tell."

Tally smiled. "I know you wouldn't. Thank you."

"You'll be handling everything today," Mariella inspected her critically. "That dress is perfect. With your ivory skin, the blue suits you. Can I do your hair?" She sent a pleading look at Nita, who yielded the comb.

Mariella worked on Tally's brown hair. Unlike Mariella's waves, Tally's hair was smooth and straight. It was long and thick, and Nita had brushed it smooth. Now, Mariella added a braid that circled Tally's head, creating the perfect resting place for her crown. Nita brought a flat wooden case and opened it for Mariella to select several sparkling hair pins.

"What jewelry are you wearing?" Mariella wore a look of concentration, as if the choice of ornaments were of utmost importance. "This is your first appearance without your father. Every detail matters." She turned to Nita. "Bring the ruby set. It will be stunning with this gown." She turned back to Tally. "Don't you think?"

"I trust your judgment," Tally replied with a smile. Mariella was likely to be correct. She was better with appearances than Tally. Right now, Tally had to figure out how to quell an outlaw uprising, discover the true motives of a popular hero, and lead a kingdom. Jewelry wasn't the first thing on her mind.

A few moments later, delicate slippers, a glittering ruby pendant, earrings, and a bracelet completed her outfit. Mariella surveyed her appraisingly. "Perfect," she decided with a satisfied smile.

It was time. At least Mariella would make sure Tally looked appropriate. All that remained was to speak clearly, stand up straight, and not make any mistakes in front of everyone.

"Hurry, my lady," Nita urged. "You need to go."

Mariella threaded her arm through Tally's. "Don't worry," she advised. "They can't possibly start without you, can they?"

Tally took a deep breath. "Thank you, Nita. I'm ready." She met her friend's eyes. "Thanks for your help."

Mariella gave Tally's arm a comforting squeeze. "Of course. I'll walk down with you."

As Tally left her room, two royal guards moved to follow her. With her arm still in her friend's, she walked down the stairs and through the passageways to the entrance of the great hall. She stopped in front of the door and drew in a long breath. Inside, she heard the low sound of hundreds of voices. She'd entered the hall a hundred times, but she missed her father's solid presence by her side. It was so much harder to do this alone. She straightened her spine and lifted her chin.

"I'll see you later." Mariella slipped away to go around to the other entrance.

At a nod from Tally, the guards opened the doors, and a fanfare announced her arrival. Every voice hushed, and silence fell as Tally crossed the room, her guards flanking her.

The crowd was a sea of faces: many familiar, many strangers, some smiling, others not. The nobility of the Seven Rivers was well represented with members from each of the seven provinces. The crowd was a mix of social classes, containing tradespeople, merchants, farmers, and villagers. The Stone Ceremony was held once every season, as tradition required, and all were welcome. No one who wished to attend would be turned away until they packed the room to the doors.

Walking slowly, her step graceful and her back straight, Tally glided to the dais holding the ancient throne of the Seven Rivers. It had stood in exactly that spot for hundreds of years, lovingly cared for and polished, intricately carved and inlaid with gems. She would not be sitting there today. It was still her father's throne. A smaller and less elaborate seat rested beside it for Tally. She stood in front of the chairs and prepared to address her people.

"I thank all of you for being here today." Despite the flutters of nervousness in her belly, her voice sounded clear and strong. "Legends tell of an ancient time when this kingdom was no more than a barren desert. Where now our lands are fertile and green, before the influence of Namradill, sand covered them. Our love for this beautiful land binds us together. We are gathered today to petition Divine Namradill for Her blessing to ensure the continued prosperity of our land. King Allenthal is not able to attend." Whispers wound through the crowd. "My father is with the goddess. He will return to us when the stonesleep is finished. In the meantime, I will fulfill my duties as Crown Princess."

A murmur ran through the crowd. Tally detected surprise and worry in it. Did they think she couldn't lead this nation, that she was weak because she was a woman? Did they think she was too young, too inexperienced to be a good leader? Hopefully, the memory of her great-grandmother as a powerful queen remained with them. Tally was her father's only child. They had known she would rule.

Still, she wondered if any of them would object. Her training had taught her to keep her expression impassive. Regardless of what anyone thought, she had to go forward.

"It's time." Her voice rang through the hall and an expectant silence fell. Servants near the tall windows pulled the drapes, dimming the light in the hall. The footsteps of two men carrying an ornate chest sounded loud in the stillness. They walked with a measured tread, their posture dignified. Not a sound came from the crowd as they crossed the room to stop in front of Tally. Each of them held one handle of the carved wooden box.

Tally unfastened the clasp and opened the lid, allowing the blue light from within to flood the room. The azure glow spreading over the faces of the crowd made them look alien. With great care, Tally reached inside and closed her fingers around the stone, lifting it out. The familiar light brightened at her touch, welling out between her fingers, pulsing in a strange irregular rhythm.

As she had seen her father do every season for her entire life, she cradled the stone, holding it against her heart. The crowd watched her, mesmerized by the radiant glow. Tally closed her eyes. Everyone else in the room faded away. She no longer saw them, and she heard nothing else but the voice of the Goddess.

My greetings, Tahlea. I stand beside you as you work to protect my land and our people. Your father is well. For the time being, he is happy in my presence, though I can tell he misses you. Your reunion will be joyful.

I shall send the plentiful spring rains to ensure that your crops will flourish. Our people work hard to till the earth, and we must take care of them.

You have enemies, Tahlea. Beware of those who profess to support you but wait for the opportunity to betray you. I shall do everything I can to help, but you must stand firm in defense of our land.

When the words faded into silence, Tally drew in a long breath, opening her eyes to see hundreds of faces staring back at her. Reverently, she lowered the stone into the chest. She closed the lid, hiding away the brilliant light. Closing the clasp, she nodded to the men holding the box, signaling them to withdraw.

"Namradill has once more offered us her protection," she said to the crowd. "She continues to guard and guide us, and we pray this city, named in Her honor, will continue in peace and prosperity." Tally paused, and the crowd cheered. "Now, eat, drink, dance. Enjoy my hospitality. I'm grateful to each of you for your support of our nation."

Short for a royal speech, but no one appeared to mind. They cheered again. Servants drew back the drapes, flooding the room with daylight once more. Tally gestured to the musicians, and they played. Several of the nobility waited near the bottom of the dais. During the planning of this event, the oldest noble families had offered their young heirs to be her partner for the first dance. Lord Marondil had won the honor, and he now smiled up at her.

With all eyes still on her, she descended gracefully and placed her hand in his. Marondil was short and fair-haired, his rich tunic straining to contain his plump body. On level ground, Tally stood half a head taller than him. She was tall enough that she'd become accustomed to looking down at some dance partners.

King Allenthal was taller than most, and she'd inherited her stature from him. While useful on the practice field, it was much less so on the dance floor. Still, Marondil gazed up at her admiringly. "You look lovely, Crown Princess."

"I thank you for the compliment, Lord Marondil." Did he have a particular reason for attempting to flatter her so outrageously? She kept her voice gracious but neutral. "You're also looking well. How is your mother feeling?"

"Better every day, thank you." He smiled warmly, his soft hand damp against hers. Other couples had joined the dance, turning in slow circles around them. Tally caught a glimpse of Mariella dancing with a handsome young stranger. They made a beautiful couple, and Mariella had turned her dazzling smile on him. Tally held back a smile. Rarely could men resist her friend's charms, and this young man looked as smitten as most of Mariella's admirers. Tally wondered who he was. A merchant? A farmer? Tally's own schedule would likely be filled with sons of the other powerful families. The older generation of the nobility had taken it upon themselves to decide who would best serve the crown by marrying into the royal family. For years, they had vied with each other to maneuver the perfect eligible bachelor into Tally's path. None of them appeared to care about her own taste or opinion.

Tally's connection to Namradill was bound to her bloodline. As she was the only heir, for the past two years, there had been mounting pressure for her to marry and produce a child. Today, this pressure created an unwelcome distraction. She wasn't ready to make any sort of decision. At the moment, there were too many other things to think about. Although, if someone came along who looked at her like the tall young man was looking at her friend, maybe she would change her mind.

Mariella reappeared, her arm in his. "Princess Tahlea, I would like to introduce Drake from Edri Province."

The young man released Mariella and bowed to Tally, taking her hand and kissing it. "I'm pleased to meet you, Princess. Mariella has already told me wonderful things about you."

"That's very kind." Tally glanced at her friend before turning her attention back to Drake.

"I wanted you two to meet," Mariella said. "I was just going to get something to drink, if you'll excuse me for a moment?" She slipped away into the crowd.

Drake looked after her for a moment before he turned back to Tally. "May I have the honor of a dance, Crown Princess?"

"Yes." It was a good opportunity to talk to him. She would have a few moments to assess whether he was a suitable companion for her friend. Taking his offered arm, she accompanied him into the dancing.

It was easy to see why he had caught Mariella's eye. He was tall and well-built. That was a relief. For the duration of this dance, at least, Tally would enjoy the luxury of not looking like she was oversized. Up close, she noticed his eyes were a vibrant blue. He was graceful on the dance floor, his movements confident. She felt a ridge of hard callus across his palm that could have come from handling weapons. Did he move this well on a battlefield? He was probably skilled with a sword.

"How long have you and the charming Lady Mariella been friends?" Drake asked, glancing toward the refreshment table where Mariella had disappeared into the crowd.

"For many years now. Since we were children; we grew up together. What brought you to the city?" Tally asked, curious about this man who appeared to be smitten with her dearest friend.

His eyes met hers. "I came to Namradan on business, but while I was here, I took the opportunity to attend the ceremony. Meeting two such charming young ladies was an unexpected pleasure. I'm honored that you agreed to share a dance, Your Highness."

"The honor is mine." She smiled. Was he truly being sincere? A subtle flicker deep in his eyes and a sardonic twist of his mouth made her wonder. She didn't yet equal her father's skill at reading people, but she already guessed that he had secrets. "Are you originally from Edri?"

He shook his head. "I grew up here in Namradan, but lately, Edri Province has been my home."

"So, you've survived the crisis happening now in Edri. It's terrible. We are taking action to prevent further trouble."

Concern filled his blue eyes. "I feel for all those who have been harmed. Personally, I've been very lucky. None of the attacks have been near me. I've been able to continue my business more or less undisturbed."

When so many people had been affected, Drake had been fortunate.

They spun in graceful turns, following the dance. "And what do you do?" Tally asked.

"I'm a merchant," Drake said. "My friend and I are just setting up our business. We are only humble traders, seeking to earn a modest living."

"Who is your business partner?"

He smiled. "His name is Andevaar."

The same man who had mysteriously appeared during every outlaw raid. A chill swept through her, and she struggled to keep her expression pleasant. If Drake noticed her reaction, he would know she had serious doubts about the man who the people had so quickly grown to adore. She had to say something. "I've heard of Andevaar. He has many admirers in Edri."

One corner of Drake's mouth quirked in a half smile. "True," he admitted. "I've known him for a long time. He's helped numerous people there, and I admire his efforts in stopping the bandits. I intend to help him as much as I can in the future."

"As do I," Tally said. "Neither I, nor my father, will tolerate such lawlessness in our kingdom."

"Of course not." Drake glanced toward the empty throne at the head of the room. "It's an unfortunate time for His Majesty to be... unwell. I wish a peaceful sleep for him."

Instinctively, she lifted her chin a little. She would have to lead on her own. "Thank you."

Drake's expression showed sympathy. "I'm sure all the people are extending wishes for his recovery. Even so, you did an admirable job presiding today. I've never attended the Stone Ceremony before. It was fascinating–almost like you were speaking with the stone."

The tradition had been handed down for hundreds of years. Why should she feel she needed to convince him now? She met his eye. "I was, yes, and I thank you for your kind compliment. In the king's absence, I must fulfill my duty."

"How do you release the power of the stone?" Drake asked, his eyes alight with curiosity.

How dare he ask such a bold question? How should she answer it? She looked back at him. "The Goddess Namradill, our Divine protector, wields Her own power. I remain Her servant. I am not here to try to control Her."

Before Drake could ask any more questions, Mariella reappeared, and Tally realized the music was ending. He bowed. "Princess, I very much enjoyed our dance and our conversation."

Tally inclined her head in reply. "As did I."

His gaze returned to Mariella's lovely features and lustrous, golden hair. His eyes lingered, tracing her slender form.

Drake was obviously interested in her friend. Tally observed the inviting smile on Mariella's face as she looked up at him. "If you'll both excuse me," Tally murmured, turning away into the crowd. Lost in each other's gaze, they didn't look after her. If Mariella wasn't going to step back and examine the situation logically, Tally would have to. Since Drake was connected to Andevaar, it made sense that he would know more about the trouble in the kingdom than he admitted.

CHAPTER 4

CROWN PRINCESS TAHLEA

TALLY ANSWERED A SUMMONS from General Kylith just after breakfast the next morning. With the usual guards shadowing her, she walked through the halls to the council chamber, where the king used to meet with his military leaders and other advisors.

As she entered, Kylith and a short dark-haired man rose to their feet. Tally didn't know him well, but she had seen Farrin before. He'd worked in the palace for many years, and she'd noticed him occasionally meeting with her father or Kylith.

"Good morning, Princess," Kylith bowed. His companion did the same. Kylith gestured to him. "You remember Farrin."

Tally nodded at him. "Of course, you've worked with my father. I'm pleased to see you again, Farrin."

"Thank you, Princess."

"Please," she gestured to their chairs, "be seated." They all sat, and she turned her gaze to Kylith.

His expression was serious. "I'm afraid it's not good news."

Tally attempted to keep her face impassive. She'd only been ruling for a few days, but none of the news she'd received yet had been good. Was ruling a nation always like this? Every moment moving from one urgent crisis to the next? She rubbed her forehead, waiting for Kylith to continue.

"Though he usually stays out of sight, Farrin is an important member of our guard. He oversees the palace guards and the staff, watching for anything amiss. Recently, he became aware of a person in the palace gathering information about the king's health and reporting it to someone out in the city."

A spy here in the palace? Her eyes widened. "Who?"

"The physician's young assistant. We've been watching her for several weeks," Farrin said. "Just yesterday, I confirmed what she was doing, and I followed her out into the city, trying to find out who she was giving the information to."

Tally's mind flew back to the day her father had collapsed. They had sent for the physician immediately. He was an old man, someone they had trusted with their well-being for many years, but his assistant? Tally remembered the quiet young woman with dark hair. "What would she hope to gain by this?"

"I fear we have enemies who would pay plenty of gold for information about the king's... condition," Kylith said.

"How long has she been in the palace?" Tally asked.

"Six weeks, your highness," Farrin replied.

Five weeks ago, King Allenthal had sent for the physician, fearing that his stonesleep would be coming soon. Had the assistant heard that? Four weeks ago, outlaws had attacked the first village in Edri. Almost as if they had been preparing their rebellion and were only waiting for the king to be asleep to begin their plans.

A sudden chill crawled down Tally's spine. Her father was a well-respected king. With him incapacitated, someone thought they could take over in his absence. They believed she lacked the power to defend her throne. Tally drew in a deep breath and set her jaw. While she lived, she would not let that happen.

She turned her gaze to Farrin. "You followed her? Who was she reporting to?"

His expression was grave. "She led us to a specific street in the city. Five different merchants have offices there. Somehow, she must have realized she was being followed and fled. We've been keeping watch and if she shows her face again, we'll arrest her." He pushed a piece of parchment across the table to Tally. Five names were listed. She recognized only one of them. Andevaar. She looked up at Kylith. "We should question all of them."

Kylith nodded. "Agreed."

"That might be harder than you think," Farrin said. "While those people own the businesses, they have holdings in other provinces, and most of them are not currently here in Namradan. Two are traveling through Ondari Province, and Andevaar is in Edri."

Tally rubbed her forehead in thought. She needed to find out the truth behind these events. Her intuition warned her they were connected. Raising her eyes, she met Farrin's gaze. "I would like to talk to each of them. Please send messages requesting they meet with me. We know that Andevaar is in Edri. We will be sending troops there to deal with the unrest, and they can carry my message. I want Andevaar to come to Namradan for an audience with me."

"Yes, Princess. I will make sure it happens." Farrin got to his feet. "Do you have any further instructions for me, Your Highness?"

"No. Thank you, Farrin."

"I will get started then." With a bow, he departed.

Tally met Kylith's eyes across the table. "Well?"

He appeared to understand her intent. "I agree with your actions."

She lowered her eyebrows. "It's *me*, isn't it?"

He raised his eyebrows. "Princess?"

She slapped her palm against the smooth surface of the table. "They think they can take over because my father is asleep, that I won't provide any opposition."

Kylith's expression was impassive. "I'm sure that's exactly what they think."

Her stomach clenched. She wouldn't give up, no matter what happened. She couldn't. There had to be a way to stop all this.

One corner of Kylith's mouth turned up. "But... they don't know you like I do. We'll find a way to show them who they're dealing with."

Tally's anxiety eased somewhat. Kylith thought she could succeed. He'd been beside her father for Tally's entire life, and she trusted his experience. She smiled slightly. "Thank you."

"Leadership is never easy, Princess, but I believe you can do this." He met her eyes frankly. "You have all your father's training, and you have Divine Namradill on your side. Whoever our enemy is, they have neither of those things."

Tally stood on the city walls, watching three companies of troops ride across the bridge and onto the road toward Edri Province.

"This will all be over soon," Kylith said. "They'll capture the outlaws and restore order."

Tally hoped he was right. Thus far, the criminals had proved adept at hiding among the ordinary citizens of Edri. They covered their faces during the raids, making it impossible to identify them. For the hundredth time, she wished she could simply talk to her father and ask his advice. When the last of the riders were gone, she turned to go back to the palace.

The royal chamberlain stood waiting for her, a long list of appointments in his hand. Instead of groaning as she wanted to, she nodded and followed him. Despite all her training, ruling a kingdom was harder than she'd expected.

The next morning, Mariella stood in the doorway of Tally's rooms, a pleading expression on her face. "Please come? I know you have meetings, but they still have to allow you a couple of hours to yourself once in a while."

Tally took her friend's arm, and pulled her into the sitting room, closing the door behind them. They sank down onto the sofa together. "What's so important about this?"

"It will be *fun*, that's what. A group of us are taking a ride out of the city for a picnic lunch. It's a beautiful day, and I know you love to ride. Several young men will be joining us."

Internally, Tally reviewed the list of young noblemen who might be attending. The idea of an outing with any of them did not particularly thrill her. But what about Drake? He was Andevaar's business partner. It would be worthwhile to speak with him again. Maybe a conversation would shed light on his friend's plans.

She met Mariella's eyes. "Will Drake be there?"

Mariella squealed in excitement and clutched Tally's arm. "Yes!" Her eyes sparkled, and she bounced in her seat.

"Have you seen him since the ceremony?"

Mariella nodded excitedly, "Several times. Tally, I can't stop thinking about him! Those eyes... they're exactly the color of the evening sky." She sighed, fanning herself with her hand.

Tally raised her eyebrows. "Don't you think this is all moving very quickly?"

Her friend shook her head in immediate disagreement. "I've never felt like this before. To be honest, when I'm with him, I wish he'd move *more* quickly. All he's done is hold my hand. He does have the most attractive hands—"

Tally held up her own hand to stop Mariella. A strand of jealousy twisted inside her. In her position, romance was a dream she couldn't confess to anyone. It seemed unlikely that she would ever meet anyone who wasn't totally focused on the fact that she was the Crown Princess of the Seven Rivers. Finding a young man who wanted to meet her simply for herself would be impossible. Her mind wandered for a moment. What would it be like to meet someone who made her feel like Drake made Mariella feel?

Tally took a firm grip on herself. Her kingdom must come first. Romance was very likely never going to happen. Still, joining the outing today with Mariella might be a good idea. If she had fallen so hard for Drake, Tally needed to be sure her friend was safe.

Tally smiled. "I'll come."

Mariella leaped to her feet and clapped her hands. "Get ready and meet us in the courtyard in an hour." She hugged Tally, running from the room to make her final preparations.

Tally's maid, Nita, appeared. "May I help you dress?"

Tally swallowed her protest that she'd rather wear trousers since they were riding. It wouldn't do to show up at a social gathering dressed as a soldier. Nita brought her a riding dress and arranged her hair. A short while later she descended to the courtyard, two faithful royal guards at her heels. One went to see that horses were prepared for them.

A group of young people had already gathered. Tally pasted on a smile as she noticed Marondil among them. "Good day, Princess!" His own smile was enthusiastic, as he took her hand

and kissed it. Several others greeted her pleasantly. She spotted Mariella and made her way to her side. Her friend smiled brightly.

"Well?" Tally murmured in her ear, "where is that handsome young man you've been waiting to see?"

Mariella didn't have to answer. Just then, Drake rode into the courtyard on a tall brown horse, leading a shorter gray animal with a white blaze on its forehead. He approached them and dismounted. "Good morning, Lady Mariella, Crown Princess." His eyes went to Mariella. "I should have asked if you enjoy riding."

"I do," Mariella insisted. "Though it's not something I do often, and…" She cast a sidelong glance at Tally. "I confess, I'm not very good at it."

Tally refused to allow a smile onto her face. She and Mariella had shared adventures and misadventures on horseback. It had never been her friend's best skill. Horses frightened her.

"I'll help you," Drake promised. "The stable master assured me this horse is very gentle. May I assist?"

Mariella looked up at the large animal uncertainly for a moment. Then, she raised her chin just a little and nodded. She seized the pommel and got her foot into the stirrup. Drake put his hands to her waist and lifted her easily into the saddle. From there, she took several long breaths, her cheeks pink.

"Ready?" he asked.

Mariella nodded. She gripped the reins more tightly than necessary, and her spine was stiff.

Tally reached up to place a hand on Mariella's forearm. She could tell her friend was apprehensive. "Will you be all right?"

Mariella nodded in determination.

With her friend settled, Tally made her way back through the group, most of them on their horses now. One of her guards held her mount's reins while the other was already in the saddle.

What must it be like to stroll out the door and go wherever you want without anyone noticing you? No guards, no fuss, no one watching your every move? A small sigh escaped Tally's lips. She'd better accept it. It was not something that was ever going to change. Pushing her thoughts into the background, she took the reins. Even hampered by skirts, she slid easily into the saddle.

The group rode out through the city gates and onto the bridge. The graceful stone arc was easily wide enough for four horses to ride abreast, while the wide waters of the great river Namra flowed swiftly beneath them, rushing toward the falls.

At the end of the bridge, they followed the wide road for some distance until they turned onto a narrow track that led past farms and woods. The spring sun shone brightly, dappled by the shadows from the large trees beside the path. Tally took a deep breath. Mariella had been right. For weeks, Tally had spent all her time fulfilling her duties. It was good to pause for a moment and breathe.

A little further up the line, Tally heard horses whinny nervously. A black dog ran out from one of the farmyards, barking ferociously as they passed. Tally directed her mount forward as she saw the dog snarling, right at the feet of Mariella's horse. The animal neighed and reared, kicking its forefeet into the air. Nearly losing her seat, Mariella held on desperately as the horse returned to the ground and bolted.

Ignoring the others for the moment, Tally urged her horse to follow her friend. Before she could get free of the group, Drake raced after Mariella. Her mount galloped in panic, her limited riding skills insufficient to control the beast. Holding her breath, Tally saw Mariella slipping to one side.

Before Mariella could fall, Drake caught up, seized her around the waist and pulled her into his arms. Tally let out a breath of relief. The others quickly moved to follow. Two of their companions pursued the panicked horse.

Tally drew up beside Drake's horse. Mariella clutched at him, shock and fear were plain on her white face.

"Are you all right?" Tally asked.

Mariella nodded, shaking, her hands gripping Drake even tighter.

"I'm so sorry," he murmured. "They promised me that horse was calm."

"It's not your fault." Her voice still sounded shaken. "I'm sure it would have been fine except for the dog."

"You're not hurt?" Tally asked.

Mariella shook her head. "Only frightened." She rolled her eyes. "And embarrassed. If I were a better rider…"

"That could have happened to anyone," Tally assured her. The others murmured their agreement.

"If we ride a little further, there's a good place to stop and rest." Drake held Mariella easily, showing no signs of wanting to release her. His concern appeared genuine. If he hadn't caught Mariella…

They rode on at a gentle walk, crossed a brook on a wooden bridge, and came to a green clearing in the woods. Everyone dismounted and several people spread blankets on the grass. Drake got off his horse and set Mariella down on a blanket.

Tally handed her reins to a guard and hurried to her friend's side. By the time she reached Mariella, Drake was already beside her, offering her water. Now, instead of looking afraid, Mariella looked mortified. "All this fuss," she muttered.

"We all want you to be safe." Tally sat beside her and put a hand on her shoulder.

The group settled and took out the food and drink they had brought. Tally stayed beside her friend, and Drake settled on her other side. After the disturbance, they gradually settled into conversation and ate. Mariella smiled at Drake. "After this, you'll believe me when I say I'm not the best rider." She glanced at Tally. "The princess is much more skilled in the saddle."

Drake met Tally's eyes, assessing. What was he trying to determine from her? From all his words and actions, he appeared deeply interested in Mariella. His gaze was different when he looked at Tally, definitely not romantic interest. It was more like he questioned or tried to measure her abilities. What exactly did he want to know, and why?

"She's good enough to ride with General Kylith." Mariella's cheeks turned pink. "I don't think he'd ever choose to invite me along."

Drake turned back to Tally; his eyebrows raised. "Don't you find a military patrol just a little *uncomfortable* after the luxuries of the palace?"

Within the folds of her skirt, her fingers tightened in irritation. Still, she refused to allow the emotion to show in her expression. Her family had led the Seven Rivers for centuries. It was her duty to take care of her people, whatever that entailed. Her own personal comfort was unimportant. She schooled her expression into one of innocence. "Not at all," she smiled. "I enjoy the fresh air."

Mariella shuddered. "Not me. I confess, I embrace a life with much less adventure."

Drake smiled, a measure of genuine warmth in his eyes. He took Mariella's hand and kissed it. "Except for today. You came through this adventure very well."

"Only thanks to you." Mariella's gaze was lost in his.

It was time for Tally to go. The two of them obviously wanted a moment to themselves. She got to her feet. "If you'll both excuse me." Neither of them objected as she slipped away.

CHAPTER 5

CROWN PRINCESS TAHLEA

THE NEXT EVENING, SEARCHING for a moment of calm after a full schedule of meetings, Tally stood alone on a balcony looking out over the gardens. The sun sank slowly, painting the clouds bright gold. Gradually the colors changed to rose and then deep purple as twilight fell. The garden paths were empty except for a single person hurrying toward the door.

As the girl neared, Tally recognized her friend. "Mariella?"

Her friend paused and looked up. Her face was bright with excitement. "Stay there. I'm coming up."

A moment later, her footsteps pattered up the stairs, and she ran across the balcony to embrace Tally. "You won't believe it!" Mariella lowered her voice, looking around to be sure no one else was nearby. "He kissed me!"

Naturally, she meant Drake. What had the two of them been doing together? It was late, far after visitors were normally admitted to the palace grounds. Mariella should have been safely resting in her own rooms. "Did he come here?"

Mariella nodded excitedly. "He came to find me. I wasn't expecting him, since he told me he had to leave the city on business, but he came." She placed a hand over her heart. "Oh, Tally, I'll never forget that moment!"

Tally smiled at Mariella's complete enthusiasm.

"He's so strong. Maybe I should be frightened of that, but he's so gentle with me." Her face reddened. "Well, not too gentle. It was like nothing I've ever felt. I thought I might melt into a puddle right at his feet. I've never met anyone like him," Mariella gushed. "Those blue eyes, and his shoulders..." she trailed into silence.

Tally's brows drew together. It wasn't Drake's shoulders she was worried about now. "How did he get into the palace so late?"

The question took Mariella by surprise, and her eyes widened. She hadn't been thinking about that, obviously. She blushed again. "I was so happy to see him I didn't think to ask. I'm sorry."

Tally took a deep breath. Her friend was in deeper than she realized. "You really like him."

Mariella grinned. "I *really* do."

Tally hated to ask the question, but she had to. "Do you trust him?" For herself, she still had many questions she wanted the handsome young merchant to answer.

"Yesterday, he saved my life," Mariella pointed out. "He could have let me fall." She took a long breath. "I know he really cares about me."

Tally hugged her friend. "I just think you should be careful. Don't let him move too fast. You are a young woman of good family and reputation, and you've been by my side since your mother died. It's been ten years already. You deserve the love of a man who will take care of you, build a family with you. Don't let this become only an affair that leaves you alone and hurt at the end. I want you to be happy."

Despite Mariella's excitement, Tally's experience made her cautious. She had seen other young women drawn into romantic affairs only to have their charming suitors move on without warning, leaving them behind. She didn't want that to happen to her friend.

Mariella hugged her back. "Thanks, Tally. You're right, of course. I confess, I don't have the willpower to ask him to step back. That *kiss*!" She closed her eyes in remembered bliss.

Tally laughed. "For your sake, I hope it all works out."

"Me too!" Her lips sank into a frown. "He's going back to Edri in the morning."

Two weeks later, a messenger from Edri Province arrived at the royal palace. Tally sat at the long table in the council chamber beside General Kylith as the guards admitted the tired, dusty man. He bowed deeply. "Crown Princess."

"Please, sit down and give us your message." Tally gestured to one of the comfortable upholstered chairs along the polished table.

The man settled gratefully into his seat. "Governor Folcan sent me. He's been using all the troops that are at his disposal, including the companies you sent to help, in an attempt to hunt down and capture these outlaws. We've had several new attacks in the last few days. Despite all the governor's efforts, he hasn't captured them. If not for the efforts of one young man, things would be much worse. Governor Folcan has come to rely on Andevaar. He has bravely stepped in to combat the attacks, risking his own safety to fight against them. Though he is young, his abilities are exceptional, and the governor placed him in command of the search for the outlaws."

Her stomach grew tighter throughout the message. Andevaar. She couldn't be the only one suspicious of this whole situation, could she? She glanced at Kylith. "If the troops we already sent have failed, it sounds like we need to send more men at once to assist Governor Folcan."

The messenger nodded. "He is very grateful for your support, and he agrees we need to take further action. Governor Folcan has developed a great admiration for young Andevaar. He felt that you should meet him, and he received your message that you wished this as well."

Tally nodded. "Yes."

"Good," the man said, nodding. "Andevaar is already on his way. Rumors of his deeds have already spread far, even here in Namradan. Before we separated in Edri, people came out to line the roads to watch him pass. Now I would guess he's only a day or so behind me."

So, the mysterious Andevaar was on his way to Namradan. This meeting would give Tally a chance to talk to him and see for herself if she could detect any sign of deceit. "Very well," Tally said. "We will prepare to meet with him when he arrives. And as soon as we finish, our army will ride for Edri."

"Thank you, Princess. I will take this news to the governor as quickly as I can." He stood, bowed to her again, and departed.

Tally looked at Kylith. "Well?"

He was rubbing the stubble on his jaw as he considered. "So, he's on his way here."

Tally rubbed her forehead. Her meeting with Andevaar had to happen, but she wasn't sure what to hope for. "Perhaps we will learn something new. We need to know the truth about these attacks."

Kylith shook his head slightly. "If what we suspect is true, he'd be the last man in the kingdom to be honest with us."

Of course, Andevaar wouldn't tell them the truth, but Tally had an idea. "I'm sure he won't. But I know someone who will." She jumped to her feet and hurried to the door. Kylith got up and followed her. Maybe he'd already figured out what she meant because he didn't question her.

A few moments later, they stood at the entrance to the king's chambers. The guards opened the door for them, and they crossed the silent space. The familiar rooms made her miss her father fiercely. He should be awake and here with her. She missed being able to talk to him. His unconscious state made the room feel like a cold, foreign place.

King Allenthal lay on his bed, as motionless as if he were dead. Only the slight color in his skin and the faint rise and fall of his chest proved that he still lived. Two guards stood at the door of the bedroom, and the old physician sat in a chair by the bed.

At the sight of them, he stood and bowed. "Crown Princess. I beg your forgiveness. When I heard about my assistant, I was appalled. I hope you didn't think that I—"

Tally stopped him with a raised hand. She took a step closer and met his eyes. "You've served the royal family all my life. Did you know what she was doing?"

He looked back at her, afraid, but still meeting her eyes. "I did not. I swear, I had no idea."

For a long moment, her gaze bored into his. "I believe that's true," she said finally. The concern in his eyes reinforced her previous opinion. If she thought he'd been part of the betrayal, she would have sent for him the moment she'd heard. Today, she saw only an old man who cared deeply for the king. "You have been faithful to our family all this time. Why would you suddenly decide to change that now?"

He took a quick breath. "I assure you, I wouldn't, Your Highness."

She glanced toward the bed. "How is my father?"

"We've watched his majesty closely, but there has been no change. He's resting just as we expected."

She nodded. "Thank you. I'm doing my best to be patient and have faith that he will be well. But today, I came for a different reason." The stone lying in Allenthal's motionless hands gave a flicker of blue light, as if it had heard her.

The old man stared at the blue glow. "He needs the stone close to him."

"I will only be a moment," Tally assured him. Stepping closer, she looked down at her father's sleeping face. She placed her hands around the stone and lifted it from her father's motionless hands. As she lifted it, cradling it close to herself, a flood of blue light filled the room.

Crown Princess Tahlea, daughter of Allenthal, it hasn't been long since the ceremony. I warned you to be wary. Naturally, you have questions.

Tally took a deep breath. It didn't seem to be necessary to speak aloud. She formed the words in her mind. *Divine Namradill, can you tell me if my father is well?*

Of course he is. The voice in her mind seemed surprised at the question. *He is with me. Did you fear I wouldn't take care of him?*

No, Tally thought. *But I miss him.*

You will have him back when the time has passed. In the meantime, you are my voice in this kingdom. Power will be given to you to protect your lands.

That was reassuring, but Tally needed more specifics. *Outlaws are attacking my people. I need to know who is behind it. Do you know who it is?*

I do. I can see all of the Seven Rivers. Your enemy is Andevaar.

A gasp escaped Tally's lips. So, it was true. The physician's assistant who had been spying in the palace had been reporting to Andevaar, not to anyone else. And even though the people adored him, he was the man behind all this trouble.

Though the people see Andevaar as a hero, without him, none of this would be happening, Namradill thought.

Tally hardened her resolve. *How do I stop him?*

His deceit must be exposed.

And how was that going to happen? Perhaps they could find indisputable proof, or the man could have a change of heart and confess. *How?*

Go to my descendant Thorvan. He will assist you.

Thank you, Divine Namradill.

Go with my blessing, Princess Tahlea.

With great care, Tally replaced the stone in her father's hands. A heavy silence settled over the room.

Kylith raised his eyebrows, crossing his arms over his chest. "Well?"

"As soon as we're finished meeting with Andevaar, you and I are taking the army to Edri. Then, I'm going into the mountains to visit the Mystic Thorvan."

CHAPTER 6

ANDEVAAR

ANDEVAAR LED A COLUMN of mounted soldiers. Governor Folcan had appointed him to command them, and, since his position was unofficial, he wasn't required to wear the blue uniform of the Seven Rivers. Against the dark army uniforms, he stood out in armor of burnished gold and a brilliant red cloak. As the road wound through small villages, the people came out to watch them pass. Word had spread. Everyone in Edri Province had heard the stories by now. They knew who he was.

The crowd cheered when they saw him. He straightened his shoulders, a rush of warmth flowing through him at their praise. The years of training, planning, and hard work were beginning to pay off. All the effort would be worth it in the end. He favored the crowd with the smile he saved for use when he wanted to charm someone and lifted his hand to wave.

Adoration was something he had never experienced before. For many years, neglect, abuse and fighting for survival had defined his life. Now, after all the hard times, the cheers were a sign that his plans were succeeding. Today, it was time to meet the princess.

They rode through the last few villages and crossed a stone bridge marking the border of Edri Province. In a couple of hours, they'd arrive in Namradan. This was his day.

The attention focused on him didn't dissipate as he crossed the border. News had traveled ahead of the army, and crowds of people lined the roads. Andevaar raised his eyes to the lofty towers of the palace. Those spires had been his first view of the city all those years ago. Standing in the center of Namradan, the graceful building had endured for centuries.

The royal family had maintained complete control of the kingdom for uncounted generations. Until now. It was time for change. Just because they held up a glowing blue stone didn't give them the right to make decisions for everyone.

The people already loved Andevaar. When he asked them to, they would support him, follow him. Someday soon, he would hold that stone in *his* hand, and they would beg him to take the throne. The pieces were all coming together.

Andevaar rode out onto the huge bridge spanning the great river. The city of Namradan lay across it. His horse's hooves clattered against the bridge stones, causing echoes that announced his arrival. He rode on, the soldiers following him. Entering the streets at the other end, masses of people lined the way as he rode toward the palace.

Amidst cheers and throngs of people, they halted in the palace courtyard. The guards were all staring at him. He met their gaze calmly. He had come here at the request of Governor Folcan to meet the princess. No one would stop him from completing his mission.

He dismounted and strode toward the gate. "I am Andevaar. I'm here to meet with Princess Tahlea. Take me to her immediately." She'd have to break from whatever vitally important thing she was doing at this moment. Perhaps she was reclining in a comfortable chair with a plate of exotic food at her elbow? Maybe she was having her hair done. It was possible she was being fitted for a new gown.

The guard nodded, and one of his companions disappeared inside the doors. Were they just going to leave him standing here on the doorstep like a peddler? Didn't they realize who he was? Maybe they did, for they opened the doors and escorted him inside.

The guard led him to a small chamber furnished with a few chairs. "Please wait here," he said.

Under the soles of his boots, Andevaar felt the softness of a patterned rug. Draperies of a fine smooth fabric hung around the window. Despite all Andevaar's plans, this was his first visit to the palace. The building was beautiful, with graceful stonework. The furniture in even this small room was finely carved, richly upholstered, and lovingly polished. He sat down, settling into the chair with a comfortable sigh. Still, all this was only a distraction from what he'd come for.

A few moments later, a servant in fine palace livery appeared with a silver tray. "May I offer you some refreshment?" He set down the tray and departed.

Gazing down at it, Andevaar took in the pitcher and glass and a selection of beautiful pastries. Strawberry tart. He fought the urge to pick it up and throw it against the wall. How dare they? These people had lived their whole lives with everything they wanted right at their fingertips when others had nothing. His hands tightened into fists.

His throat was dry from the ride. He lifted the glass and sipped a pale delicious juice, the perfect mix of sweet and tart. Lovely. It must be nice to live in such luxury. The princess probably never even had to ask for anything.

Years ago, King Allenthal threw a party when his daughter turned five. Andevaar had been one of the nameless, unnoticed people in the crowd watching a slender little girl with a serious face and long dark hair walk forward and lift her hand in an imperious wave. An exquisite gown draped her small form, and a silver circlet rested on her head. King Allenthal, looking powerful and self-important, had stood behind the girl. His smile had invited the people to love the child as much as he did.

It wasn't that simple. Back then, she had been an innocent child, and now, she was grown and held the power of a kingdom in her hands.

A voice disturbed his memories.

"If you'll follow me, Sir?" the servant spoke from the doorway.

It was time.

The servant guided Andevaar through the marble passageways to the door of an enormous hall. She would meet with him in the throne room? Pretentious. Well, he wouldn't cower, if that's what she intended.

His head erect and his shoulders square, Andevaar strode up the long room. Tall windows let in light from both sides. A raised dais at one end held the ancient throne of Seven Rivers. It was elaborately carved and trimmed with gold and gems. He'd expected to see her seated in it. Instead, his eyes moved to a smaller, plainer chair to one side, where a girl with long dark hair and the same serious expression he remembered from his youth watched him approach. She wore a gown of deep green velvet and long gloves. Gems glittered at her throat and wrist, and a silver crown settled into her hair.

A large man in a military uniform stood at her shoulder. The scar along his face made him recognizable. General Kylith. By all accounts, he was a valuable friend or a dangerous adversary. He wore several weapons, and if rumor could be believed, knew how to use them well.

Andevaar stopped at the edge of the dais and bowed. The princess didn't deserve his adulation, but the occasion required it. He wasn't here to start a disturbance today. It was her place to address him first. For a long moment, they met each other's gaze.

Her eyes were a deep brown, her skin ivory, and her expression impassive. Though she was still young, she had obviously had years of practice concealing her thoughts and emotions.

Finally, she spoke. "Governor Folcan speaks very highly of you. I invite you to introduce yourself."

Her voice was clear and smooth. Arrogant.

He kept his own tone confident. "My name is Andevaar. It has been my honor to serve the people of Edri Province in their hour of need."

She inclined her head in acknowledgment. "The governor is very grateful for your service. We are all grateful for what you've done to help."

He bowed again. "I appreciate the opportunity. Since I was fortunate enough to be nearby, I did what I could. When most of these attacks occurred, your highness's soldiers were not on hand to protect the people. I felt I must offer my aid to those in distress."

At that comment, he caught a slight tightening of her jaw. He wanted to sneer. Of course, she'd sent troops, but his plans had been well-laid, and her soldiers were far behind him.

Her eyes met his. "How did you manage to be present at attacks in so many varied locations?"

He allowed the ghost of a smile to lift his mouth. "I am a fortunate man, Your Highness. Luck is certainly a factor. But my business takes me to many places. I travel extensively to establish trade."

Did she believe him? Those cool brown eyes gave nothing away.

"I see." Her tone was neutral but lacked any warmth.

He went on. "I'm only a humble merchant, Your Highness. I wish nothing more than to enjoy peace and run my business. Unfortunately, many of my friends and neighbors have been the victims of these brutal attacks, and they looked to you for protection. When no relief came, I did what I could."

She gave no obvious reaction to the censure in his words. Could she tell he was trying to goad her? Perhaps her jaw tightened a little more, while her slender fingers gripped the arms of her chair.

Her chest rose in a long slow breath and her hands relaxed until they lay smoothly against the dark wood. "We will not allow this violence to continue."

He nodded toward her. "I applaud your efforts, of course. You took action as soon as word of the unrest reached you. Yet, the attacks continue. They will go on unless you stop them. It's possible they will expand beyond the borders of Edri soon. I have put myself and my friends at substantial risk all over *my* province in order to keep the people safe."

"Your efforts are praiseworthy, and you have our gratitude. I assure you, I will not rest until we find a solution." Her piercing gaze met his. "Can you tell me who is behind the attacks?"

He rubbed his chin in apparent thought. "There is a man who leads them: a formidable fighter, always seen mounted on a black horse. He wears the image of a hawk on his tunic. Many of the people call him by that name."

"Do you know who he is?"

"How would I find that out, Your Highness?" Andevaar met her eyes. "I have faced him in battle several times, but he covers his face. If we might locate his horse, that would be an important clue. The animal is distinctive."

"And he fights well?"

"He does."

She was silent, sending another long look at him. "But not as well as you?"

Maybe she was trying to provoke a reaction from him. He wasn't going to give her one. "I have managed to defend myself so far. I do the best I can. My goal is to find him and reveal his identity so he can face the justice he deserves."

She nodded. "That is our goal as well. We appreciate your help. Since you have such a gift for finding the outlaw, I will send two dozen of my own guards to help you."

Andevaar nodded at her with the appearance of gratitude. She wanted to know what he was doing, and she thought sending more of her own men to watch him would give her information. Let her send them. He would make sure they saw only what he wanted them to see. He smiled politely at her. "That's very gracious of you."

She didn't react. Her face remained impassive. "If you find any information that may lead to the capture of this criminal, I ask you to report to General Kylith."

"Very well, Crown Princess. I will pass any information I might discover along to him."

Regally, she rose to her feet. She was taller than he expected, but maybe it was just the steps between them. "Andevaar, I thank you for your service to our kingdom and for meeting with us today." She nodded to him and then swept from the room. The velvet folds of her gown fell gracefully around her as she went to the side door and disappeared. His audience was over. But what did that matter? Soon, the other provinces would love him as much as Edri did. When Crown Princess Tahlea failed to capture the outlaw, the people would be forced to look for another option. He would be ready.

CHAPTER 7

CROWN PRINCESS TAHLEA

T ALLY PACED SLOWLY ALONG the portrait gallery, her hands clasped behind her back. She paused before the painting of her father, stern and regal, inside his gold frame. "How would you have handled *that* man today?" She wished she could hear his answer now. After reviewing the meeting with Andevaar endlessly in her mind, she still wasn't sure how it had gone. Not well. She had felt herself behaving stiffly, constantly striving not to react to Andevaar's less-than-subtle barbs.

She had never before encountered anyone so arrogant. It was in his walk, the commanding stride that assumed others would get out of his way. His burnished gold armor and red cape had only enhanced her impression. He expected every eye to follow him. She couldn't blame them if they did. He was tall and his presence commanding. Dark hair brushed his shoulders, framing a strong jaw covered by a short beard. His eyes were his most memorable feature, dark and piercing. They noticed everything. Had he cut through her defenses and read her emotions?

Hopefully not, but how could she know for sure? She had hoped in vain that he would give something away during their conversation. Well-accustomed to reading people, she had intended to gather information about his motives. Instead, he had attempted to push her into displaying her worries and fears about the unrest in her kingdom.

She hissed in frustration and moved past the portrait of her grandfather to the picture of her great-grandmother, Queen Tahlathea. The artist had painted her as a young woman, though there were other likenesses of her as she aged. She'd ruled the Seven Rivers until she was nearly eighty. In the painting, the queen stood straight and tall, a crown on her head and a scepter in her hand. She appeared supremely confident and commanding.

Tally reached out to touch the frame. "You never let anyone intimidate you, did you?" she murmured. "You ruled with power. Was there ever a moment when you weren't sure what to do?" The painted eyes of Queen Tahlathea gazed serenely back at her.

Smiling slightly at her own foolishness, Tally lowered her hand. For now, she must be the princess her people needed. One day, she would be queen, though hopefully not for many years. She would rule because it was her duty. There was no room for doubt or for some arrogant young man to try to destroy her. She could not allow that to happen.

Familiar, firm footsteps came along the hall behind her, and she turned to face Kylith.

He bowed and straightened to face her. "Andevaar is gone, Princess, already on his way back to Edrithil."

"Were you able to find out anything else about him?"

Kylith shook his head. "Nothing we didn't already know."

Her lips tightened. "Either way, it's time. We'll ride at dawn."

He cleared his throat. "You already know my feelings. I only want to keep you safe."

He did not approve of her plan to visit the mystic, and he'd made his opinion very clear. She understood his reasons. He felt she'd be more secure here in Namradan than riding with the army. His opinion hadn't changed her mind.

She raised her eyes to meet his. "I know how you feel. But I cannot leave the fate of my kingdom to anyone else. I won't. I trust you and the guards to keep me safe."

His eyebrows lowered and his jaw tightened. "How can I do that if you leave the protection of the army and travel into the mountains? It would be immediately obvious that you'd gone somewhere."

Tally put on a sweet smile. "Not if someone takes my place."

He shook his head. "Another girl wearing your clothes won't fool anyone if they get close."

She met his gaze. "It will be your job to make sure no one gets that close."

Kylith's expression darkened. "Are you talking about Mariella? Have you considered that you might put her in danger? And what about the risk to your own safety? Out in the mountains with only a few guards, anything could happen. What would the rest of us do without you? We have no other heir."

"I'll be careful," she promised. "I'm trusting you to keep Mariella safe, and I'll keep Gerran close. He'll make sure nothing happens to me."

"You know I don't agree," Kylith growled. "But the final choice is yours, Princess."

She nodded. "Good. We ride at dawn."

"Very well." His expression sank into a frown as he stalked away, leaving her alone as the evening light shone through the high windows in the gallery. With a last glance at her great-grandmother's portrait, she walked in the opposite direction.

Just down the hall from her own quarters, Tally knocked on the door of Mariella's rooms, and her maid answered.

"Come in, Princess," she invited, "I'll let Lady Mariella know you are here."

Mariella appeared a moment later, dressed in a soft white nightgown covered by a thick robe. "Tally? What is it?"

Tally took a deep breath. "Maybe we should sit down?" They moved to the plush sofa and seated themselves.

Mariella's eyes widened. "Is something wrong? You look like you're trying to share bad news."

Tally shook her head quickly. "No, nothing like that. I need to ask a favor of you. I spoke to Divine Namradill."

"At the ceremony?"

"No. I went to visit Her two days ago."

Mariella put a hand to her chest. "What did She tell you?"

Tally's fingers tightened in her lap. "Maybe some of it is bad news. She told me that Andevaar is behind the attacks in Edri."

Mariella gasped, her hand flying to her mouth. "But that can't be! He's Drake's friend, and he's been saving people. He can't be the one attacking them. That doesn't make sense."

Putting a hand on her friend's shoulder, Tally bowed her head. "I'm sorry. If it's true, and they really are friends, this news doesn't reflect well on Drake."

"I'm sure it's only some kind of misunderstanding," Mariella protested. "Drake would never be involved with something like that. He's an honest businessman, not a criminal."

Despite her friend's protest, Tally went on. "I hope that's true, and I'm sorry to speak ill of either of them, but I have to discover the truth. I'm leaving in the morning to do just that. I wondered if you would be willing to go with me?"

Mariella's eyebrows rose. "What? Me? I would do anything to support you... but..."

"I'm sorry to have to ask this of you, especially after casting doubt on the motives of the young man you care for."

Mariella's expression softened at the mention of Drake. She was thinking of him. That was obvious.

Tally wanted to stand by her friend. "I promise, I won't form any final opinions about Drake until we get to the bottom of this," she said. "But I have to protect my people, and I cannot ignore the instructions given to me by Divine Namradill."

Mariella smiled slightly at her promise. "Thank you for that, Tally. I hope you're wrong about Drake. The more I get to know him, the more I like him, and I can't imagine he'd do anything bad. What did the goddess tell you to do?"

This was the difficult part of the plan. "She told me to visit the Mystic Thorvan in the mountains above Edri. It would take a few days to reach him and return, and I'm hoping to make the journey in secret."

Shock appeared on Mariella's face. "But if you leave the army, won't everyone know you're gone?" Realization suddenly washed over her. She held up her hand, palm toward Tally. "Don't tell me."

Tally nodded.

Mariella's face paled, and her lips trembled. "So, you don't want me to simply go with you. You want me to *be* you while you're gone?"

"I wouldn't ask if the situation wasn't serious." Tally put a comforting hand on her friend's arm. "General Kylith and his men will protect you every second. If no one realizes that I'm gone, there will be much less chance of something happening while I'm out there with only a few guards."

Mariella shivered. "What if something happens to you out there?"

"I'll make sure it doesn't," Tally promised. "All we have to do is travel to Edri. Who knows, you might even see Drake there." Maybe if they did, they could learn more about his true character and motives.

Mariella looked thoughtful. "That's true." She looked around the comfortable room. "I've been here all these years with you, and you've almost never asked me for anything. What kind of friend would I be if I refused your request, after all you've given me?"

Tally hugged her. "You never had to do anything to earn my friendship. You'll have it no matter what. Thank you, Mariella."

Mariella groaned. "We'll be on horseback the entire way!"

"We could take a carriage," Tally said. "But I would prefer to ride, especially with the army."

With a resigned sigh, Mariella nodded. "Everyone knows you'd rather be on horseback. So, if I'm going to be you..."

Tally and Mariella both survived the first few days of riding in dresses. They traveled side by side, while Gerran and the other guards surrounded them. The extra caution seemed ridiculous as they rode along peaceful roads and through quiet villages. The peace was only an illusion. Tally's lands were in turmoil. Occasionally, they passed buildings or fields that had recently been burnt. No doubt the result of raids by Hawk and his outlaws.

When the army stopped for the night, they pitched a tent for the ladies, and, so far, aside from long hours in the saddle, they had endured little discomfort.

Once the evening meal was over, Tally and Mariella retired to their tent. In the light of a lantern, Tally loaded her gear into a backpack: food, a leather waterskin, rough wool blankets, and other necessities. Mariella watched her. "You'll be careful out there?"

Tally smiled. "I promise."

Mariella held up a long brown wig they had brought to complete her disguise. "I never pictured myself with dark hair."

"You can have your own back in only a few days." Tally checked her sword belt and added a knife.

Staring at the weapons, Mariella bit her lip. "They don't expect me to... act like you? I can't fight, and if I get off my horse, everyone will notice I'm suddenly four inches shorter than I'm supposed to be."

Mariella was a good friend to agree to this plan at all. Tally shook her head. "You won't have to do anything. Just look like me, ride along, and Kylith will keep his men around you. No one else will get near you. He'll do the same when you get to Edrithil. Once you're there, you can be yourself again. Kylith will make sure no one sees the princess."

Mariella gave a determined nod. "It will be all right. We can do this. Only... Tally, please be careful?"

In the dark before dawn, Tally dressed in trousers, a blue army tunic, and light armor. She buckled her weapons around her waist and shouldered her pack. Mariella watched her from the warmth of her blankets. "Be safe."

Tally bent to grip her friend's shoulder. "You too. I'll see you soon."

In the starlight, Tally slipped through the silent camp. Gerran and two other men waited for her beside four saddled horses. He handed one set of reins to her, and she led the horse to the edge of the camp. The guards watched them pass silently. None of the sleeping soldiers stirred. They led the horses a little way from the last guards before they mounted, moving at a slow pace away into the predawn darkness.

The narrow road rose steeply before them. Soon, Tally could look back and see the whole encampment spread out beneath them. She was heading toward the secluded mountain valley where the Tower of the Mystics had stood for hundreds of years. It hadn't seemed hard to find on a map, but the reality might be very different. What would her father's old friend Thorvan do when they got there? Namradill had sent Tally to him, expecting some kind of solution. Would he be able to provide one?

The day became clear and bright, and the horses sweated as they climbed. The faint trail wound into the woods. It was cooler beneath the trees, but the thick vegetation offered many places to hide or set up an ambush.

Gerran's eyes scanned their surroundings constantly. Holding up his arm, he signaled the group to stop. "This way!" he hissed, turning to one side. He slid off his horse and pulled the animal off the road into a thicket of young trees. Tally and the others quickly followed him. They stopped in the middle of the growth, where branches would hide them from sight. Gerran held his finger to his lips, ordering silence.

For several long moments, they all waited, hearing no sound but bird calls and the rustle of leaves in the breeze. The sound of voices carried faintly through the woods.

"He said to watch the road," a man's voice said.

It sounded like someone was already searching for them. Their departure was supposed to be a secret. Tally's lips pressed together in frustration.

"...don't see anyone. Maybe we passed them."

"No. The others spotted them down below. They can't be far from here."

Tally's eyes flew to Gerran. He was shaking his head and cursing silently. Someone had discovered their departure. Maybe they didn't know she was with them. Maybe they were only guarding their territory. Maybe.

They remained in their hiding place until everything was quiet. "We need to stay off the road," Gerran said. "Everyone keep your eyes open. If they find us, we're going to be outnumbered." He fixed the other soldiers with a hard stare. "Our job is to protect the princess, no matter what."

The two, a quiet soldier named Ervan, and Will, a lean man with red-brown hair, nodded. "Understood," Will said.

They mounted again, following Gerran on a winding route that more or less hid them from sight. They hurried on as the sun sank behind a distant ridge and the light faded.

In the gathering dark, Tally pulled her horse to a stop behind Gerran. He was staring into the woods. A gleam of orange light flickered from a campfire. They heard the distant murmur of voices. Gerran pointed into the woods, directing them to the right, and the four slipped away into the gathering dark.

It was nearing midnight when they finally stopped in the shadow of a rocky outcropping. A patch of thick grass provided good grazing for the horses. Tally sat down beside Gerran with her back resting against a boulder. For a long moment, they were all silent, munching on cold food from their packs.

"They're already looking for us." Gerran glanced at Tally. "We hoped that wouldn't happen. Maybe they have more spies than we thought."

"How much farther is it to the tower?" Will asked.

"Another couple of days." Gerran rubbed a hand over his face. "I hope that as we climb higher, we'll encounter fewer people in the woods."

"Unless they're following us," Tally pointed out.

Gerran rested his head against the rock and closed his eyes. "I hope not. Get some rest. We'll divide the night into three watches."

"Four," Tally protested.

Gerran grinned. "Since the goal is to guard *you*, what would be the point of that?"

She crossed her arms over her chest and met his gaze. "My eyes work just as well as anyone else's."

The others laughed. "I'm sure she's right," Will said.

Tally stared at Gerran expectantly. "I hope you're not disrespecting my ability to watch for trouble?"

He shook his head. "Princess, I wouldn't dare. Four watches. I'll wake you when my turn is up."

They made it another day and a half before trouble found them. As the day faded into afternoon, they rode beside a stand of thick trees when a shout rang out behind them. A band of raggedly dressed men armed with swords and axes stepped from the cover of the branches to block their way.

"Just come with us," one man said, raising his weapon. "If you don't fight, we won't hurt anyone."

Tally heard several horses coming up behind them. The heavy forest growth blocked escape on one side, and a steep ravine cut to the other. Putting a hand on her sword hilt, Tally looked behind them to see a troop of horses, at least a dozen, if not more.

"Ride!" Gerran yelled, urging his horse off the brink of the steep slope. Tally followed, her stomach dropping as she looked down. Bracing herself against the stirrups and leaning far back in the saddle, she held on as the horse skidded and slipped in the loose earth and stones. She hoped Will and Ervan were behind them, but she couldn't look. All she could do was stay in the saddle, keep her balance, and hope the horse didn't miss its footing and roll.

Her mount stumbled twice but kept its feet. They came out at the bottom, she and the animal both panting. There wasn't time to rest. Will and Ervan made it safely off the slope just behind her. "This way!" Gerran urged his horse on. He followed the narrow floor of the ravine downward for a moment, until it branched, and he turned his horse into the other fork and headed up the new path.

Loose rock filled the gully, making treacherous footing for the horses. They picked their way through. At this pace, the outlaws would catch up. Already, she could hear voices behind them. The sides of the draw grew gradually shorter until they came out into the forest. The trees were large and widely spaced, with little undergrowth, which was good for riding but not so good for avoiding pursuit.

Gerran picked up the pace, and for a few moments, they left their enemies behind. When the riders behind reached the open forest, they picked up speed as well. Shouts echoed through the trees. Gerran urged his horse forward, and Tally followed him.

They rode as fast as the horses could manage. Finally, they had to stop and rest the animals. Moving behind a group of boulders, they dismounted, watching the slope below them. After a few moments, a rider came into view. He appeared to be searching for them or for any sign of their passing. He wandered to the left and then the right, but, somehow, never came any nearer.

"What's he doing?" Tally hissed. "Why doesn't he follow us?"

Another rider appeared, then several more. None of them rode up the slope toward them. For an hour, they watched the searchers comb the woods without ever coming in the right direction.

Gerran bumped her with his elbow. "Let's go."

They led their mounts to a small stream where they all drank. Still hearing no close pursuit, they mounted and rode on at a slow pace. They were drawing close to the stark, bare mountain peaks. At this high altitude, occasional snowfields remained from the winter chill. Yellow flowers bloomed in the damp earth, springing up immediately when the snow retreated.

Coming over a rocky rise, they rode into a sheltered valley hidden at the base of the peaks. A round tower built of gray stone drew Tally's gaze. An unlikely structure in the middle of the mountains. Distinctive. This could only be the Tower of the Mystics. Tally saw no sign of human habitation other than the tower itself.

They rode up to a door made of thick, rough planks bound with rusted iron. It didn't appear to have been opened in some time. Gerran knocked, his heavy fist making a dull sound against the hardwood. No response came. He knocked again, not receiving any other result. He lifted the latch and shoved the door open. It moved unwillingly, just wide enough for him to enter.

"Hello?" he called.

Inside, it was utterly silent. Tally followed the others into a round room ringed by a staircase built against the outer wall. Thick dust lay undisturbed over everything. Gerran circled the room, his boots leaving tracks. He returned to stand beside her.

"Check upstairs," he ordered the others. "See if you can find anyone."

The two soldiers climbed the staircase, their weapons ready, but they returned after only a few moments. "There's nothing here," Will said.

Gerran looked at Tally.

"He has to be here somewhere." Tally rubbed the hilt of her dagger as she thought. Could he have left? Where might he have gone?

"I think it's been years since your father saw him," Gerran said. "Maybe he's dead."

A thread of worry worked its way through her mind. Namradill wouldn't have sent her to the tower unless Thorvan was here. But what if something had happened to him? The outlaws weren't very far from here. Maybe they had already found the old man alone and captured or killed him?

They walked back out into the late afternoon sunshine, pulling the door closed behind them. "We'll make a wider search of the area," Tally said.

Gerran nodded, and they headed back toward their horses. Tally had one foot in the stirrup when she saw a man, nothing more than a motionless shape beneath one of the ancient trees.

She removed her foot and put it back on the ground. "There's someone there." She pointed.

CHAPTER 8

CROWN PRINCESS TAHLEA

GERRAN STAYED AT HER side, his hand on his sword hilt, as Tally walked toward the gray figure in the shadow of the trees. The others hurried to join them.

A man in a rough wool cloak came forward to meet them. His hair was gray, his back slightly stooped, and his stride was careful and slow. He didn't appear to be bothered by the sight of the well-armed soldiers but came toward them without hesitation. When his eyes met Tally's, he smiled warmly.

"Crown Princess Tahlea." He greeted her with a bow. "I came to Namradan to celebrate with King Allenthal on the occasion of your fifth birthday. You've grown since then."

One corner of Tally's mouth rose. "Perhaps a little. You must be Thorvan."

"Yes, Princess." The old man smiled again. "You and your friends are welcome here. How may I serve you?"

She glanced back down the hill. "Outlaws nearly caught us not far from here. Have you seen them? They aren't far away, and I worry they will find you here. You would be in great danger if they attack."

His gaze sharpened. "I know where they are. But *they* don't know I am here."

"If they search the area, won't they find you?" The thought of a single old man confronted by a dozen ruffians wasn't pleasant.

Thorvan smiled and shook his head. "They can't find this valley."

"Do you mean they haven't yet?" Gerran asked.

Thorvan shook his head. "No, I mean they *can't* find it. Did you observe they couldn't follow you too close to the edge of my land?"

Tally's mind flew back to their pursuers ranging back and forth but seeming unable to find the path ahead. "You prevented them from finding their way?"

The old man waved his hand dismissively. "Of course. No matter how they might search for a way in, no one enters this valley without my permission."

That was impressive. Tally had been so worried about the old man, but it seemed that he wasn't in any danger. She searched her memory for anything else her father had told her about the power of the Mystics. They were the literal descendants of Namradill in her physical form, having a portion of her power passed down to them through the generations.

Tally looked into Thorvan's serene blue eyes. "Divine Namradill told me to seek you out. My father spoke very highly of you. He said you might help, if our land should be in need."

"Of course," Thorvan replied. "I will do all I can. Please, follow me. We will find rest and refreshment, and you can tell me everything." He turned away into the forest.

"I thought the tower was your home." Tally pointed at the stone structure.

Thorvan turned back and glanced up at it. "It *is* imposing. But it's not very comfortable. Bring your horses and follow me."

Tally breathed a sigh of relief as he led them through the forest. She had arrived safely, found Thorvan, and he was willing to help. For the moment, none of them were in danger from the outlaws within his valley. A hard knot of tension in her neck eased a little.

They led their mounts along a mountain path until they entered a grove of enormous trees standing in the shadow of steep cliffs. Their steps were nearly silent as they walked on a thick carpet of fallen needles. The air was warm and fragrant with the tang of pine trees.

Evening was falling. Coming suddenly out into the golden light, Tally saw a lovely green meadow and a little cottage and barn tucked against the rocky slope of the mountain. Two horses grazed contentedly inside a pasture surrounded by a fence built of unpeeled logs.

"Your horses may rest here," the old man gestured, opening a gate. Tally and the others led their mounts inside. In only a few moments, the animals were grazing contentedly, and Thorvan led them toward the house. "Please, come with me. You also need to rest and eat."

They followed the old man to the door of the cottage. He opened it for them, inviting them in. It was a cozy little place, with a stone fireplace, a tiny loft overhead, and a rough wooden table scrubbed spotlessly clean. A young man with curly brown hair stirred something in a pot suspended over the fire. Thorvan introduced him. "My grandson, Toban."

Toban bowed to Tally and smiled, his expression good-natured.

Tally returned the smile. "I'm pleased to meet you, Toban." She was glad the old man didn't live here alone. While this place was beautiful, she was sure it could be lonely.

Thorvan drew back a chair for Tally. "Please, be comfortable."

She took the offered seat. There were only three chairs around the little table, but the old man seated Will and Ervan on sections of log near the fire. Gerran sat down beside Tally. With all of them inside, the little place seemed even smaller.

"We can talk after we eat. You must be hungry," the old man said, taking a stack of wooden bowls from a shelf. He handed them to Toban, who filled them and passed them around.

Tally's stomach growled at the sight of food, and whatever they'd been cooking smelled delicious. She accepted a bowl and spoon gratefully. "Please eat," Thorvan said, cutting thick slices from a loaf of brown bread.

For several minutes, they all ate. He'd served them a stew with tender meat and vegetables. His bread was excellent. None of them had eaten a hot meal for days, and they all ate with enthusiasm. Tally accepted a second slice of bread. The old man appeared unusually prepared, considering that four sudden guests had appeared.

When she'd finished chewing, she turned to Thorvan, who was seated across from her, calmly finishing his meal. "Thank you for your hospitality. You're very kind to feed us. How many people live here?"

Thorvan smiled serenely. "Just the boy and me, and..."

A small child burst into the cottage and ran to embrace Thorvan. Strands of fair hair escaped her braid, and she clutched a fistful of rapidly wilting wildflowers. "Look what I found! If I put them in water now, they'll be all right, won't they?"

Thorvan took down a cup from the shelf. "Get some water and you can put them in this."

As the little girl took the cup, she spotted their visitors. Her eyes looked enormous in her small face as she surveyed Gerran and his weapons. She stepped closer to Thorvan and gripped him. "We have guests, Leya," Thorvan explained, putting a reassuring arm around her. "This is Tahlea, Crown Princess of the Seven Rivers."

Leya stared at Tally in wonder. "Are you a real princess?"

"Yes."

The child shook her head. "You can't be."

"Why not?" Tally asked.

"Princesses wear pretty dresses and crowns." The child eyed Tally's boots and army tunic critically.

Many people in her life seemed to have that expectation. Tally lowered her voice confidentially. "Don't worry. I have them, but I left them back in the city. There's no way to get here except riding, and that's very hard to do in a dress."

Leya appeared to accept that answer. "That's true." She came closer and looked Tally in the eye. "You're beautiful like a princess, even if you aren't wearing a dress." Her gaze became penetrating. "I think you're a good princess."

Tally smiled. "That's a very kind compliment coming from such a fair maiden."

Leya giggled. Thorvan put his hand on the girl's shoulder. "My dear, now that you've met the princess, you can take your flowers outside to arrange them. Toban can help you, if you wish."

"Yes, grandfather." The child skipped to the door and disappeared. Toban rose and followed her. Thorvan smiled fondly after them.

"Your granddaughter?"

"In a manner of speaking," Thorvan said. "Even though I live in this remote place, I maintain contact with many people. Sometimes, children are born with an unusual concentration of the blood of Divine Namradill in their veins, which suggests the possibility of them becoming mystics as they grow up. I knew of Leya soon after she was born, and when her mother died, it was my honor to take her into my care."

Tally looked toward the pot of stew. "Only three of you live here, and you just happened to prepare food for all of us?"

Thorvan's blue eyes twinkled as he met her eyes across the table. "Have you no respect for a mystic? I knew you were coming."

Tally's eyes widened. She should have realized. "It's still very kind of you to feed all of us." She looked toward the two soldiers sitting near the hearth.

Will cleared his throat and got to his feet. "We appreciate your hospitality, Mystic Thorvan," he said politely. "We'll check on the horses." He jogged Ervan with his elbow, and they headed out the door.

Tally turned back to Thorvan. "Do you know why I came?"

He took in a long breath. "I believe so, but tell me anyway. What guidance have you received from Divine Namradill?"

Tally met his eyes. "She told me a man named Andevaar is my enemy."

The old man's eyebrows raised. "And what has he done?"

At the mention of Andevaar, Tally felt all her muscles tighten. "I believe he intends to seize control of the Seven Rivers. He's already gained great influence in Edri. Mysterious bandits have attacked our people, and, somehow, Andevaar is there just in time to rescue them. What can the people do besides be grateful to him? I think he caused the whole situation."

Thorvan regarded her thoughtfully. "There have been many troubles in Edri, but, recently, it has grown quiet."

"There's no more fighting because he's won. Everyone in Edri adores him as a hero. Even Governor Folcan. They're all on his side." Tally fought the urge to jump from her chair and pace the room.

Thorvan rubbed the gray beard on his chin. "Have you met this man?"

Tally nodded. "Once." Not something she would easily forget.

"What was he like?"

Tally gritted her teeth, remembering the subtle attacks behind his apparently gracious words. "He doesn't wish me well. I felt he was polite only on the surface."

"Did he anger you?"

What a strange question for the old man to ask. She met his eyes, trying to discern the meaning behind the question. Even though his tone had been perfectly mild, Tally felt her temper rise again. She couldn't allow that to happen. Her father had trained her for years not to speak hastily. Now she needed to put the good of her kingdom first.

Taking in a long deep breath, she smoothed her expression. "I confess, he made me angry. But my own feelings aren't important. He means to conquer my people, and I can't stand by and allow that to happen. Innocent people have already died, and the rest look to me for protection. Divine Namradill revealed that Andevaar is behind all this trouble, and I believe Her. There is other evidence that also points to him."

Thorvan nodded. "The Goddess is wise. She sees much more than any person could, and she has protected the Seven Rivers for centuries. You're right to listen to Her."

Tally rested her forearms on the table and leaned forward to look at him. "She told me to ask for your help, and I know my father trusted you. What can I do about Andevaar?"

Thorvan sat back in his chair; his expression was thoughtful. "So, you believe that all the trouble stems from this one man? That he made himself appear a hero?"

"I do." Tally said. "It's all just too convenient." She exchanged a glance with Gerran who remained beside her. He listened quietly, but his eyebrows drew down in anger. Andevaar's men had already put them in danger on their way here.

"But, of course, he's not acting alone," Thorvan said. "If we remove him, there will be others."

"Yes," Gerran said in agreement.

"True," Tally admitted, "but with him gone, we can unravel the rest of it. Could you use your powers to…" she cleared her throat and shifted in her chair, "get rid of him?"

The old man raised his bushy eyebrows, and Tally felt a twinge of guilt in her belly.

She squared her shoulders. "Not for me," she said firmly. "I would not ask it for myself, only to save other lives and for the good of my kingdom."

"Could you bear this man's blood on your hands?" His expression was serious.

"I don't want to hurt anyone, but if killing him saves the lives of my people, then yes." She gathered her determination. "Whatever it takes to help my people. I am charged with protecting them."

It was better to have one life lost than lose many more, she knew that, but the thought was horrible. She shook her head. "There must be another solution."

"I agree," Thorvan said. "When so many people love him, if you cause harm, you'll make him a martyr."

Thorvan was right. The last thing Tally needed was the people's hero dead or locked up. It would only unite his allies to fight harder for him. There had to be another way. "How do we stop him without making a martyr of him? Do your powers offer a solution?"

"Perhaps," Thorvan said, rubbing his chin. "But we can only use my mystic's power for healing or defense. I cannot simply strike him down."

They looked at each other silently for several long moments. Finally, Thorvan's blue eyes lit up, and he grinned. "I have an idea. I can create an enchantment. It will not *harm* him exactly. Instead, he will lose his memory, his past, his ambitions, all of it. I feel certain that the Goddess would approve of this plan. I cannot cast any enchantment that She would not sanction."

Tally stared back at him, her eyes widening in surprise. "You can cause him to forget everything?"

"Of course," Thorvan said. "Well, not everything. He would still remember the basic skills needed to live life. But he won't remember who he is. Or anyone else."

"Would it be permanent?"

The old man rubbed his chin, considering. "Is that what you want?"

A wave of hope surged through her. Thorvan's plan might work. It could be the solution she needed so badly. Tally attempted to analyze the situation from every angle. What reason could she have for returning the man's memories later? The facts swirled around in her head: Andevaar, the people of Edri, unknown attackers, burnt farms, a hero who had saved them and tricked them into placing him in command of all the soldiers in the province. How could Tally possibly anticipate every potential result of this plan? But she had to make a choice. Her eyes met Thorvan's.

"I suggest this," Thorvan said, rubbing his hands together. "I will create the enchantment and bind it to your hand. When you touch his skin and say 'praeteren,' it will take effect. It will not be instant, but, within a couple of hours, his memory will be entirely erased. The change will remain permanent unless *you* remove it. If you touch him again at a later time and say 'memini,' his memory will return."

Tally stared at Thorvan. His suggestion was unconventional, not what she'd expected. She'd pictured arresting Andevaar and throwing him in the dungeon for treason. Even with the power she wielded as a princess, she couldn't do that without more proof. If she took such shameless advantage of her position, it would breach the trust her people had built in her family over hundreds of years.

How was Thorvan's suggestion any different?

Either way, she had to do *something* about Andevaar. She was sure the spy in the palace had been gathering information for him, and Namradill had told her he had caused all the unrest. She needed a solution. Which choice would cost the fewest lives, cause the least suffering? "What would you do, Father?" she murmured, imagining King Allenthal's motionless form lying with the blue stone on his chest.

"He trusted you to make the right decision," Gerran said.

Gratitude warmed her, and she smiled at him, appreciating his confidence. She turned back to Thorvan. "It's been difficult with my father in stonesleep. I relied on him."

The old man nodded. "That's only natural, and I understand. Perhaps he isn't as far away as you think. I have sensed his presence intertwined with Divine Namradill. King Allenthal is a good man, and this time will allow the Goddess to teach him. Because of Her, your family has ruled wisely and fairly for centuries." The mystic's eyes were kind. "His time with Her will be extraordinary."

Tally looked back at him. What was her father experiencing at this very moment? What was it like to be with the Goddess? "Extraordinary..." she repeated.

"Well, what would you like to do?" he asked.

Tally took a deep breath. She turned and met Gerran's eyes beside her. "We've been friends for a long time. What do you think?"

He lowered his eyebrows, his hand straying to the hilt of his sword. "So, are we firm on the decision that killing him is not an option?"

"Not now," Tally said. "We need to expose his lies first."

"If he forgets all his lies, how can we expose them?" Gerran asked.

That was a good point. She rubbed the back of her neck as she thought. "It would be on us to expose them once he forgets. At least he could no longer carry on the deception. It would give us a foothold."

"There would be no way to get him to confess anything if his memories are gone," Gerran said.

That was also true. She turned it all over in her mind. Perhaps Thorvan had some foresight with his gifts, but she didn't. She turned back to the old man. "Do you know, in advance, if this will work?"

He smiled gently. "The future is clouded. Sometimes, with only a moment's thought, people leave a path they have been on for years and choose a new course. Every decision affects the people surrounding it."

She adjusted her question. "Will this choice help my people?"

"It will," Thorvan assured her.

Tally took a deep, steadying breath. How would she know if she was making the right decision? If only there were more time to decide, more facts to gather. This situation forced her to take immediate action. Namradill had sent her to Thorvan. For now, his idea seemed like the best plan. Tally decided to take his suggestion. She lifted her hands and dropped her palms flat against the table. "We will do as you say."

"Very well, we'll begin at once. Wait here," Thorvan said, getting to his feet. He went to a cabinet at the back of the room and searched through it, pulling out a shallow wooden bowl and several other items.

Tally exchanged a curious look with Gerran.

Thorvan returned to the table with the bowl in his arms. He set out bunches of strange herbs, a stone, and three candles. "Do you remember the words? Practice them before I have enacted the spell. It's all right to say them before we begin. They won't do anything yet." He lit the candles.

"Praeteren," she said clearly. "Praeteren."

"And the other?"

"Memini."

He nodded approvingly. "Be sure you commit them to your memory."

"Will it work on anyone?" Tally asked curiously.

"Yes, the enchantment will affect anyone you are touching when you say the word. So, I urge you to wait until the proper time. Each of the words will work only one time. You must be sure you have the right person before you use it."

A sudden worry came to her mind. "What if I can't find Andevaar?"

He looked up from his work. "You must leave this valley to complete your task. If you are right about his plans, he will find you." Thorvan resumed his seat opposite her, his blue eyes were penetrating under his heavy brows. "Are you ready? It is impossible to predict every consequence of using magic. Every enchantment is a serious thing."

It was Tally's duty to accept responsibility, and she was prepared. "I understand."

"Very well. Give me your hand."

Tally extended her right hand across the table. Thorvan had set his candles in a triangle around the bowl. He reached out to touch the stone set in the bowl, which was surrounded by leaves. It had seemed like an ordinary stone before, a dull gray. At the old man's touch, it glowed blue.

Instantly reminded of Namradill, Tally almost gasped, but she clamped her lips together and held still. This stone was much smaller, its light fainter. Thorvan grasped it between two fingers and picked it up. His lips moved as he spoke silent words. Standing slowly, he held the stone above her palm.

The blue light fell onto her palm. It was not just a glow, but a distinct pattern of symbols: an outer circle, with two concentric inner circles. Between them were figures, strange runes made of glowing blue light. In the center lay an image like a star with many points. It was beautiful. Her palm felt hot, and her skin tingled.

Thorvan held the stone there for several long moments. The image rotated slowly on her hand until he finally lowered the stone to touch her skin. There was a hissing sound and a sudden flash of blue light; she felt a minute shock against her skin, like a tiny spark of lightning. Then, the light was gone, and the old man held an apparently ordinary bit of rock between his fingers.

Tally glanced over at Gerran, who stared at her hand with wide eyes.

"The power will remain there, in your hand, until you're ready," Thorvan said. "Do not forget the words."

"I won't." She drew her hand back across the table and stared at her palm. No sign remained of the beautiful pattern. Her hand looked just as it had before, the skin cool again, the strange spark of power hidden.

"It's already growing dark," Thorvan said. "You and your friends should rest here tonight before you ride back."

Tally was eager to be on her way, but an uninterrupted night's sleep without watching for outlaws sounded blissful. "You are very kind, but there are four of us." She looked around the little cottage.

"There is fresh hay in the stable loft, and I have extra blankets."

"Thank you, Thorvan. We appreciate it. The stable will be perfect. That way, we won't disturb anyone when we leave early tomorrow."

"As you wish, Princess Tahlea."

She smiled at him. "Thank you for helping me, for helping our kingdom. I hope your efforts will save many more lives."

"I hope so too," he said, "and I am always here should you need me."

CHAPTER 9

ANDEVAAR

INSIDE THE MOUNTAIN FORTRESS of Sathar, Andevaar heard the clattering hooves of horses arriving and hurried out into the courtyard. Drake was there, dismounting beside several of their men. A glance at his face informed Andevaar that they had succeeded. All their hard work was about to pay off. Excitement welled up in him, and he strode to meet his friend.

The other riders led the horses toward the stables, leaving no one nearby. Still, Andevaar couldn't risk anyone hearing them. He raised his eyebrows in an unspoken question. Drake nodded. Triumph flooded through Andevaar, and he wanted to shout.

"Follow me." Andevaar crossed the courtyard and entered a passageway. He lit a lantern, and they descended a flight of stairs coming out in a hall with several doors leading off it. Andevaar opened a door and ushered his friend inside. In the soft glow of lantern light, they wound their way through stacks of crates and boxes to the back of the room. "Take one end." He gestured toward a crate, setting down the light. Together, they slid the large wooden box away from the wall to reveal a small, inconspicuous door. Andevaar took the keys out of his pocket.

He grinned and handed one to Drake. "There are only two. Don't forget where you put it."

While Andevaar fitted the key into the lock, Drake watched over his shoulder. The door opened to reveal a small space surrounded by the stone of the wall. Drake knelt beside him, opening a leather satchel and removing something heavily wrapped in cloth.

This was it. They were about to win a kingdom.

Drake placed the bundle carefully into the space and set the empty satchel beside it. Andevaar locked the door securely. Each of them taking an end, they slid the large crate back into place, hiding the door.

Andevaar's key hung on a leather cord, and he put it back around his neck. "No one saw you?"

"No one," Drake assured him. "I've been to the palace before. While I was there, I learned everything I needed to get in and out. I gave the king your regards."

Andevaar grinned. "I appreciate that. He didn't object when he found out we planned to take his daughter?"

Drake assumed a thoughtful expression. "He didn't *say* a word." Drake slipped the precious key deep into his pocket. "Where is she now? Have your spies brought news?"

Andevaar folded his arms across his chest, smiling. He hadn't expected the princess to be so rash. It was a turn of events he would never have planned for. Crown Princess Tahlea had left her army behind and sneaked away into the mountains with only a few guards. She must be more arrogant than he suspected to believe she could depart without anyone seeing her.

Over the last several months, Andevaar had placed two dozen of his most loyal men within the king's army. It had been worth it. "She's out here in the mountains, not far away."

Drake's eyes widened. "Why? What is she doing?"

Andevaar shrugged. Why would she place herself in such a vulnerable position? She couldn't possibly have a good reason. Maybe it was only poor judgment. He'd been right to set his plans in motion just as the king went to sleep. "Some of our men nearly caught her a few days ago. We have patrols extending along the mountainside in both directions. They will find her. Once we have the stone *and* the princess, it's over. We've won. Go back to Edrithil and make sure no one has cause to suspect us. I should have her within a few more days, and then I will return to work with Governor Folcan."

CHAPTER 10

CROWN PRINCESS TAHLEA

TALLY AND HER COMPANIONS made camp as the sun sank peacefully on the horizon. They had left Thorvan's two nights ago and, so far, the path had been clear. Still, Gerran kept watch while the others cared for the horses. Once the animals were picketed and grazing placidly, Tally gathered with the others to share a meal.

Chewing her ration of jerky, Tally sat with her back against a rock. When she finished, she took out her blankets and wrapped them around herself. The mountain night cooled quickly.

"Get some sleep," Gerran advised from where he had resumed his post, watching. "I'll make sure we change the guard. Rest now, and you can take the last watch."

Tally curled up with her back against the rock. "Wake me immediately if you hear anything," she ordered.

"I will, Princess."

Night wind whispered in the treetops, while the last bright shades of sunset faded and the stars came out. The bright points of light looked close enough to touch up here in the thin mountain air. For a long time, she stared at the sky. She was tired, but her mind ran in circles.

How was she going to get close enough to Andevaar to enact the spell? What if he discovered that she'd done something to him before he lost his memory? Her mind spun, reviewing a long list of things that could go wrong.

Restless horses awakened Tally from a light slumber. One of them snorted uneasily, and when she turned to look, the row of animals all had their heads up, alert and uneasy, staring off into the dark forest. Tally slipped out of her blankets and put her hand on the hilt of her sword. The night was black and silent.

"Gerran!" she hissed. The other sleeping forms started awake at the sound, reaching for their weapons. A shout of warning from Will, who had been standing guard, rang through the camp. A moment later, the dark shapes of men were everywhere. The soldiers jumped to their feet, drawing their weapons. Gerran moved to Tally's side, taking position to protect her.

Yells echoed through the woods and the sound of weapons clashing surrounded them. Outlaws. Tally needed to reach their leader, but she couldn't simply stop fighting and allow them to harm her friends. Enemies attacked from all sides, and she fought hard to defend herself. Ervan knocked down an outlaw and turned to meet Gerran's eyes. "There's too many," he said. "Will and I can hold them back while you get her out of here."

She wanted to object, but Gerran pulled her away from the others. Only one direction appeared free of enemies. His voice was tense as he ordered, "Come with me!"

Tally gripped his arm as they slipped through the dark, away into the forest. The shouts and cries grew fainter behind them. As they hurried between the dark trees, Tally stopped suddenly.

She heard something ahead: voices, a group of people. Standing beside Gerran with her back against a large tree, she waited, trying to force her rapid breathing to come and go silently.

Gerran held his sword ready. He also heard the enemies ahead of them. His voice was only a whisper, but Tally heard it. "I need you to go."

"No," she protested. "If they know who I am, they won't kill me. You should leave me and run."

Gerran's voice was grim. "I can't do that."

Another large band of attackers had followed them from the camp, and now they were stuck between the two groups. She caught Gerran's urgent command just before the clash of weapons sounded in the dark. "Run."

Tally bolted away into the dark, with underbrush scraping at her legs and branches whipping her face. After she put some distance behind her, she slowed, focusing on quieting her movements. She stayed in the shadows of trees and vegetation, slipping soundlessly through the brush.

Had Gerran been hurt or killed back there? Just because he had told her to go didn't make her feel any better about leaving him behind. In the distance, the sounds of pursuit came. She hurried on as fighting continued in the night, sometimes louder, sometimes almost gone, until it broke out in another place. Finally, Tally heard nothing at all. Had she lost them? She needed a place to hide until it was safe to look for her friends.

Creeping through the dark, she found a large fallen log. It lay on the ground, but as her hands traced along its length, she found a hollow that left a space between the trunk and the forest floor. She slid her body into the space and held still.

She hadn't been in her refuge long before several sets of stealthy footsteps approached. Silent and motionless, she heard them pass her and then return. A pair of boots stopped, and a man stood right beside the log without discovering her.

The searchers didn't speak, but she could tell that there were a lot of them. There were too many for one person to fight. Were they looking for *her* specifically or had she and her companions simply been in the wrong place at the wrong time? She heard the soft sound of their boots on the forest floor as they searched.

Some of the adrenaline remaining from the attack faded, leaving her tired and cold. Gerran had fought an entire group of them just to give her a chance to run. She couldn't let his efforts be in vain. Now she had to do what she could to get away. She still heard outlaws nearby. If she tried to move, they would find her. She needed to remain free in order to help the others.

Tally clenched her hand around the hilt of her knife. The gray light of dawn filtered through the woods. Her hiding place wouldn't stand up to a thorough search in the daylight. Where could she go? A sudden crunch of boots on the pine needles decided for her.

A rough hand seized her shoulder and dragged her from beneath the log. As he pulled her upright, Tally raised her knife and held the blade against the man's throat. "Who do you serve?" she demanded, pressing the blade against his neck just hard enough to break the skin.

He swallowed hard and released her. "The -the Commander."

"What's his name?" She took a step toward him, increasing the pressure on his neck.

"Please! They call him Hawk. He ordered us to find you. He told us any girl hiding in the forest would be the princess."

So, this man served the masked leader of the outlaws. That wasn't really a surprise. Tally increased the pressure of her blade. "Where is he now?"

"F-Fortress at Sathar, down the mountain."

Four of his friends were coming slowly up behind the man. "Stay back, or I'll cut his throat," Tally warned. "Back up."

Several pairs of hands seized her from behind, jerking her away from the first man. Hot anger tore through her, and she twisted the blade, leaving him with a nasty cut. She kicked, connecting hard and taking one down, while she tried to jerk her knife hand free. Tally dragged her wrist from their grasp, striking one in the side. More hands seized her.

They knocked her to the ground and pinned her against the dirt, twisting the knife from her grip. "Hold still, Princess," a rough voice ordered. Hands with a vise-like grip pulled her wrists together behind her and tied them. She struggled with all her strength. She couldn't stop fighting. If they took her, she couldn't help Gerran.

They dragged her back to her feet. In the new morning light, she could see them more clearly. At least a dozen men surrounded her. They were all armed, and many wore bits of armor, but no sign of a uniform or anything that might identify their allegiance. Who was this man they called Hawk? The fact that they called him commander seemed to indicate an organized military structure. Perhaps if she found him, she would find Andevaar, or at least news of his location.

One outlaw stepped forward to face her. He wasn't a large man, but his eyes looked cold and curiously blank. She couldn't detect a shred of emotion anywhere in his expression. "Princess," he sneered. "I'm sorry the commander couldn't be here to greet you himself."

"Who are you?" she demanded.

An icy smile twisted one corner of his mouth. "I don't have to tell you anything, but my name is Hargen." He bowed mockingly. Straightening, he seized her arm in a painful grip. Another outlaw clasped her other arm, and they marched her off through the woods.

Everything looked different in the daylight, but Tally picked out the route she'd taken during the night. Where were her friends? Her eyes darted frantically through the trees, dreading to find what she was searching for. A man in a blue tunic came into view as they passed a stand of small trees; he was lying unmoving on the ground.

"No!" her voice sounded strangled. "Gerran!" She struggled against her guards. "Let me go! He needs help!" Maybe he wasn't dead. He didn't move or respond to her call, and blood covered his face and several other places on his body.

"He's dead already," Hargen hissed beside her. "Another word from you, and I'll go back and make absolutely sure of it."

Her stomach dropped, and she stopped struggling. Gerran had been protecting her. It was her fault he lay there covered in blood. She had to find a way to help him.

The outlaws only gripped her tighter. Tally fought a sick churning in her stomach. She kept hearing Gerran's voice over and over in her mind, telling her to run. Why had she left him to face them alone? She shouldn't have gone.

On they marched. It took quite a while to reach the place where Tally had camped with her guards. As she desperately scanned the ground, she saw two more crumpled figures. They had come to protect her. How could she find the strength to lead if being Crown Princess meant watching others suffer and die for her?

An endless day passed, walking down the mountain. The tight cords dug into her wrists. Being bound filled her with simmering anger. They hadn't even allowed her to try to help her friends. There was no way to know if they were dead or only injured. She couldn't stop thinking about her companions, even though she badly needed a moment of privacy, a drink of water, and something to eat. Her captors had given her none of these things. At least she was alive and unhurt.

As the sun set, they came to a well-worn path leading into a rocky ravine. They followed the canyon until they stopped before a high stone wall with a strong gate. Inside, a single tower rose. Her captors marched her up to the entrance. Someone must have been watching, for it swung ponderously open and they all went in. The door swung shut with a dull thud behind them. This place would not be easy to get out of.

Three stone buildings surrounded an open courtyard paved with flagstones. The outer wall defended the rest of a narrow gorge. Now inside, she could see that the canyon went back a long way before it came to a dead end against high cliffs. There were many hastily constructed shacks and other tents and temporary structures.

The men dragged Tally toward one of the buildings and through the door. The place was filthy and furnished with only a rough table and benches.

A skinny, balding man got up when they entered and came to stand in front of her. He smiled, revealing dirty teeth, and the expression didn't reach his eyes. His voice was a menacing rasp. "Good evening, Princess. You must dress for your meeting."

"Meeting with whom?" she demanded. Would they take her to Hawk? Maybe he would give her some clue where Andevaar was. For a moment, she felt the skin of her palm tingle. She needed to find him soon.

The man did not answer her question. Instead, he nodded to Hargen, who still held her. Hargen unbuckled her belt, letting it and the empty sheaths of her knife and sword fall to the floor.

The brush of his fingers against her caused a flash of revulsion. "Don't touch me," she snapped.

The skinny man's smile grew wider. He held up a ragged, foul-smelling garment of indeterminate shape. "Your wardrobe, Princess."

Tally stared at him furiously. Surely, they didn't expect her to cooperate. Hargen drew a dagger and held the point of it against her throat. His breath burned against her ear while his hand clamped around her arm and the keen point of the blade against her neck stung. "Such soft skin," he whispered. "I would very much enjoy killing you."

Her stomach twisted in revulsion. The knife point reminded her that struggling wasn't an intelligent option at the moment. She concentrated on keeping her body still.

"I'll give you a chance to change your clothes by yourself." The skinny man looked her up and down, his gaze lingering offensively on her body. "Only one chance."

The desire to kick him was powerful. Tally wrestled down the urge. It wasn't wise with a knife at her throat. She could handle the bald man, and maybe Hargen, but she wasn't egotistical enough to think she could beat them all; there were more of them just outside.

"That armor must be so uncomfortable," Hargen said, pushing the knife point further into her skin. "Let me help." Her skin crawled as his fingers undid the buckles at her side and pulled the stiff leather over her head.

"I'm going to free your hands now," the bald man said. "You'd better behave. An entire army waits just outside. There's no way out of this valley except through the gates. You would not get out alive."

Hargen lowered the blade of his knife from her throat and slid it between her hands to cut the ropes. She felt relief and stinging pain as her numb fingers came back to life. She wanted to fight, but how would that go? For now, it was better to go along. So, she stood there rubbing her wrists.

The skinny man held out his arm with the ragged, shapeless tunic over it. "Well?"

Tally stared at him furiously. She reached for the rough garment and pulled it over her head.

"Oh no," the man protested. "Remove the other first."

The urge to attack them flared up even stronger.

Tally removed the blue soldier's uniform and tossed it onto the bench. She felt her cheeks color as the men leered at her in her chemise. Trying not to give them the satisfaction of a reaction, she forced her face into the serene expression she used when she had to make public appearances. She picked up the foul-smelling, ragged tunic and pulled it over her head. It was a shapeless bag of fabric that hung down past her hips. Lovely.

"Boots," the man ordered, a wide smile plainly showing that he was enjoying the entire process.

Tally glared at him as she unlaced her boots and pulled them off.

"And now the rest." He pointed toward her pants and stocking feet.

When it was all done, she stood there, legs and feet bare. She'd never left her room with this much skin showing.

"Very good," the bald man said. "They ordered me to be sure you weren't concealing any weapons."

"I can do that," Hargen said quickly, taking a step toward her.

Tally met his eyes. "Don't touch me," she snarled.

But the bald man nodded to him, and he seized her arm while his friend gripped her from the other side.

The bald man made his search, and Tally clenched her jaw at the feel of his hands on her skin. He took his time with the task, his fingers lingering against her flesh. No one had ever dared to touch her like this before. She longed for an entire company of loyal soldiers at her command to protect her and force him to stop. The door banged open, interrupting him.

"Bring her," another guard said, and they took her back out into the open. She dearly missed her armor and weapons. She felt exposed walking around with her arms and legs bare, and vulnerable with no shoes. There were more outlaws here than when she had crossed the courtyard before.

These were the men who'd been attacking villages. They knew who she was. Demanding that they respect her office would only make this worse. They didn't care. Instead, she resolved not to show any sign of weakness.

Outlaws filled the space, shouting and jeering at her. Tally clenched her jaw and stared straight ahead. The ranks of men closed in all around her until she and her escort were pushing through the crowd. Hands grabbed at her, not polite about where they touched her. A few swift kicks removed some of them, but there were more. She felt her face flush with embarrassment, and anger rose in her. No one had ever treated her so disrespectfully before. By the time they crossed the open space, she felt dirty.

At last, they reached the doors of one of the stone buildings, and they pulled her inside, leaving the disorderly men behind. The room was lit with torches. Her guards took her to one end and stood, one on either side of her, gripping her upper arms.

Relief flowed through her to be away from the crowd. She felt small, wishing for the power to strike down the offensive men who saw her only as an object.

For several long moments, they all just stood there, plainly waiting for something to happen. The door opened again, and a figure in a dark hooded cloak entered and paced the room until he stood before her. In the dim light, she caught no glimpse of a face.

"Your Highness," the cloaked figure bowed. "You look lovely." He paused and appraised her. "I must say, it's gratifying to see you dressed so... appropriately. Would you care to take another stroll outside?"

Tally felt her cheeks heat in fury, and she ignored his question, striving to keep her face impassive, not giving anything away. "What do you want from me?" she demanded.

"Much. After all, you do have *everything*." Sarcasm was heavy in his voice.

A chill went down her back at his words. "Who are you?"

He took a step nearer where the light was brighter and threw back his hood.

Andevaar.

CHAPTER 11

CROWN PRINCESS TAHLEA

WITH GUARDS ON EITHER side of her holding her in place, Tally stared back at Andevaar, working to keep the shock from her face. He was here. Namradill had been right about him. Not that Tally had doubted the Goddess, but now there was no question. She had found him.

What could she say to him?

Some great artist might have sculpted his features, from the arrogant expression he wore to the straight nose and strong jaw. His dark eyes were cold and matched the icy sneer on his lips as he slowly took in her appearance. Untidy tendrils of her hair escaped her braid and fell against the disgusting tunic. His gaze traveled along her body, her uncovered legs, and ended on her bare feet.

He nodded to the guards, inclining his head toward the door. They released Tally and moved to shield the exit. She stood still as Andevaar stalked closer. Tally felt like prey, and he was a predator, circling before he struck. She fought to remain still as he walked around her, examining her from every angle before returning to face her.

One corner of his mouth quirked up in something between a sneer and a smile. "I must say, Crown Princess, I've never seen you look better."

Hot anger flared up inside, and she pushed it back, trying not to let it show in her expression. "What do you want?" She repeated her question.

"First, your cooperation."

How could he even *think* she would go along with his plans? She bit back a furious reply.

His cold eyes met hers. "How it must aggravate you to lose control when you've been in charge all your life. You live in a palace, surrounded by servants who fulfill your every whim. You have no idea what really happens in your kingdom."

Her hands tightened into fists, but she remained silent, meeting his eyes. She drew in a slow silent breath through her nose and forced her hands to uncurl, one finger at a time. He was only trying to provoke her. Despite being completely in his power at the moment, she couldn't allow him to control her emotions or her decisions. She forced her voice to sound calm. "Tell me what you see happening in my kingdom."

"You claim to care for your subjects, yet you do nothing when they are suffering."

Tally raised her chin. "I have always done everything I can to help them! I must answer to the Goddess Namradill, and it's my duty to protect them."

He shook his head in protest. "You sit in your palace, never lifting a finger, and claim the Goddess has given you the right to rule. Namradill is only a stone! All you do is hold up the blue rock, and that gives you the power? Anyone else could do that just as well!"

Her eyes widened. He didn't know how wrong he was. "She isn't just a stone!"

He leaned offensively close to her. "I forgot. She's a stone who speaks to you. Only no one else can hear it. That makes you insane *and* a tyrant!"

Her hands had tightened again so hard that her nails dug into her palms. She was *not* a tyrant. "That's not true," she ground out the words. "Our people have a deep faith in Divine Namradill. She has protected us for centuries."

Andevaar laughed coldly. "Your family has kept that lie going for a long time. It's time to admit that the whole thing is only a pretense allowing you to stay in power."

Despite her efforts to remain calm, his words affected her, and her body shook with fury. By the satisfaction mixed with anger in his expression, she realized it had been his goal to make her upset. She had to stay in control, if not of the situation, at least of herself. Forcing her voice back to a neutral tone, she met his eyes. "What is it you want me to do?"

"Well, Princess," he bowed sarcastically, "I have come to this meeting prepared to offer you three choices. The decision is entirely yours. I will accept any of them."

She waited for him to present his options. Whatever he tried to make her do, she had to be brave and protect her people. Nothing was more important than that.

He gave that icy half-smile. "First is to leave this land, permanently. Renounce your throne, and I will see you safely to the borders. You may take your invalid father, or whomever you like, with you. If you leave, no more lives will be lost in the fighting."

Her eyes widened in disbelief. Did he think she would give up so easily? "I will not abandon my people." She did not know what would happen to her father if she moved him. He was vulnerable during his strange rest, and he needed to be guarded, not undertake a difficult journey.

Andevaar went on, his voice cold and confident. "Your second option is to keep fighting. I promise you will never find all my servants. I have loyal followers in many places, and my power grows daily. This war would waste many lives. I believe you object to people dying on your behalf?"

Her eyes didn't leave his, and she kept her voice even. "Third?"

He offered his hand mockingly. "You may accept my hand in marriage. Our legal union will place *me* on the throne, and rule of the Seven Rivers will be *mine*. Don't worry, I will make sure you are comfortable. You can continue to live in the luxury that is so important to you, as long as you don't get in my way. If holding a blue stone in your hand makes you the king, I can do that. We'll make arrangements to take care of your father."

Tally's whole body tensed. Obviously, he still believed that Namradill was merely a stone. If the Goddess didn't accept him, he couldn't appoint himself King of the Seven Rivers. And how could Andevaar think Tally would ever marry him? She glared at him. "Why do you think I would accept your terms?"

He seized her arm, pulling her uncomfortably close to him. "Because you have to. No matter what you decide, you won't keep the throne, little princess." His dark eyes bored into hers.

Refusing to look away, she put her palm tight against his forearm. "Praeteren!"

He didn't react to the word. For a long moment, neither of them moved.

Then he blinked, looking away. When he spoke, his tone was brusque. "We're finished here." He waved his hand in dismissal and the guards came forward to grip her arms. "You may go, Princess. I have urgent business with Governor Folcan at Edrithil, but I'll be back in a few days. You can let me know your decision when I return." Without another word, he left the room. She heard his heavy boots cross the stone floor and the door open and close behind him.

He thought he had won. Maybe he had. How was she going to stop his plans? There was no one here to help her. When the spell took effect, he wouldn't remember his ultimatum, but Tally was still a prisoner, and she needed a way out.

The guards gripped her tightly. Instinctively, she struggled, but they only increased the pressure. One of them laughed. "Hold still," he growled. "Fighting won't do any good. You're not getting away." He was a large beefy man with a scraggly beard clinging to his thick jowls. His unkempt hair grew in a fringe around a shiny bald patch on the top of his head.

They escorted her out into the courtyard. Tally heard the clatter of horse hooves on the stones and the heavy boom of the gate shutting. Andevaar had gone, leaving the courtyard empty.

The two guards marched her to one of the wooden plank shacks. The one who had ordered her to hold still leaned close, and she smelled the sour odor of someone who rarely washed. He spoke in her ear. "Andevaar ordered us to make sure we kept you in your place, Princess. I'll be back."

If he hadn't gripped her securely, she would have jerked away at the feel of his hot breath on her ear. He laughed at her attempts to free herself. They reached the entrance of the small building, threw her inside, and shut and barred the door behind her.

Panting, Tally sank to the floor in the dark building. The big man promised he'd be back. What had Andevaar ordered him to do to her? Unable to see anything, Tally made a quick exploration of the room using her sense of touch. If she could find a way out, she didn't intend to be here when he returned.

The place wasn't large, and as her eyes slowly adjusted, she could see a little in the faint light leaking between the gaps in the rough planks of the wall. The room was cold and empty except for a few stones on the dirt floor. She searched the cracks and corners for any means of escape. Finding nothing, she sat down and pulled her knees up to her chest, trying to preserve as much warmth as possible.

Despite the cold, she felt relief in the temporary solitude. Her mind raced through a list of possible solutions, trying to identify one that might work. If she couldn't stop Andevaar, he would seize control of the Seven Rivers. Had the spell worked? She reviewed the moment in her mind. Her palm had touched his arm, and she was positive she'd said the word correctly. Thorvan had promised that, within a couple of hours, Andevaar wouldn't remember anything. Was he out in the forest right now, having forgotten everything? Would his friends discover that something was wrong with him and come to her demanding answers?

Alone with her churning thoughts, the night was long and cold. Several times during the dark hours, Tally heard footsteps and hushed voices. Her stomach tensed whenever she heard anything. When would the big outlaw come back?

In the pre-dawn dark, Tally woke from a light doze to hear heavy footsteps approaching. She scrambled to her feet, watching the entrance. Someone removed the bar, and the door opened, allowing in the orange glow of torchlight. Against the flickering light, the shape of a man loomed black in the doorway. "Good morning, Princess."

From his voice, she recognized him immediately as the guard who had brought her here last night. Tally glared at him. "What do you want?"

He gave a low laugh at her tone as he looked her up and down, his eyes lingering on her bare legs. "Dressed in rags, locked inside a fortress, unarmed, not a friend in sight, and, still, you sound stuck up."

"Leave me alone," Tally ordered.

Ignoring her command, he moved nearer. "I don't have to do what you say."

She backed away until her back bumped into the wall. "What did Andevaar order you to do to me?"

He grinned. "Only to make sure we guarded you, kept you secure and as *comfortable* as possible."

Icy fear flooded through her. Comfortable? Last night, Andevaar had offered her his hand in marriage. If she accepted, it would be nothing more than a transaction. He would leave her alive as agreed, but he would grant her no consideration, no honor. That was more than plain since he'd sent this man to attack her.

The outlaw took another step toward her. He was big, heavily muscled, but wearing extra weight around his middle. A quick scan revealed a knife at his belt, but no other weapons on him. She watched him as he approached, his large hands reaching for her. The sour smell of his body wafted toward her.

As his hands touched her arms, Tally seized the front of his shirt and brought one knee up hard into his crotch. As he doubled over, she struck his nose with the heel of her hand, causing him to drop to his knees with a bellow of pain. She leapt toward the door, but several other outlaws blocked it. No escape there.

Breathing hard, the big man looked up at her, his brows lowered in fury. Blood streamed from his nose over his mouth and jaw. He wiped at it with his sleeve and got back to his feet. This time, he came more carefully, watching her before he grabbed for her. She dodged out of reach, and he sprang to follow, seizing her arm. Tally aimed another blow at his face, but his brawny hand blocked it. When she brought her knee up, he turned his body, deflecting the attack harmlessly to the side. She wrenched her arm free of his grip and backed up, seeking more space to defend herself.

There wasn't anywhere to go in this shack, and he lunged at her. She dodged to one side, but not fast enough. He struck her, pinning her against the plank wall. His impact had enough force that she heard a few of the boards crack. The rancid smell of his breath hit her face, and the acrid odor of his body surrounded her. He pushed himself against her, his hands roaming. She twisted, trying to escape, but she didn't have room to strike him with any force. One beefy hand gripped her jaw, pulling her face up. Ignoring the blood on his face, he kissed her.

His lips crushed against hers, hard and demanding. This had to stop. It was unbearable. With all her strength, Tally twisted free, jerking her body to one side, partially escaping his grip. She could taste blood on her lips and feel more of it smeared around her mouth.

The light from the doorway gleamed on the edge of his knife. "Stop fighting me," he demanded, brandishing the weapon. "I won't hurt you if you stop."

Hot fury surged up through her, and she seized his wrist in both hands. He attempted to twist away, but she kept her hold, matching his movements. His other fist struck her jaw, knocking her head back. For a moment, she couldn't see, but she still refused to release his wrist. His second blow to her face loosened her grip, and he drove the knife at her, the blade cutting into her shoulder.

Fiery pain exploded through her, and she felt hot blood flowing.

As he raised the blade again, she managed to resume her grip on his wrist. She twisted to the side to deflect another blow from his fist and drove her knee into his crotch. It was not as potent as her first attempt, still, it drew a grunt of pain.

His free hand jerked one of her hands loose, allowing his blade to strike her again.

Outside, a shout came from the courtyard. "Where is Saller?" A man's voice demanded furiously. "Saller! Get out here."

Abruptly losing focus on Tally, the burly man backed away. His expression had changed to one of terror. He stumbled toward the door, making another hasty attempt to clean the blood from his face. A moment later, Tally was alone, breathing hard, clamping her hand over the cuts to slow the bleeding. The guards outside shut and barred the door.

Putting her eye to a crack between the planks, she tried to see what was happening. She couldn't see much, but she saw the bulky form of the big man crossing the courtyard. All the other outlaws were quiet as he came to face another man. Tally recognized him as Hargen, the man who had threatened to make sure Gerran was dead.

"What were you doing in there?" Hargen demanded.

The man he called Saller hastened to respond. "I—I'm sorry. I was only bringing the princess her breakfast."

Tally heard a blow.

"I'm sorry!" Saller groaned. "It won't happen again, I swear!"

She heard a cry of pain, and the big man dropped to his knees. Hargen's cold voice filled the now-silent courtyard. "Hawk left *me* in charge until he gets back. He has a plan for the princess. It doesn't include *you* getting your hands on her. She's valuable, more valuable than your worthless life." For a moment, Hargen looked down at him. The icy sound of his voice carried, even though he spoke quietly. "Next time, I'll kill you. And I'll take time to enjoy myself while I do it." He spoke louder, as if addressing the crowd. "Stay out of there. No one harms her until we're finished."

Tally sank to the floor against the wall, holding the throbbing cuts on her shoulder and trying to catch her breath. With the back of her hand, she scrubbed at the blood left on her face. As she got up and reached for the water bucket, desperate to clean herself, she realized she was shaking all over.

CHAPTER 12

THE MAN WITH NO NAME

H E WOKE WITH THE morning sun in his eyes. Blinking, he raised his head to see a lush green forest surrounding the clearing where he lay. No one else was in sight. Slowly, he sat up. Although he saw no apparent danger, he felt the instinct not to remain lying here in the open, and he hastened into the cover of the thick trees. Under their concealment, he sat down and rested his hands on his knees.

It was time to go. He needed to go... he was on his way to...

Where? He searched his mind for memories and found nothing.

Looking carefully around for anything that might offer information, he scanned the woods. He couldn't tell if he recognized this place or not. Rubbing his forehead, he tried to recall where he had been going. It must have been important. But he remembered nothing.

What had he been doing?

He took a deep breath. There had to be something. His existence had not begun a few minutes ago when he opened his eyes, had it? Attempting to quiet his mind, he looked around at the peaceful woods. There must be something there in his past.

He couldn't shake the feeling that he'd been in the middle of something significant.

Closing his eyes, he turned his face toward the dappled sunlight, feeling the warmth on his face and the light illuminating his eyelids. Peace. Warmth. He breathed deeply again. After several long relaxing moments, he realized he was thirsty, and he walked up the hill toward the sound of running water. Looking down into the still water of the tiny pool, he didn't recognize the man who stared back at him. Untidy hair hung down around his face. The eyebrows were heavy over very dark eyes. Dark stubble covered the lower part of his face. His nose was long and straight.

He stared into the reflection of his own eyes. What kind of man was he? Was he looking at the face of a friend or brother, or a solitary person who faced life alone? Did anyone care about him? He shook his head, threw a stone into the pool, and sat down on a rock to search himself for more information.

He wore tough clothing well suited to being in the woods. His boots were sturdy and well-made. They fitted him very well, seeming to indicate someone had made them to fit. He was not a beggar then, if he had paid the cobbler. He searched his pockets and found them empty. Beneath his shirt, he found a leather cord. Pulling it out, he saw a key. It must belong to something valuable if he'd carried it so close. With no way of knowing what it might open, he tucked it back out of sight. At his belt, he wore a sheathed dagger and an empty sword scabbard. He opened his hand and examined the lines of callus across the palm that seemed to show he was accustomed to using his hands. Fighting? The empty sheath showed he'd been carrying a sword, a weapon never used for any purpose other than battle.

Was he a soldier? Had he been fighting for some significant cause?

He couldn't remember.

His stomach growled, informing him it had been a long time since his last meal. He got to his feet. If he had no other purpose, filling his belly would do for the moment. As he moved quietly through the woods, the man saw the boy before he was aware of being watched. The lad was splitting firewood, swinging the ax in an easy arc to land solidly in the section of log.

Was this young man an enemy? A friend? A stranger?

He kept his hand on the hilt of his dagger as he approached. The boy stopped chopping and watched him come, his face open and friendly, except for a hint of wariness as his eyes took in the hand on the knife hilt. He held the ax casually in his hands.

The man faced the boy. "Who are you?" His tone sounded less friendly than he'd intended. Surely this young man meant no one any harm. Trying again, he took a deep breath, and relaxed his shoulders, and allowed his voice to sound more pleasant. "Forgive me, I don't know where I am."

The young man grinned. "I'm Toban. You've just crossed into my grandfather's lands."

"I'm pleased to meet you, Toban." His voice still came out as a menacing growl. That wasn't right. Toban had offered him a friendly smile. He forced his tone to sound kinder. "It *is* good to meet you."

Toban set down the ax and came forward, offering his hand. It took great effort to abandon the knife hilt and extend his hand. The young man shook it. "And you are?"

"I'm—" He paused. Of course, he knew the answer. He knew. Only he didn't.

For an awkward moment, his mind searched frantically. He did not like the idea of telling this friendly young man he didn't know his own name. A name flitted through his mind. It seemed to belong in a dream, or in the distant past, but it seemed right.

"I'm Flint," he decided. Yes. The name felt right, though at the same time, he was certain he'd been called something else. Exactly what, he couldn't recall.

"Well met, Flint." Toban grinned. "I was just about to head back to the house for breakfast. Would you like to join me?"

Flint paused. It felt very unusual for someone he'd just met to offer him food and friendship, but he couldn't detect any hint of harm or deceit in Toban. Flint's stomach growled, deciding for him. "I would be very grateful."

Toban picked up an armful of firewood and headed off. Flint picked up his own load and followed. As they left the cover of the trees, he saw a small, sheltered valley tucked against towering mountain peaks. The morning sun lit fresh grass. A sparkling stream flowed down from the rocky edge of the mountain, crossing an open green meadow. The place was beautiful. Flint didn't remember ever being anywhere that felt so peaceful. Maybe he didn't recall ever feeling peace. He took another deep breath.

Ahead of him, the boy walked with a springy gait, displaying youth and good spirits. He set down his load of wood in a box outside the door of a snug little cottage, and Flint followed his example. The boy opened the door. "Grandfather? Set out one more plate."

Following the boy's beckoning, Flint entered the cozy room, having to duck slightly under the doorway. A gray-haired man was busy setting food out on a rough table. While Toban was taller than the old man, neither of them came past Flint's chin.

I'm tall, he realized. Was he this much larger than everyone else?

"Welcome," the old man said. "My name is Thorvan. Who are you?"

"He said his name was Flint," Toban supplied helpfully.

A small child appeared, darting from a corner to hide behind Toban and peek out from behind him.

Thorvan came nearer and gazed intently into Flint's face. It felt as if the man's penetrating blue eyes could see into his very soul. He was being evaluated. Slowly, a smile spread across the old man's wrinkled features. Flint must have passed some sort of test.

"I'm very glad you're here, Flint," the old man said. "Please, sit. You must be hungry."

Thorvan and Toban took seats across the table as Flint sat down. The tiny girl crept slowly closer to him. She wore her fair hair in a braid, though strands were escaping it. Her dress was homespun, and her little feet were bare. Despite her apparent shyness, her blue eyes met his directly. He could feel... something as she gazed at him. A strange sensation he couldn't name. She was so small. Even seated, he looked down at her. She watched him for another long moment, her eyes wide, before she fled to Thorvan and clung to him.

"Leya, this is Flint," Thorvan said, pulling over another chair and seating the child beside him. He looked back across the table. "My granddaughter, Leya."

"I am pleased to meet you, Leya," Flint said. She returned his gaze but didn't speak.

Toban passed food around, and they ate fresh bread and roasted meat. The food tasted wonderful. Toban had a hearty appetite, which made Flint feel more comfortable as he cleaned his plate for the second time. Finally, they all pushed back their plates and looked at each other.

"Now, that's better, isn't it?" The old man's voice was kind.

Flint smiled in reply. "Much better. Thank you." It was much easier to think once he had met the demands of his stomach.

"Of course, you're welcome here," the old man said. "Where are you going?"

Flint's mind spun in circles at the question, never coming up with an answer. He didn't know. Was it wise to reveal his weakness to these people? He took a deep breath. No. It was only his foolish pride that wanted to hide any sign of ignorance. What good was pride when he didn't know who he was? There was no reason to try to lift himself above anyone else. He decided to be honest. "I don't know where I'm going."

"Do you mean you haven't made plans?" Thorvan asked.

Flint shook his head. "No. I can't remember anything before waking up in the forest a few hours ago. I don't know who I am, or what I was doing before that."

"You said your name was Flint," Toban protested.

"At the moment, I didn't feel ready to tell you I don't know." He sighed. "As I think about it, there's no reason to hide it. Whoever I was is lost to me now. I chose a name that seemed right and called myself Flint."

"It's a fine name," Thorvan said, his arm around the little girl. "Is that what you would like to be called for now?"

Flint nodded. "It will do well enough until I remember more."

"So... you recall nothing." The old man gazed at him thoughtfully. "If someone out there is looking for you, we have no way of contacting them at the moment. The forest has many dangerous men in it. You'll be safe here as long as you don't leave the valley. What is it you'd like to do? If you remember nothing, you can choose to do anything."

Flint met the old man's blue eyes. He had the feeling that he'd been doing something very important and that he'd stopped, his task unfinished. What had it been? He searched his mind but still came up with nothing.

"What do you think is the best way a man can spend his life?" the old man asked.

The question startled Flint. "I... I don't know. That question will require a lot of thought before answering."

"Wisely spoken," Thorvan said with a smile. "I would like to help."

Flint didn't think that people usually came forward to help him. It felt unfamiliar. But the offer felt good. He could tell the old man meant it sincerely, but he still had to ask. "Why do you want to help me?"

Thorvan met his eyes frankly. "I feel you could serve others. You are a strong young man, and you have many abilities that could protect and benefit those you care about."

Flint's eyes widened. Those he cared about? Who did he care about? He didn't know what to say in response.

"Perhaps someone who knows you will come looking for you and be able to reveal more. In the meantime, it would be my honor to assist until you decide what to do," Thorvan said. "Toban feels the same."

Flint looked back, considering. He glanced at Toban, who gave an encouraging nod.

"There is always plenty of work to do around here," Thorvan said. "You may repay our hospitality by helping with it."

That sounded more than fair. "Very well," Flint replied. "I will gladly accept your offer, while I try to remember my past and think about the answer to your question."

"Good, good." The old man got to his feet, patting Flint on the shoulder. "There's not much space in here," he gestured to the little room, which held the table, a tiny loft, a bed in one corner and two chairs by the fireplace, "but I have plenty of bedding. Toban can help you make a place to sleep in the hayloft."

With an armful of blankets, Flint followed the boy to the stable, wondering whether sleeping in borrowed blankets on a bed of straw was far beneath his station or a welcome improvement over sleeping in the woods.

They made up a bed in one corner of the hay loft, spreading the blankets on a thick layer of fresh straw. "Thank you... for helping me," Flint said to Toban as they climbed back down the ladder.

"I'm glad I can," Toban said. "It feels good to help. You'll see."

Flint had plenty of opportunities to find out during the rest of the day. They cleaned the stables, worked with a young horse Toban was training, and mended a hole in the roof of the cottage. By the time the sun sank behind the distant mountains, they were both starving again.

They washed their faces and hands in the basin outside the door. Flint could see the sun setting through a few soft clouds. It was beautiful. Thorvan's little granddaughter, Leya, came around the corner of the cottage and stopped in her tracks, staring up at him. She looked frightened at first, but she didn't move, watching him gazing at the sky.

"The colors make you happy," she observed.

Flint realized it was true. He felt satisfied with the day's work. Today in this place felt like a fresh beginning. The tasks he had completed had given him new experiences. The peace of this place had allowed him to take a deep look into himself. The child was right, the colors did make him happy. Despite not remembering his life, he didn't think he'd felt happy for a long time.

The little girl came closer and stood facing him. "Why are you so big?" she asked, craning her neck to see his face.

"I don't know." The beginnings of a smile lifted one corner of his mouth. The expression felt new on his face. Maybe he didn't smile often. He looked down at her. "Why are you so small?"

Her eyes widened, and she giggled. "I'm five years old. Every person who is five is small. Didn't you know that?"

Being around children didn't feel familiar to him at all. He met her eyes gravely. "I didn't. I'm glad you are here to teach me."

She rewarded him with a sweet smile and took his hand. "I'll help you."

They went inside and sat down at the table. In companionable conversation, they ate together. Thorvan proved to be an excellent cook, though he had only simple ingredients to work with. The food tasted good to Flint, and he wondered how it compared to what he usually ate. Was he used to plenty or to lack? His body felt well and strong. He'd obviously not been starving. Maybe it was only the warmth of companionship around the table that felt unfamiliar.

When they had finished eating, they washed the dishes. Leya appeared to have some skill in the task, and she didn't hesitate to instruct Flint. While the job felt vaguely familiar, he accepted her guidance.

With the work done, they sat by the fire for a while. Toban worked on mending and cleaning the horse's tack, while the old man picked the seeds from some kind of dried herb. Leya sat on the hearth playing with a collection of simple toys made of wood. Flint stared into the fire and reviewed what had been a very strange day, maybe the strangest in his life.

Now, it was the only day he remembered.

The little girl yawned as she played, and Thorvan went to the corner of the room and pulled a trundle bed out from beneath the larger bed. "It's time to sleep, Leya."

"I'm not tired," she insisted, a yawn interrupting her words. Even so, she carefully replaced her toys in a wooden box, then went to Toban and hugged him. "Good night, Toban."

He smiled warmly and returned her hug. "Good night."

She turned away from Toban and looked at Flint. For a long moment, no one moved, as she looked at him appraisingly.

Appearing to have decided, she ran to Flint and threw her arms around him. "Good night, Flint."

He'd never felt anything like the sweetness of small arms around his neck. Unwise or not, she trusted him with her presence and her affection. The child was completely sincere in everything she said to him. "Good night, Leya." He wanted to thank her for her acceptance, but what could he say?

She kissed his cheek, giggling as his stubble tickled her, and then she ran to Thorvan, wishing him good night just as enthusiastically. He tucked her into bed, wrapping the blankets around her.

It was time for Flint to retire. He got to his feet, wished them good night, and went out into the cool, silent night. For a while, he leaned against the wall of the stable and stared up at the stars. They came out, one by one, twinkling. A soft, fragrant breeze moved in the pine trees. Flint sighed. The sense of calm in this place felt entirely new to him. Maybe it ran deeper than just forgetting his troubles.

He searched his mind, trying to find any memory. Did he have a family? That idea was startling and felt very foreign. He didn't think he did. Did he have friends who were wondering where he was? Duties undone? Enemies?

Somehow, the last felt more familiar, but if he had enemies, he didn't remember who they were, and they weren't here now. It was time to let go of feeling angry. Looking within himself for resentment, he allowed it to dissipate and allowed the peace of the night to seep into him. He didn't need to have enemies anymore. Thorvan's question came back to him. What *was* the best way to spend your life?

Whatever answer he discovered, he hoped it included the quiet serenity of the mountains. Flint went inside to his bed of straw, wrapped the warm blankets around himself, and fell into a deep slumber.

A tall, dark-haired man wearing old, patched clothes walked out the door of a tiny cottage with a bundle in one hand. When he turned to smile at someone behind him in the doorway, a little boy ran from inside, throwing his arms around the man's waist. "Don't go, Father." His small arms clutched the man, and he buried his face in his shirt.

The man dropped his bundle and knelt to embrace the child. "It won't be for long," he promised. "I'll save as much money as I can and come home when my enlistment is up."

"Couldn't you find another job here?" the boy asked, pulling back to meet his father's eyes.

"I tried," the man said. "I've been trying since we lost your mother. I kept looking, hoping something would come up, until all my savings were gone. The king is offering good wages to soldiers, and I need the work."

The boy nodded slowly. "The king is lucky to have your help. You're strong and very brave." He touched the hilt of his father's dagger sheathed at his waist, rubbing his fingers over the metal cast in the shape of a lion's head. "You can use grandpa's knife if you need to fight."

"I need you to be good until I get home. Be brave, Flint." He held the boy close for another long moment before he shouldered his bundle and went off down the road. The boy watched him go until a bend in the road hid him from sight.

Flint woke with a gasp in the dark before dawn. The dream had been so real. He felt like he'd been standing right there, watching the ragged man walk away. *Be brave, Flint.* Who was the man who had left? Flint should know him. The man had the same dark hair he, himself, had, though his features were different. The boy in the dream had called him father. Flint searched his memory and found nothing more. The dream must offer some clue to his past. The man had called the boy Flint. Was he seeing his own father? Had he remembered the name from the distant past, or were the man and boy strangers to him? He lay there reviewing every detail until the light of dawn filtered into the stable and the birds sang.

By the time Flint had been in Thorvan's valley for a few days, Leya appeared to adore him, and Toban had become a good friend. While the little girl had tagged along with them, Toban had produced a bow, and they took it into the meadow to practice. "If you can use a bow, we could go hunting," the young man suggested. "Can you shoot?"

Flint shrugged.

Toban demonstrated knocking an arrow, drawing the bow, and taking aim at a stump two dozen paces away in the grass. As the arrow struck the center, Leya clapped her hands, and Toban grinned. "Your turn." He handed over the bow.

Even though he didn't remember using one, the weapon felt familiar in Flint's hand. Knocking an arrow, he drew and fired, easily landing the shot beside Toban's. So, he could shoot. It must be something he'd done before.

Leya clapped again. "Can I shoot it too?" She skipped forward and put her hand on the bow next to Flint's. Her little arms were too short to reach the grip and the string at the same time. He held the bow, and she placed her fingers to pull the string. He arranged his hand around hers and set an arrow against the string. "Are you ready?"

She nodded, concentrating. She pulled. Her efforts barely moved the string, and he pulled gently. She released the arrow, his hand following hers. The shaft flew in a brief arc and plunged into the grass well short of their mark. Leya didn't seem to mind. She laughed in delight and clapped her hands. "I did it!"

Flint couldn't help but smile.

Toban laughed and praised her. "That was a good shot! You might need a little more practice before you're ready to hunt."

"That's all right, I'm going to play now, anyway." The child skipped away, heading back for the cottage.

Toban looked at Flint and gestured toward the two arrows stuck in the target. "I have another bow. Are you ready to hunt? The deer won't hold still like a stump."

Flint grinned, ready to accept the challenge.

Chapter 13

Crown Princess Tahlea

ONFINED IN THE MISERABLE shack inside the outlaw fortress, two days passed quietly. At intervals, they brought Tally food and water, but no one entered the room or tried to bother her again. The pain of her injuries eased a little, and she passed the time as usefully as possible. She discovered that during Saller's attack, three boards had cracked. One fissure was an arm's length from the end of the plank, and the damage had created a long splinter. Trying not to make a sound, she slowly worked the piece loose.

When it finally came free, she had a slender spear of wood as long as her forearm. If she could distract the guards, she might be able to lift the bar on the door from the inside. Night fell, and quiet settled over the compound. Tally reviewed possible ways to divert the guards. Two of them stood just outside the door.

Before she came up with a workable plan, the sound of men shouting and feet hurrying broke the quiet. Tally put her eye to the crack. Men were running, gathering horses as if they were preparing for a fight. Had General Kylith discovered her capture or come to search for her when she didn't return on time? Could it be someone else entirely? Either way, this was exactly the distraction she needed.

"Go see what's happening," one guard said. The other man ran off toward the gates. With one gone and the rest of them distracted, this was her chance.

She couldn't see the other guard from her vantage point, but she knew he was still there. She would have to hurry. The noise outside worked to her advantage. Taking the sliver of wood, she inserted it into the crack between the door and the frame. Slowly, she lifted. The bar moved a little. It was heavy from this angle, but she maintained pressure until the bar fell away, allowing her to push the door open. Her gaze quickly found the guard. If not for the confusion happening around them, he would surely have heard the noise. As it was, his back was toward her as he looked at the milling mob of riders.

Picking up a rock from the ground, Tally slammed it hard into the back of his head. He crumpled to the ground with a thud. Quickly, she assessed if anyone had heard, but the camp was turning into chaos. She dragged him swiftly back into the shack. He offered no objection as she pulled his boots from his feet. Unbuckling his belt, she jerked it free, and her nose wrinkled in disgust at his scent.

Tally had no other choice. In her current outfit, she had no chance of escaping undetected. As repulsive as she found the idea of wearing this man's clothes, she had to do it. She unfastened his trousers and tugged them down, refusing to be squeamish. The rock had done its work, and he didn't move. His shirt, jacket, and boots followed. A moment later, dressed in dirty, ill-fitting clothes, and with the guard's weapons belted around her waist, she pulled his hood forward to shade her face, replaced the bar on the door, and hurried toward the gathering riders.

Several men were saddling horses, while other men gathered and mounted. Tally joined the line, took the offered reins, and mounted swiftly. She kept the hood pulled low and didn't look at anyone directly. A large company of horsemen milled around in the open space before the gate. Hargen rode to the front, raising his sword.

"The king's army is coming," he yelled. "They haven't found our fortress yet. We need to stop them before they do. Ride!"

A little of the tension in Tally's middle eased. Kylith was coming. He was leading his men up the mountainside, and if she could only reach them, she'd be safe.

The gates opened, and the horses condensed into a column and rode out the gates. Tally joined them. The cuts on her shoulder ached, and she was stiff and sore from her captivity in the cold drafty room, but it felt good to be riding again.

The horses poured out into the forest with only the light of half a moon to guide them. She hoped no one would look closely enough to recognize her among the riders. All she needed to do was keep herself safe until she reached her friends.

The outlaws rode steadily downhill. Tally could see the forest thinning until it opened into grassy hills. The moon shed enough light to make out the dark shapes of an army. Her army. It must be General Kylith.

Ahead, she saw the light of several torches between the trees. A large group of outlaws on horseback gathered the riders into orderly companies. Tally had no other choice but to ride forward with everyone else when all she wanted was to break away and get to her general.

"You men, join the first company on the left, and you—"

Tally's stomach clenched as she recognized the man's voice: Saller. She didn't look at him, instead she kept her eyes on the leather reins in her hands.

"Look at me when I'm talking to you!" he yelled. He urged his horse directly at Tally until their mounts were side to side. He jerked the hood from her head, and she looked up into the face of the same man she'd fought with two days ago. His nose had swollen badly.

"It's the princess!" Saller shouted. "She's escaped!" He grabbed for her reins, but she jerked the horse to one side and dug in her heels. The animal leapt forward. She punched one outlaw who tried to block her path. In a moment, she was past them, and the light of the torches faded into the trees. Riding as fast as she dared in the moonlight, she fled downhill.

The sound of shouts behind her and the pounding of hooves drove her to even greater speed. An outlaw with a drawn sword charged toward her from the side. Tally drew her stolen weapon and met his attack. The clash of steel on steel rang out. She had no trouble parrying his clumsy attack and, in only a moment, she had landed a slash to his upper arm and another across his leg. Pain made him slower. Urging her horse forward, she locked blades with him and dumped him out of the saddle.

The delay had allowed the others to catch up. Turning her horse, she urged the animal down the hill. The ground was uneven and treacherous in the dark. For several moments, she pulled away from the pursuit. She'd begun to hope she might outpace them when her horse stumbled.

Her mount lurched horribly beneath her, and the horse went down, sending her to the ground. She rolled to absorb the shock. When she came to rest, she couldn't breathe for a moment. There wasn't time to recover. The outlaws were coming fast. Tally searched the ground, retrieved her sword, scrambled to her feet, and ran.

The first few riders passed her and pulled up in front of her. She bolted to one side into a growth of slender trees, too close together to allow horses between them. There was less light under their leaves, and she tried to move quietly, but it didn't take long for her to hear footsteps all around her.

An outlaw appeared, swinging his sword at her. She blocked the stroke and attacked him. He had more skill than the last man, but he was nowhere near as good as Gerran. She cut through his defenses several times to wound him. He yelled in pain as her sword struck his leg. When she ran, he didn't follow. She came to the edge of the patch of woods but couldn't stay under cover. The pursuit was coming, and she had to move on. Tally sprinted out into the grassy meadow, heading down toward her friends.

A group of outlaws were close behind her, and another closed in from the side. The moonlight glinted on their raised weapons. She would have a fighting chance if she faced them individually, but there were too many.

She blocked the slash of the first man, only to feel hands seizing her from behind. As she kicked at them, grunts of pain rewarded her efforts, but several powerful hands gripped her sword arm. "No!" she yelled, fighting them with all her strength. They closed in, gripping her from all directions, wrenching the weapon out of her hand. They pushed her to the ground, twisting her arms behind her and holding her down.

The sound of weapons clashing and shouting erupted around Tally. Several of the men holding her against the ground released her to join the conflict. She pushed and kicked against her remaining captors, but they held tight as a group of horses rode up and stopped near them.

"It's the general!" One of the outlaws gripping her hastily drew his weapon and joined his friends. From where she lay on the ground, she couldn't see much, but she heard the ring of weapons, and the man collapsed to the ground a few paces away.

The last two pairs of hands holding her vanished. Relief flooded through her as she recognized General Kylith's deep voice.

"General!" she shouted, rolling onto her back.

He dismounted and hurried over to her, going to one knee beside her, his sword still in his hand. "Princess? Thank the Divine! Are you hurt?"

"Nothing serious." Her shoulder was scraped and bruised from her fall from the horse, and the cuts from her encounter with Saller had reopened. But it could have been so much worse.

Kylith offered his hand and helped her to her feet, pulling her into a fierce hug. "I've been going out of my mind with worry! After the attack, Will escaped. He was hurt pretty badly, but, somehow, he made it down the mountain and came to me with the news. We didn't know if you were dead or where they might hold you. They could have done anything to you."

Tally hugged him back, grateful beyond words for his faithful support. "I'm so happy to see you, General. We have to find Gerran and Ervan. They're both hurt. I know where they are, but the outlaws wouldn't allow me to help them. Gerran was fighting them. He told me to run—" Her stomach twisted. "It was days ago now. What if he's dead?"

Kylith hugged her again. "We'll find them. I trust Gerran's judgment. You did the right thing by listening to him."

"I can show you where they were." Tally started back up the hill.

Kylith's eyes widened in alarm. "No! You're not leaving here. Just tell me where you were. I'm not sending you out there again, no matter how many guards you take."

"But we have to find them before it's too late!" she protested. "What if it already is?"

He put a comforting hand on her shoulder. "We'll find them. I promise. Just tell me."

Tally gave him all the information she could, describing exactly where they had camped, and the direction she'd gone when the fighting had separated them. Then she waited, hoping that Kylith would find her friend, pleading to Namradill that he was still alive.

Remaining with the soldiers, Tally waited on the mountainside where they had met the outlaws. Small skirmishes continued to erupt in different places throughout the night. Just before dawn, word came that they had found Gerran and Ervan alive.

It was growing light again when a strong escort brought the wounded men down the hill. Gerran was in the saddle, though another soldier rode with him, holding him up. Tally sighed with relief, but worry flooded through her when they got close enough to see blood on his forehead and matted into his hair.

She ran to meet them and reached up to take his hand. "You're alive!" She met his eyes. "I was so afraid they'd killed you."

"No," he scoffed, his voice weak. "I'm not that easy to kill. Only a dozen of them attacked. Not bad for an old man."

Despite his joking tone, Tally could see the tightness in his expression. There was more blood on his arm, side, and one leg. She gripped his hand. "Thank you."

He nodded, not making any flippant remark this time. "I'm so relieved to see you safe."

"You too. I'll see you soon, then." Tally released his hand to allow them to continue their slow progress.

"We're ready." Kylith handed her the reins, and she got on the horse and followed Gerran.

The morning grew hot, and a dry breeze that belonged in a desert came up from the valley. As they left the battlefield and rode down the hill toward their camp, Tally felt the stress and sleeplessness of the last several days. She brushed beads of sweat from her forehead. Despite the heat, she had to concentrate on bracing herself against the incline as they descended. Otherwise, she might have fallen asleep in the saddle. She barely remembered reaching the camp and passing the guards at the perimeter. As she dismounted, the general escorted her to her tent. Tally found the cot inside and fell asleep without even taking her stolen boots off.

Tally opened her eyes to see the tent canvas above her. She blinked and stared at the fabric as her memory caught up. Sitting up slowly, she watched the fading light that looked like sunset. The day was still unseasonably warm, clinging to the heat even as the sun sank. Had she slept the entire day away? Wrinkling her nose, she looked down at her dirty, borrowed clothes. She held up one hand and saw the raw places where they had tied her wrists. Gingerly, she touched her damaged shoulder and the bruise along her jaw. Her muscles complained loudly when she moved, and her stomach growled. Grimacing, she got to her feet.

"Tally!" Mariella rushed from the far side of the tent to hug her. "You don't know how worried I've been! Even General Kylith, who I thought was actually made of stone, looked ready to crack." She stepped back, eyeing the horrible clothes. "What are you wearing? Tell me everything." Her eyes stopped on the bruise on Tally's jaw and the cuts on her shoulder. "What happened?"

Tally put a hand on Mariella's shoulder. "Don't worry about me. I'll tell you the full story soon, but, first, I need to check on Gerran."

Mariella beckoned. "I'll show you where he is. Come on."

They hurried to a nearby tent and Tally looked inside. A glance revealed several cots, some occupied. She went to the one where Gerran lay. He appeared to be sleeping, his head now neatly bandaged, and his other injuries tended. She recognized Ervan lying in the next bed.

The army medic was a gray-haired man with kind eyes. "How are they?" she asked him.

"They hit Gerran on the head pretty hard," he admitted. "Still, the leg wound is the most serious, but he'll pull through just fine. Don't worry, Princess."

"And Ervan?"

Anxiety tightened the medic's expression. "I've done all I can. Now we will wait and hope. Try not to worry.

"I can't help worrying about them," she protested. "They got hurt protecting me." Mariella put an arm around her.

"They were both doing their jobs," the medic said firmly. "It's not your fault."

Tally couldn't escape responsibility so easily. Every man in this army served the Seven Rivers. It was her duty to keep all of them safe. She stared down at her faithful teacher and bodyguard. He made no movement except for the regular rising and falling of his chest.

Tally needed to end this conflict. What if Gerran or the others died trying to protect her? Her mind flashed back to her conversation with Andevaar. He knew she didn't want any of her people to suffer. No one's life should be wasted in this pointless fighting. Andevaar had started all of this. He could not be allowed to continue it.

"Gerran will be all right," the medic assured her. "He's strong, and he'll recover. I have high hopes that Ervan will too. For now, go find something to eat. You must be hungry. You can check on them again later."

Tally's stomach growled at the suggestion. "All right."

She left the tent with Mariella at her side. Tally needed to wash, but the smell of supper wafting through the camp was too enticing. Soldiers stood in several lines to receive portions of stew from large kettles. Mariella handed her a bowl and spoon.

The girls took their turn in line, receiving their servings. They saw General Kylith seated around a tiny fire with several other men. His broad form cast a dark shadow against the flickering orange light. They sat down beside him, the others making room for them. For several moments, no one spoke while they concentrated on eating. The stew was nothing fancy, but it was hot and filling, and after the stress of the last few days and sleeping through today's meals, Tally was famished.

She finished her bowl and the remaining half of Mariella's. Satisfied warmth grew inside her.

Kylith turned to her as she finished. "I hope you got some rest?"

She swallowed her last bite. "Yes, thank you. I'm feeling much more myself. Your arrival this morning was timely. I'm very grateful."

He put a comforting hand on her arm. "Lady Mariella has done an excellent job making it appear that you never left."

Mariella sent Kylith a grateful look. "I'm just glad we have her back safely."

Kylith looked at Tally. "I'm grateful I got there when I did." He rubbed his jaw. "We received disturbing news while you were gone. The outlaws crossed the pass into Ondari Province. In the last two weeks, they have attacked several towns, though the messenger said that the last few days have been peaceful."

Tally hoped the recent peace meant that Thorvan's spell had worked. It did not surprise her that Andevaar's schemes had moved to the neighboring province. That had been his plan all along. She needed to know if the attacks had stopped when she cast the spell. Where was he now? Had his men begun searching for him? With his memory gone, he wouldn't have completed his journey to Edrithil. What would his supporters do when they found him? Surely, without his memory, he wouldn't be able to lead them.

"I hope I've found a way to stop him," Tally said. "Are we meeting with your leaders?"

Kylith eyed her disreputable outfit. "Yes, as soon as you freshen up a little. Your luggage is still in your tent. I have sent a basin of hot water there as well."

She felt the corners of her mouth turn up at the bliss of the thought but she couldn't afford to think only of herself. There was much to be done.

"Thank you, Kylith," she said. "You can gather everyone while I'm cleaning up."

"Of course, Princess."

CHAPTER 14

CROWN PRINCESS TAHLEA

Evening deepened over the army camp, bringing the welcome cool of night, and Tally was now blessedly scrubbed. She had bound up the knife cuts on her arm before dressing in her own clean clothes and the extra boots, which she had packed at the last minute, just in case. She found General Kylith and his leaders gathered in the command tent. Eight men sat around the table when Tally arrived. They all stood as she entered.

She nodded to them. "Thank you. Please, sit down. I realize that my trip into the mountains was dangerous, but it was... educational." She took a seat at the table.

General Kylith stared at her in disbelief. "Educational? Princess, forgive me for speaking so frankly, but we came far too close to losing you. Namradill is our protector, and without an heir to your bloodline, that protection would be gone. When the outlaws took you, we didn't know if they would kill you, or try to ask some enormous ransom, or—"

Or try to force her to marry her enemy in order to place him on the throne. Tally held up her hand to stop him. "You arrived in time."

Kylith's eyes widened, but he didn't interrupt her.

Tally explained what had happened. "They attacked our camp. My guards did the best they could, badly outnumbered."

General Kylith's brows knit in concern. "Were they looking specifically for *you*?"

Tally nodded. "Yes. No one *should* have known I would be there, but they seemed to know exactly who they were looking for. Our enemies have spies in this camp."

Kylith stared back at her, sharing her realization. Someone among their ranks was a traitor. Tally couldn't help a quick glance around the table. She knew each of the faces. These men had served her father all her life. She looked each of them in the eyes. "All of you have been with us for many years. I trust you. But we must be on our guard and discover who is reporting to our enemies."

"Yes," Kylith agreed. "I will increase the number of guards around the camp, and we will keep our eyes open. Now," he turned back to Tally. "Tell us what happened."

"They took me to a stronghold in the mountains," Tally told them. "It was well guarded, with high walls and a strong gate."

Kylith rubbed his jaw. "There's an old fortress at Sathar. Is that the place?"

"A narrow valley with a wall running across the canyon, and a single tower?"

He nodded. "That sounds like it. How did you get out?"

Tally smiled slightly. "I actually have you to thank for providing a distraction at exactly the right time. When you advanced up the hill, the outlaws gathered to stop you. In the confusion, I escaped the room where they had locked me and borrowed clothes and weapons from the guard."

"Borrowed?" Kylith asked with one eyebrow raised.

Tally smiled graciously. "After I hit him on the head, he didn't object. I pulled a hood over my face and joined the outlaws preparing to meet you. I rode with them down through the woods. Unfortunately, someone recognized me along the way. You know the rest."

"Did you see Andevaar?" Kylith asked.

Her mind raced back to the terrible choices he'd offered her. "Yes, and his plans are exactly what we expected. The province of Edri is only the beginning. He plans to gather more influence until he seizes the throne. He intended to keep me prisoner until I made an agreement that would place him in power."

Kylith's eyebrows lowered. "As we feared."

"What about Divine Namradill?" a captain asked. "Does this man realize that She will not grant Her favor to a usurper?"

"He doesn't believe it. Any of it. He thinks it's all a trick. He doesn't acknowledge the power Divine Namradill holds over the Seven Rivers," Tally said, "or Her connection to the royal family. We can't let him succeed. That was the main reason I went to the Mystic Thorvan."

"Was he able to offer any help?" Kylith asked.

Tally nodded. "His solution was... unusual, but I hope, effective. Thorvan pointed out that part of Andevaar's plan is to win the hearts of the people. If I simply caught him and executed him, he'd become a martyr, and we'd have even more unrest. Instead, Thorvan created an enchantment to cause Andevaar to forget everything."

For a long moment, they all stared at her with wide eyes. Shock, confusion, and uncertainty all crossed their faces. Kylith was the first to recover. He rubbed his chin thoughtfully. "So, the plan is that, with his memory gone, Andevaar will forget his ambitions."

"That's what we're hoping for."

"But wouldn't you have to get close to Andevaar to use the enchantment?" the captain asked.

"It's already done," Tally said. "When we met at Sathar, I had the opportunity, and I took it."

"So, he has already forgotten?" Kylith asked. "Where is he?"

Tally shook her head. "I don't know. He said he was riding back to Edrithil, but I don't know if he made it."

"Even if he remembers nothing, his men could still use him as a figurehead," Kylith pointed out.

"That's right," one captain said. "If they have him, they will remind him who he is, and force him to help them."

They were right. They needed to find Andevaar. Where was he?

Kylith drew in a long breath and laid his hand on the table. "We will all think about this and meet again in the morning to discuss plans."

The next morning dawned bright and hotter than any Tally had ever felt, even in midsummer. Not far above the horizon, the sun was already blazing down. The heat was enough to dry up the grass and shrivel the leaves on the trees. Tally had just left her tent with Mariella at her side when a powerful gust of wind tore through the camp, shaking the tents.

Tally looked at the horizon. A thick cloud rapidly bore down on them. She'd never seen a storm like it before. The color was all wrong, brown instead of the blue gray of rain clouds. An icy tendril of fear curled in her belly. Something was very wrong.

A few moments of frenzied activity filled the camp. The soldiers did what they could to secure tent lines, belongings, and horses. Kylith came toward them. "Come to the command tent." Tally and Mariella went with him. They were nearly there when the storm struck.

The wind roared through the camp, carrying thick, choking dust and stinging particles of sand, instantly reducing visibility to nearly zero. Tally continued the way she'd been going. She could no longer see Kylith, but his arm reached out to guide her. She stumbled into the tent as he pulled the flap shut behind her.

Coughing and brushing sand from their faces, they stood, catching their breath.

Tally had never seen a sandstorm before. She'd never even heard of one, except in old stories of the desert. Legends told that the sands had covered this land too until Namradill had given Her blessing. Why would the goddess allow such a storm into the lands under Her care?

Two more men entered the tent, a blast of dust accompanying them. They closed the flap behind them, doing their best to keep out the storm. One of them was a guard, the other she didn't know.

He stepped forward. "An urgent message, Crown Princess."

Tally's hands tightened into fists, and her eyes flew to the strained expression on the messenger's face. "What is it?" A sliver of fear twisted in her chest. "Is it my father? Is he all right?"

"The king is... safe, for now," the man said slowly, and Tally felt the color drain from her face. His look told her that, somehow, safe was not good. He leaned closer and shared his message quietly. "Namradill has been stolen."

A shiver ran through Tally's entire body. For a moment, her lungs felt frozen, unable to draw in a breath. This couldn't be true. Namradill had been secure in her father's hands. There were guards everywhere, around the clock. She met the man's gaze, wanting to shout but forcing herself to speak quietly. "Are you telling me that someone just walked in and took the stone?"

The man nodded.

Tally stared back at him. "Some criminal took it from my father's hands while he slept? They could have killed him! How did this happen? Where were the guards?" Another shiver skittered down her spine. Whoever had taken the stone did not wish her well, or the king, or anyone in the Seven Rivers. Her father had been completely vulnerable.

The messenger's face paled. "We have doubled the guards and searched every corner of the palace several times. We found nothing to reveal who did this or where they are."

Who else would have stolen the stone but the man who wished to seize the throne? Tally searched her memory of their confrontation. Had he said anything implying he meant to steal the stone? He'd mentioned that anyone could hold it in their hand and be the king, but that was all. Still, she should have realized. Her breath quickened, her mind spun, and her stomach froze into a ball of ice.

Tally hadn't been in charge of the Seven Rivers for long, and already she'd made a mistake so monumental that it could destroy her entire kingdom and claim her father's life. He couldn't survive long without the stone.

It *must* have been Andevaar or one of his supporters who took it. The plan must have already been in motion before her encounter with him at Sathar. The stone was precious, and they would have had a plan for hiding it. Tally did not know where it was. And she had just erased the memory of the man who did.

Glancing toward the canvas flap that provided the only exit from the tent, she fought a surge of longing. She'd take a horse and ride so far and so fast that no one would ever find her again. She wouldn't have to face the disappointment and loss her subjects would suffer.

Inhaling deeply, Tally mentally shook herself. She was the Crown Princess of the Seven Rivers, and she would not run. She would do everything in her power to find a solution.

Kylith knelt beside her chair and put his large hand over hers. "Are you all right?"

She opened her mouth, wanting to explain everything in a rush, wanting to ask him to help her find a solution. She closed it again. Mariella sat beside her, and the messenger was still there. A few of Kylith's men were also present. Taking in a calming breath, she met Kylith's eyes. "I'm all right, but we have a serious problem. Unless we find Divine Namradill, this storm might be only the beginning." She turned to the messenger. "How long ago did this happen? Is there any other information that might help us?"

He shook his head. "Six days ago. I'm sorry, Princess. I wish I did. Everyone has been searching the palace, looking for any clue to the stone's whereabouts, as well as trying to discover who did this. They are watching the king closely, and so far, his condition remains unchanged."

She met his gaze directly. "We cannot afford to have our king's life in danger. Tell them to increase the guard even more. The king will be all right for a time, but it won't last. If we hope to save his life, we must find the stone."

The man nodded, shifting nervously on his feet.

"Thank you for bringing me this information. I know it couldn't have been easy." She turned to Kylith. "Is there somewhere he can rest until the storm passes?"

Kylith nodded to a guard, and they slipped out. The other tents were only a few steps away. They would find their way despite the storm.

Dragging a chair over to Tally, Kylith sat down. He still gave off an aura of calm. That was helpful, since she wanted to yell in frustration.

Her eyes stung with angry tears. "I've made the biggest mistake of my life." She shook her head, gazing down at her hands in her lap.

He placed a hand on her shoulder. "Sometimes we make decisions using the best information we have, only to learn more later and see things very differently."

That was a vast understatement. Most people's mistakes didn't destroy entire kingdoms. "I used the spell on Andevaar. By now, his memories are long gone. The stone is too important for him to have trusted it to any of his followers. He would have planned a place to hide it, and now he doesn't remember where it is."

Kylith's jaw tightened as he thought it through. "It can't have been Andevaar himself who stole it from the palace."

"No," Tally agreed. He'd been at Sathar with her. Who would he trust to bring him the stone? The outlaws weren't nice people. If Andevaar shared the location of something so valuable with them, they would steal it.

Mariella spoke up. "Drake is his friend, but he couldn't have been involved in this! He can't know what Andevaar is really like. How could they be friends if he did? Drake wouldn't steal Namradill."

Tally wasn't nearly so sure. The two men were business partners. "We should speak to him. Do you know where he is?"

Mariella shook her head. "He told me he had business here in Edri Province, but I don't know where exactly. I hoped we might find him at Edrithil."

"I think that should be our first step," Kylith said. "He might be in the city. And we can speak with Governor Folcan and search for anyone who might have seen Andevaar or Drake."

For two days and nights, the wind shrieked, and dust coated everything. No one made any attempt to travel during the storm. The sand blasted anyone unfortunate enough to be outside for any reason. Soldiers sheltered in their tents. Many had coaxed their horses into lying down and staked out their tents with the animals' heads inside the meager shelter.

It was difficult to get any rest. Finally, Tally wrapped her head in her jacket to muffle the sound and keep out the fine particles. She lay in her cot, the blankets now gritty with sand, and the tent walls flapping in the wind raging outside. Edrithil was a starting point, but there was little chance Andevaar was there. He'd left Sathar. Without his memory, he could have gone anywhere. He was probably wandering lost somewhere in the mountains. Without shelter, he might not have survived the storm.

No. He was alive, somewhere. If they couldn't locate Drake, she had to find Andevaar, return his memory, and force him to reveal the stone's location.

Sleep eluded her as the possibilities roamed through her mind. Simply finding him wouldn't be enough. She needed a way to ensure his cooperation. Which would be what? She remembered the hard set of his jaw, those cold eyes, the satisfaction on his face as he'd tried to take everything from her. He would probably rather die than return the stone to her.

If the outlaws found Andevaar, they would take him back to Sathar. If they did that, Tally had no way to get inside without leading her army up the mountains to attack the walls. Many lives would be lost if she did that. She would choose that option only as a last resort.

With his memory gone, Andevaar wouldn't recall a reason to return to Sathar on his own. He was still somewhere in the wilderness, and she needed to find him before the outlaws did. She couldn't take the entire army with her. A small group would be better. They could search, staying hidden to avoid the outlaws. Kylith wouldn't like it, but Tally had to go after Andevaar.

CHAPTER 15

FLINT

URING THE NEXT SEVERAL days, Flint spent a great deal of time in the woods. He enjoyed the silent peace of the trees and the small flowers blooming beneath his feet. Something about the wilderness solitude soothed Flint, and he spent hours at a time watching the quiet passing of animals or listening to the wind in the trees.

Finding a rock high on a ridge that overlooked the rest of the woods, Flint sat for a long time in silence. How long had it been since he examined himself? Perhaps there were advantages to forgetting his past. His memory now felt like a vast lake. The surface was entirely calm at the moment, though he could no longer see into the depths. While he didn't remember the circumstances, there was pain inside him. Loss.

He couldn't remember their faces or names, but he sensed that he'd lost people. He didn't think he'd allowed anyone into his heart for a long time. The emotion gathered into a tight knot in his chest.

Though he couldn't remember, he concentrated on gathering the sorrow from inside himself and allowing the weight of it to dissipate and the soft breeze to carry it away. At this moment, his memories were entirely out of reach. It was time to let go and move forward.

Flint didn't move for a long time, but when he did, he stretched and smiled. He went off through the forest feeling that a heavy weight had been removed.

As he followed the trail back toward the cottage, the sun sank into clouds of a strange brown color. He looked out over the valley, and a chill ran down his spine. He'd never remembered seeing weather like that before, but maybe he had in the past and couldn't remember.

It was a storm, coming fast.

Flint ran to the corral and led one horse toward the stable. Toban came just behind him with the other. They had nearly reached the stable doors when the wind blasted through the meadow carrying fine, driving sand with it. The horses whinnied and pranced as it struck. Flint pulled open the door, and they led the animals the last few steps into the barn. He shut the door behind himself and leaned against it.

"What kind of storm is *that*?" Toban asked, brushing dust from his face. His question confirmed that the wild weather didn't seem to belong.

Flint had never seen anything like it. "This storm should be in a desert, not a mountain valley."

Toban nodded, his brow furrowed in concern.

When they finished caring for the animals, they went back out into the storm and ran for the cottage. The dust was so thick that they couldn't see where they were going and found the building by blundering blindly along the familiar path.

They shut the door on the harsh wind and tried to catch their breath, coughing to clear the dust from their lungs.

Inside, no one moved. Thorvan sat motionless in a chair, staring into the fire. The flames bent one way, then the other, as the wind blasted down into the chimney. He didn't look up as they entered. Leya sat near the fireplace, her eyes huge in her little face.

Even though he hadn't been here long, Flint already respected the old man's insight and experience. He'd never seen Thorvan appear anything other than calm and relaxed. Maybe the storm was more serious than Flint had thought.

Flint went to Thorvan and put his hand on the old man's shoulder. "Are you all right?"

It was a long moment before Thorvan replied. He laid his hand over Flint's and gripped it. "I'm all right. Just... worried."

"About the storm?" Flint asked. "We made sure all the animals are in."

"This isn't an *ordinary* storm," Thorvan said.

CHAPTER 16

CROWN PRINCESS TAHLEA

AFTER THE STORM ENDED, they wasted two precious days while Folcan's men searched Edrithil for any word of Andevaar or Drake. At the end of the second day, when there was still no news, Tally had given up waiting.

In the middle of the night, she slipped out of the Seven Rivers army camp. She had donned someone else's leather armor. It didn't fit like her own and so disguised the shape of her body. She wore a plain dark tunic, with a hood wrapped around her head, covering the lower part of her face.

Kylith selected ten soldiers, led by a man named Arrick, to guard her. She wished Gerran could have been among them, but they had left him in Edrithil to recover. Arrick and the others were all men Kylith had known and trusted for years. Tally didn't want to think about what would happen if any of them were traitors.

During a secret, huddled gathering in the dark, Kylith had explained that their mission was dangerous, and that they needed to protect Tally but also keep her hidden among them. They all left their uniforms behind to further hide their identity.

Outlaws roamed the woods, prepared to attack anyone wearing a blue army tunic.

"Thank you for agreeing to join me," Tally said, looking around the tight circle and meeting each man's eyes. "The only reason we're attempting something so risky is that our kingdom, the lives of our people, depend on our success."

"You can count on us, Princess," Arrick said.

From the bottom of her heart, she hoped she could. She hoped she wasn't leading them to death and injury. What cost would they pay for following her? The thought that she might not bring them all home again caused a sick churning in her stomach.

They rode upward for two more nights, drawing near the place where outlaws had attacked her camp before. They would go the rest of the way on foot. Past that point, it became too difficult to hide the horses. Tally made sure they remained strictly out of sight during the daylight hours. As they kept a careful watch on the terrain, they spotted small groups of armed men from time to time. Nothing about their dress or gear identified who they served, but they must have come from the outlaw fortress. There were no other villages nearby, and there were too many of them to be simple hunters.

The men appeared to be combing the woods systematically. They must be searching for her, or for Andevaar. From what Tally knew of their plans, they needed him. All their plots centered on making him a hero and supporting him as he attempted to seize power. It was too late to go back and try to place someone else in that position.

As she watched a group of outlaws disappear into the woods, Tally let out a quick breath of relief. If they were still searching, they hadn't found him yet. There was still a chance she could get to him before they did. If they located him and took him back inside the walls of Sathar, it would require an army to get him out. Battle, blood, death. She had to locate him before the outlaws did.

Hiding by day and moving stealthily by night, Tally and her companions made their way higher. The closer they got to Sathar, the more danger they were in, but that was where they hoped to pick up Andevaar's trail.

Tally and her companions slipped soundlessly through the dark forest. A small group of outlaws huddled around a fire. Tally needed information if she were to succeed. Maybe these three could provide it. She gathered her men around her and quickly explained her plans. Moving silently, they crept through the underbrush toward the outlaws.

Attacking in a rush, they seized them from behind, attempting to keep their victims from crying out. They dragged the struggling outlaws deeper into the brush to ensure no one would see them.

Arrick took out a long dagger and held it against the throat of one outlaw. "If you cry out," he hissed. "I'll kill you so quickly, you won't know whether anyone heard you."

The outlaw nodded, his eyes wide in fear.

The soldier removed his hand. "What are you doing in the woods?" Arrick asked.

"Hunting." The word ended in a choked gasp as the point of Arrick's knife pierced into the man's skin.

"The truth!"

"Please!" the man begged, beads of sweat standing out on his forehead. "They ordered us to find Andevaar. We've been looking for days, but we haven't found him."

"Where was he last seen?" Arrick demanded.

The outlaw twisted, attempting to pull himself away from the knife point. "I don't know! No one saw him. They showed us the place where they found his horse wandering, but that's all they found."

A burst of excitement flooded through Tally. It wasn't much, but it was something. Arrick looked over his shoulder for her instructions. "Have him show us the place they found the horse."

"Take us there," Arrick ordered the man.

"I—It's dark," the man pleaded. "How am I supposed to find it in the dark? It will be daylight in a few hours, wait—"

"No waiting." Arrick's voice was hard. "We're going now." He nodded to his companions. "Bring the others."

They needed to find the place before dawn. Tally looked up at the sky, gauging how much dark remained. Dawn would increase their danger, especially with captives. She kept her hand on her weapon in case her companions needed help.

For hours, they walked. The first gray light of dawn was just lighting the east when their captives stopped. "This is it." The man pointed toward a wide meadow with a little stream flowing through it.

"Are you sure?" Arrick growled.

The outlaw nodded vigorously. "Yes. This is the place. We found the horse here alone, but no other sign of Andevaar." He twisted in Arrick's grip. "You have what you want. Now let us go!"

Arrick looked toward Tally. If they released the outlaws, they would tell their friends they had seen them, and the hunt would tighten around them. What else could they do? She would not order her men to kill them in cold blood. They needed the outlaws to stay quiet, at least until she and her friends had moved on.

Moving to stand beside Arrick, she murmured in his ear. "Do you think there's anything else they can tell us?"

He gazed at the man he'd questioned, assessing. "Maybe. But I think we have what we need." He glanced up at the sky. "Either way, we need to move on."

"I agree," she said. "Bind them, somewhere out of sight. Their friends will find them, but it will give us time to get away from here."

They moved their captives beyond the edge of the clearing into an area of thick undergrowth. It was getting light now. They needed to move. One of the captive outlaws struggled, despite the knife at his throat. He rolled, causing the soldiers to loosen their grip for a moment. Away from the blade, the man yelled.

A moment later, they heard footsteps approaching through the brush. Tally drew her sword. Several outlaws burst out of the thick cover and ran toward them, raising their weapons and shouting. Arrick and the others released their captives, who bolted to join their friends.

Raising her blade to defend herself, Tally stood with the others. The attack crashed into them, and the ring of metal on metal filled the woods. The outlaws were about equal in numbers to them, but Kylith had trained his soldiers well, and their skill surpassed the untrained ruffians. A man swung his sword at Tally, and she blocked the blow, returning one of her own that struck his arm below the shoulder. He gasped in pain and pulled back. Three of the attackers were on the ground when the others broke and fled.

Tally and her friends needed to get out of sight. They quickly lost themselves in the thick cover and ran through the woods, seeking a hiding place. A short while later, they stopped at a rocky outcropping. The spaces between the rocks were just large enough for them to slip inside.

It was a good hiding place. They remained there, motionless and concealed. Several groups of outlaws came into sight throughout the day but didn't come close enough to find them. From her place, pressed uncomfortably against the stone, Tally let out a breath of relief each time they moved away again.

The evening deepened around them, causing a quiet stillness to cover the woods. Hesitantly, Tally slipped from her hiding place. "Arrick and one more, come with me. The rest of you stay here."

Arrick slipped out to join her. "Remain here unless we're attacked," he instructed the others. They moved silently back toward the clearing where the man had reported finding Andevaar's horse. "What are we looking for, Princess?" Arrick asked quietly.

"Anything that belonged to Andevaar. We need to discover where he went."

The trees surrounded a meadow open to the sky. Combing through patches of thick brush, lush grass, and searching clumps of rocks, they covered the entire clearing carefully, finding nothing. Exhausted, her shoulders slumped as they went back to their friends. It was nearly midnight when they reached the outcropping again. They desperately needed rest and better light if they were going to find anything.

"We'll stay here tonight," she said. "Everyone sleep in turns. We'll search again in the daylight."

If she hadn't been so exhausted, Tally might not have slept, curled between the unforgiving rocks. Despite everything, her body demanded rest, and her eyes closed.

The morning dawned bright and cloudless, unseasonably warm for spring. Arrick and three others made a circle through the woods surrounding their hiding place. When they returned, reporting all was quiet for the moment, Tally returned to her search of the clearing.

While the rest of their group remained hidden, she, Arrick, and two of his men searched the area again. They spent hours combing the thick grass and looking through the rocks along the stream. Tally walked slowly along the edge of the running water. It wasn't a large stream, but it gathered into a few deep pools. Peering down into one of them, she caught sight of something reflective in the morning light. She dropped to her knees, staring down into the deep clear water.

Arrick came to join her. "What is it?"

Tally pointed to the water. "There's a sword, down at the bottom of the water."

He looked down, his expression confused. "Why would anyone drop their weapon in there?"

A man who had lost his memory might. He might have dropped it in the fast-moving water, and the current could have swept it into the pool. Tally stared down, trying to recall the details of the blade Andevaar had been wearing when they met. At the time, she hadn't focused on it, but there had been gold on the hilt, which could match the gleam of precious metal she saw now.

A tendril of hope grew inside her as she rose. "It could be his. Let's go further and see if we can find anything else."

The four of them moved up the hill, following the course of the water. Beyond the edge of the clearing, the woods closed in again.

As they climbed slowly, combing every thicket, Tally sweated in the warm sun. Near the middle of the day, she walked through a patch of brush and felt something under her foot. The texture didn't match the rest of the undergrowth. She bent low and saw a brown leather satchel.

Her heart rate sped up at the sight, and she pulled the bag from where it had caught in the thick bushes.

"Princess!" Arrick hissed.

She caught the warning in his tone and slipped down into the brush, out of sight. A group of a dozen outlaws, all armed, were apparently searching. Barely breathing, she remained hidden until they were gone. The other two soldiers emerged from hiding a little higher up the hillside. Tally needed to keep searching. They were so close. First the sword, now the satchel. If they could avoid detection for just a little longer, perhaps the trail would continue.

"We should hide until dark," Arrick said. Tally wanted to protest, but she knew he was right. There was no sense in putting her men in danger. For now, she had to be satisfied with the clues she had.

She followed Arrick until they found a thick growth of bushes beside a large boulder. It provided excellent cover and a view of the surrounding forest. "I'll stay with the princess," Arrick said to his men. "You two go down to the rest of our men. Wait until dark, and then bring them here to meet us."

With a nod of understanding, they slipped away, quickly vanishing between the trees.

Soon, everything was quiet. Tally turned the small satchel over in her hands. She opened it and found a folded piece of parchment inside. While the seal had been broken, she recognized it belonged to Governor Folcan. She skimmed the message.

It expressed gratitude and gave instructions to return immediately to Edrithil. None of that was important. Her heart pounded as she saw it was addressed to Andevaar and signed by Folcan. This bag had been Andevaar's. A messenger would have delivered a sealed letter. Someone had already done so. Andevaar had opened and read the message and had been on his way to complete his tasks when the spell had taken effect. Like his sword, he'd forgotten its importance and left it behind.

Why would the man move up the hill instead of down? There was no way to answer that, but if Andevaar continued long on this course, he'd come to the edge of Thorvan's lands. Maybe he was still there, wandering aimlessly along the border if the mystic didn't allow him to find the little valley. Why would Thorvan allow such a dangerous man inside?

Maybe Andevaar wasn't far away now. If they didn't find him soon, she'd continue on into Thorvan's valley and see if he could provide any aid in finding Andevaar. She shook her head. She didn't want to ask for help, not so soon after enacting the spell. Maybe her judgment was poor after all. Unease twisted inside her. She was supposed to be the ruler of the Seven Rivers, not a little girl who couldn't make up her mind and didn't know what to do.

Tally slept for a couple of hours in the warm afternoon sunshine. When she woke, she sat up and took her turn watching while Arrick slept. When night fell, she wanted to be on her way again, but they had to wait for the others.

While Arrick watched, she slept again. It was past midnight when the others reached them. "Were you followed?" she asked as their companions slipped into the hiding place.

"No, Princess," a soldier reported. "We saw several groups, but they didn't see us. There are more outlaws in this area every day."

Arrick nodded at that. "If we're going to keep you safe, we need to leave."

"We can't!" Tally protested in a fierce whisper. "We *have* to find Andevaar."

"The outlaws are bringing more men to this area all the time," Arrick said. "Finding him won't help if they capture you."

As much as she didn't want to admit it, it was true. If she planned to save her father's life and her people, she needed to be free to do it. They could continue up the mountainside. "We'll move toward the border of Thorvan's lands. We'll be safe there."

Taking advantage of the darkness, they moved up the slope. Tally passed the thicket where she had found the satchel. Andevaar must have come this way after the spell. If they continued on his trail, maybe they'd find another sign.

They moved on until dawn. In the growing light, Tally spotted something up ahead, just visible beneath the underbrush. A bit of dark leather, too smooth to belong in the wilderness. When she pulled it out, she saw a boot.

"Take it with us," Arrick advised. "We have to get out of sight."

They settled themselves into a small rocky hollow to wait out the light of day. Tally pulled out the boot and examined it. It was well-made, and very familiar. It couldn't be.

Beside her, Arrick stared at it. He took it, holding it against his own larger foot. "Are we following Andevaar? What man has feet this small?"

Tally took the boot back and placed it beside her own foot, displaying a perfect match. "It's my boot."

Arrick's eyebrows raised. "How is that possible?"

"They took my boots when I was at Sathar." She turned it over in her hands. It had been easy to recognize it. She wouldn't be the only one who would. "Kylith would recognize it. Maybe Andevaar planned to use it as proof that they captured me."

"Yes," Arrick said. "That would be a good reason for him to carry it with him."

They were on the right track. They had to be.

Evening deepened over the silent woods. As the sun set, Tally and her companions slipped from their place and started up the hill. A sudden shout echoed from between the trees above them. Outlaws. She couldn't see them yet, but they were on the steep incline above.

Rocks rolled down the slope, dislodged by the men's feet. Tally and the others slipped off to one side. In the fading twilight, they ran, staying in a group. More shouts echoed through the woods. It wasn't just one group out there. Tally could hear outlaws approaching from several directions.

She came to a sudden stop at the brink of the steep ravine.

Too quickly to allow a chance to flee, several men charged out of the brush at them. Tally and her friends drew their weapons and met the attack. A tall, bulky man with pale hair thrust his blade at Tally. She parried easily and drove him back. He was very strong, but not fast. She could evade his attack easily. Arrick and the other soldiers held back the surrounding outlaws. But the forest floor provided uneven footing to fight on, and they were being pushed to the edge of the steep rocky ravine. Tally and the others held their ground, fighting fiercely on the brink.

More yells echoed through the woods. A larger group of outlaws arrived to support their friends. Two more fighters joined the one already attacking Tally. She parried as quickly as she could, trying to hold them all off, but three opponents spread her defenses too thin. A sword point pierced her right thigh, and she clenched her jaw against the burst of fiery pain. Trying to take weight off the injured leg, she twisted to one side, and another blade penetrated her back to one side of her spine.

Two of the attackers were still coming. She raised her blade to hold them back, but their combined force pushed her backward. Her feet slid toward the edge of the ravine and a loose rock gave way. Tally almost didn't realize she was falling until her sword fell from her hand and landed farther uphill than she had just been. The jarring impact knocked the breath from her lungs, as her left shoulder, her arm, and then her head collided with stone and gravel. Finally, her fall eased into a slide until she came to rest in a pile of scree.

For a moment, pain drove all thought from her mind. Every part of her body hurt, but the outlaws wouldn't wait. Gasping, she dragged herself up. The sword wound on her thigh bled heavily. With shaking hands, she tore a strip from the hem of her tunic and bound it.

Yells and the clash of battle rang from the top of the ravine, but no one was near at the moment. It wouldn't take long for them to come looking for her. Moving silently as darkness deepened, Tally crept along the bottom of the ravine.

Her leg burned like fire, but, for the moment, it still obeyed her will, and she kept moving. As the shock of the fall wore off, the pain coalesced into the worst injuries: a sharp burning in her thigh and back and a wicked throbbing in one temple and her arm, just below the shoulder.

She couldn't stop now. If she rested, the outlaws would overtake her. They were probably already following her.

Tally kept going, eventually finding a way out of the ravine and into the forest. The sounds of pursuit faded into the darkness behind her. A wall of rock loomed above her, and she followed it. Unable to go further, she stopped before a small space between two boulders. Easing herself into the opening, she slid further inside until she was out of sight. Resting her throbbing body against the cool stone, she was aware of nothing more.

An animal snarl and a sharp pain in her ankle woke her. Coming suddenly back to awareness, she realized something moved near her feet. A vicious growl that sounded like a wolf came through the dark. It must have followed the scent of blood to her. Tally gripped the hilt of her dagger still at her belt. When the black shape lunged closer, she struck at it and heard a yelp.

Panting, Tally held the knife ready. How many of them were out there? Another of the pack leapt into the crack. The animal's paws landed on her chest, its weight driving her back against the rock, its jaws snapped for her throat. With her arm beneath the wolf, she thrust upward with her blade, connecting with its unprotected belly. She smelled its fetid breath and felt its teeth along her jaw as it yelped in pain. The animal was powerful, and it struggled, trying to free itself from her blade. Shaking with effort, Tally held the blade firm, barely keeping her grip on the knife as the wolf struggled.

Its yelps turned to whines until it collapsed on top of her. Tally lay, trying to catch her breath with the hot weight of the carcass lying on her. All her injuries were burning. Another wolf growled by her feet, and she fought to shove the dead wolf away. Its limp weight refused to budge. Tally gripped her knife and waited.

CHAPTER 17

FLINT

WHEN THE STORM PASSED, the days were clear and hot. No rain fell. Several times, Flint found Thorvan staring at the sky. Though the old man had said nothing more about the weather, he still seemed preoccupied. Flint paused beside Thorvan as he looked out toward the horizon where the sun was setting.

"Are you all right?" Flint asked.

Thorvan drew in a long breath and nodded, lowering his eyes from the distant view. "Yes."

"You look worried." Flint eyed the lines at the corners of the old man's eyes and the crease between his brows. "Is there something I can do to help?"

Putting a hand on Flint's shoulder, Thorvan smiled. "I think there might be. But you've already provided so much help to me and my grandchildren. Perhaps I shouldn't ask more of you."

Flint smiled in return. "You helped me too." He'd enjoyed the old man's wisdom and humor and his unusual insights. If he needed something now, what kind of man would Flint be to refuse? "What would you like me to do?"

Thorvan looked toward the sunset, where the edge of the valley dropped off sharply. "A short while before you arrived, the daughter of an old friend of mine came to ask for my help. She left here on an urgent errand, and I fear she's in trouble. Below this valley, outlaws fill the woods. I'm an old man, and I don't want to send Toban to help her. He's young and strong, but he has no experience dealing with men like that."

Flint was silent for a long moment. He opened his hand and stared at the lines of callus along his palm. "You think that I do." He drew in a long breath. "Who do you think I am?"

The old man smiled. "I think you're my friend, a kind young man who helped fix my roof and care for my horses. I believe you can do a great deal of good in the world. And I believe you have the strength and skills to protect someone, should those outlaws attack them."

Flint stared out into the darkening forest. The old man's answer hadn't been specific, but he decided it was good enough for now. "When should I leave?"

In the distance, so far away they could barely hear it, a wolf howled.

"Can you go at once?" Thorvan asked, staring into the dark toward the sound. "Her name is Tally. She has long dark hair, and she's tall."

Flint headed for the stable. His dagger was already at his belt. He grabbed two blankets and a clean shirt, rolled them up, and picked up the bow and quiver Toban had lent him. He met Thorvan on the doorstep. The old man held out a pack. "Thank you for doing this."

Toban always insisted that it felt good to help other people. When Flint saw the gratitude in the old man's expression, he agreed. He stuffed the blankets into the pack with the provisions Thorvan had included. He slung the pack and bow over his shoulder and walked across the meadow into the darkening woods.

The quiet of the forest surrounded him. He heard nothing but the whisper of the wind in the trees. The usual nocturnal birds and insects were strangely silent as he moved down the slope.

He walked for several hours, and midnight had passed when Flint stopped to rest. He'd seen no sign of anyone yet. Even the wolves had gone quiet. He hadn't heard them for a while. In the daylight, he could look for tracks. Maybe he could search in both directions from the path he'd taken to see if anyone had walked through recently. It would be easier than trying to find one person in the vastness of the mountains. Setting his pack and bow to one side, he rested his back against the trunk and closed his eyes.

The little boy brought an armful of sticks across the room and stacked them beside the fireplace. A white-haired woman, bent with age, stirred something in a bowl. They both looked up as they heard a knock at the door.

The boy scampered across the room to the door, while the old woman followed, leaning heavily on a cane. Opening the door, the boy faced a man in a dark blue military uniform. For a long moment, they stared at each other. The soldier wore a grim expression.

"Are you Jothan's son?" the man asked the boy.

The boy looked from his serious face to the large envelope in his hand. He nodded. "My father went away to serve the king. Did you see him? Do you know where he is and when he's coming back?"

The man on the threshold cleared his throat and bowed his head. "I'm very sorry to have to tell you this, but he's not coming back. There was an accident. Jothan was killed."

The boy' face drained of color. The old woman stood behind him and gripped his shoulder. "No!" he gasped. "There must be some mistake. It can't be..."

The man at the door handed him the envelope. "I served with Jothan. He was a good man, a friend. I'm very sorry."

The boy stared at the envelope in his hands, tears running down his small face.

Flint woke to the howl of a wolf. The animal wasn't far away. Shaking his head, Flint tried to clear away the remnants of the dream that had seemed so real. He felt the boy's heartbreak, the stabbing pain of loss. It surrounded him, making his own chest ache. Rubbing a hand over his face, he came gradually back to the present. Dark forest surrounded him. Another wolf howled.

From his time hunting, he knew the packs avoided people. Toban had told him they stayed well away unless someone was injured. Flint's stomach twisted at the thought of a person alone and injured in the woods at night. Even with his brief experience, he'd observed that the mountains could be harsh. He got to his feet, trying to shake off the thought. The pack might be gathered around the carcass of a deer or some other animal.

Slipping soundlessly through the dark, his eyes adjusted to the faint light of moon and stars. He headed toward the source of the howl.

As he drew near, he saw that the pack had cornered something. The animals formed a semicircle at the base of a wall of rock and, from time to time, one of them made a tentative lunge forward. The boldest of them leapt toward the crack in the rock but retreated, yipping in pain. Whatever was hidden there still lived and obviously objected to becoming supper for the wolves.

Flint picked up two palm-sized stones. With a yell, he jumped forward, throwing them at the wolves. The first stone struck one hard. It yelped and jumped. The rest of the pack looked around uneasily but then broke and fled into the woods.

Cautiously, he approached the crack in the rock. At first, all he saw was the carcass of a wolf, but that couldn't be all. When the last wolf had attacked, something had retaliated. He drew close enough to see that the body of a person lay covered by the lifeless form of the wolf.

"Are you hurt?" Flint asked. The faint light gleamed off the blade of a knife. He backed up. Apparently, he had *not* found the girl Thorvan had sent him to look for. Maybe this man knew where she was. He'd do what he could to help. "It's all right. The wolves have gone. Can I help you?"

"Who are you?" the figure hissed.

"My name is Flint," he said, making his voice sound as soothing as possible. "I won't harm you. I heard the wolves and I only want to help."

The knife blade still faced him, but the weapon shook a little.

"You're not an outlaw?"

"No," he answered immediately. He rubbed his forehead. At least he didn't *think* he was an outlaw, but maybe he was and didn't know it. Thorvan knew the outlaws were in the forest near his valley. Did he recognize any of their faces? Would he have told Flint if that was the case? "I promise, I only want to help."

In response, the knife fell back.

Flint dragged the limp carcass free, revealing the human figure dressed in armor and leather boots, lying beneath it. "That's better, isn't it?" he asked.

He heard no answer. He'd thought the wounded man believed his offer of help, but in fact, he'd passed out and dropped the knife. Flint picked up the blade and stowed it safely in his pack. He'd been through this part of the woods, and he knew of a hidden hollow in the rocks not too far away. He'd be able to kindle a fire there without the light being seen.

Dragging the unconscious figure out from between the rocks, he checked for signs of life. His fingers found a pulse beneath the chin, and he heard the soft sound of breathing when he put his ear near the injured man's mouth. He was obviously hurt, but in the dark, there was no way to tell how badly.

Bending down, Flint dragged the unmoving body over his shoulder and stood up. Not too bad. The voice had sounded young, even in a whisper, and the man had a thin build. Good. He was easy to carry.

Flint walked for a while, hearing nothing more than a couple of distant howls from the wolves. When he reached his destination, he set the injured man down. Quickly gathering wood, Flint started a small blaze in the shelter of the rocks. Stone surrounded them on three sides, and loomed overhead, while thick brush screened the opening. Inside, lay a sheltered space, now lit by the glow of the little fire.

The night was cool, and the unconscious man already shivered. Flint pulled blankets from his pack and wrapped them around him. In the fire's light, he attempted to assess the injuries. A large patch of blood surrounded a makeshift bandage on one thigh.

Flint groped in his pack for a clean shirt, cutting it into strips with his knife. He untied the crude bandage, now soaked with blood, and pulled the torn trouser leg back from the wound. It looked deep.

He recognized a sword wound when he saw it. Whoever this young man was, he had seen battle. Had the outlaws attacked him? Flint might find out what had happened after the injured man rested.

Flint wondered once more about his own past. Blood and battle seemed familiar, but why would he choose such a life over the peace of the wilderness?

Binding up the wound, Flint continued his investigation. In the flickering firelight, he saw blood on one sleeve, just below the edge of the young man's pauldron. Loosening the leather strap, he lifted the shoulder plate back. With his knife, he widened the hole in the sleeve.

Something had struck the arm. Black bruising ran from shoulder to elbow. The worst of the impact had pierced the skin in several places that still oozed blood. Was it broken? With great care, he felt the bone. The injured man groaned at his touch but didn't wake. Flint felt up and down again but couldn't find a fracture. Taking one of the cloth strips he had made, he wrapped the arm.

Turning him onto his side, Flint saw that something had pierced his back, leaving a rent in the leather armor. Unbuckling the straps, he slid it carefully off over his head. He raised the shirt to examine the wound when the figure suddenly stirred. The injured man gasped and wrenched himself away from Flint's hands.

"It's all right," he said soothingly, raising his empty hands to show he meant no harm.

The wounded soldier slid as far away as possible in the small space and pulled his knees against his chest, staring wide-eyed at Flint.

"You're hurt," Flint said. "I was only trying to help."

"I'm fine. It's nothing."

Flint stared back. It had been very dark in the forest and now he could see more clearly in the firelight. The eyes that met his were dark, with gracefully arched brows and heavy lashes. The hood had fallen back, revealing glossy dark hair in a long braid. Soft wisps had come loose. Flint's eyes scanned the face and then traced the shape of legs and hips, and his mind put all the pieces together.

A woman. Maybe she was the girl Thorvan had sent him to find, after all.

She stared at him as if he was about to leap for her throat as the wolf had done. Her hands went to the empty sheath at her belt, obviously searching for her weapon.

"You don't need it now," he said firmly. "I'm trying to help."

Slowly, her eyes took in the fresh bandages on her thigh and arm. "You did this?" Her tone was incredulous.

"Yes."

She took in a long breath. "Thank you for helping me." Her dark eyes examined his face.

He felt the need to offer some sort of introduction. "My name is Flint."

"Tally," she answered.

He smiled slightly. He'd found her.

Her eyebrows rose in shock, but eventually they lowered, as she continued to watch him as if waiting for him to attack.

They couldn't sit there all night. She needed help. "You took a sword in the back," he said. "Are you going to let me see it?"

"It's not too bad," she insisted, her jaw set.

He stared at her, his eyebrows raised. When he didn't move, she finally conceded.

"Fine." She turned her back to allow him access to the wound.

He sat down cross-legged behind her. "I need to see it." It would be better to give her a warning.

She nodded.

Moving slowly, he pulled up the fabric of her tunic. Underneath was a white chemise of fine, smooth fabric. He felt his face heat. This girl was a stranger, and he shouldn't be looking at her underclothing. Mentally, he shook himself. He wasn't here to ogle. Blood soaked the delicate, pale fabric. For a moment, he couldn't decide what to do. The garment was close fitting. He could not slide it aside, but he needed to treat the wound. He took out his knife and cut through the bottom part of the fabric, which allowed him to lift it away from the injury.

The cut was halfway down her back, about three fingers from her spine. He cleaned it with water and cloth. Blood had soaked down her back, but the flow had almost stopped now. He held a soft pad of cloth against it, wishing he had something to soothe the damaged flesh. It had to be painful.

"I need to keep this in place." He cut a long strip of cloth from the remains of the shirt. Holding one end against the wound, he passed his hand around her side. She hissed between her teeth and seized the end with her good hand, wrapping it across her ribs, and handing it back to him. They repeated the awkward process again before he tied the ends securely.

He'd tried to touch her as little as possible, since it obviously bothered her. Her pale skin looked soft, smooth, and perfect between bruises and the sword wound. He finished his work and pulled the fabric back down into place. She turned around to face him, her eyes still following his every motion.

"Thorvan sent me to look for you, to help if I could." He hoped telling her would allow her to trust him, even a little.

She shook her head. "That's impossible. You don't know Thorvan."

Why was it impossible? Maybe she knew of a reason that he didn't remember. "Thorvan? He's about this tall, gray hair," Flint touched his shoulder. "Kind eyes. Knows everything."

One corner of her mouth lifted in a faint smile. "That sounds like him. But..." Her voice trailed into silence.

When she didn't finish her thought, he continued his work. The side of her head, beginning above her eyebrow and running toward her ear, had a jagged cut. He began cleaning it. The strands of her hair felt like silk against his calloused fingers. His eyes traced the graceful curve of her slender neck. How had he not noticed sooner? Despite the trousers and the armor, now that he knew, it was impossible not to notice that she was a woman. "Are you hurt anywhere else?"

"My ankle. Right side."

She brought her feet around closer to the fire. With her good hand, she reached for the laces and began untying them.

It looked like a slow process with one hand. "May I help?"

"If you wish," she murmured, leaning back against the rock and closing her eyes. He loosened the laces and pulled off her boot and sock. A long, swollen bruise was already turning purple along her shin and down toward her foot. Several bloody puncture wounds surrounded her ankle.

"Wolf?" he asked.

She nodded wordlessly. He cleaned and bandaged the injuries as well as he could.

By the time he finished, she was shivering again. He spread a blanket along the ground near the fire. "Come and rest. It will be warmer here."

Using her good arm and her good leg, she slid herself over onto the blanket. She tried to get comfortable without lying on any of her injuries, finally settling on her right side. Her face was still tight with pain. She moved her injured arm, trying to settle it.

"Here." He rolled his cloak into a ball and slid it under her elbow. "Better?"

"Thank you," she murmured.

He covered her with the other blanket.

The boy watched a large wagon pull up to the back door. His eyes widened at the sight of so much food. Rows of crates and barrels filled the wagon bed. There were stacks of warm, soft blankets and an enormous basket of feather pillows. When no one was watching, he reached out to touch them. He'd never felt anything so soft.

A heavy hand landed on his shoulder. He turned to see the master, a big man with a long nose and heavy brows. "Don't touch them," he ordered. "You might leave dirty fingerprints. We don't need them, anyway. They'll bring a fine price at market, and it's better to save the money for our future needs. Now, go inside."

The boy returned to the shabby dining room and sat on the hard bench beside the other children. Their faces were thin and haggard. All the children dressed in the same shapeless, ragged gray clothing. A child stood on a stool, dipping a ladle into a pot. The other children shuffled past in a line, each holding out a bowl for the one behind the pot to pour a thin soup into it. The pot was empty before the last child came by. Several of the others poured a little of their own meager ration into her bowl.

The meal was silent, and they shivered in the chilly room. The master watched them from the doorway. "Clean up!" he ordered. "This house belongs to the king, and you have to clean up after yourselves." The children scattered, two running to the pump in the yard for water, others gathering the dishes, sweeping the floor, and heating wash water.

When the man had watched them finish the cleaning, he pointed up the stairs. "Now, bed! And if I hear a single sound, someone will get a beating."

The children went to a long room with rows of narrow beds, each with a lumpy straw mattress and a single thin blanket. The boy lay on his bed, huddled into a ball against the cold. None of the children dared speak. Rules were rules, and there were lots of rules there. No one wanted another beating.

The boy faced the wall. Whispering under his breath so no one else could hear. "Can you hear me, father? I miss you, but I hope you're with mother now. Why did you have to leave me?"

Flint woke suddenly in the gray pre-dawn light, remembering the pain and loneliness of the dream. No child should have to live like that. Trying to shake off the sorrow he felt, he looked around. He hadn't meant to sleep, but the girl had been so still, he must have dozed off. Nothing remained of his little fire but ashes. His eyes flew to the other side of the hollow. She was gone.

How had she even moved, injured as she was? Where had she gone? Even the boot he'd removed to tend her ankle was gone.

Despite his limited experience, it had been obvious that she'd been frightened of him. He couldn't deny that it made sense. She was a girl alone and hurt. They didn't know each other, but he'd hoped to ease her fears when he said Thorvan had sent him. Obviously, she hadn't believed him.

The forest was dangerous for someone in her condition. Flint had to find her, even though she didn't want to be found. She needed help. As he gathered his things, he realized she had taken his bow. He scattered the ashes of his fire, shouldered his pack, and followed her trail out into the forest.

CHAPTER 18

FLINT

H E FOLLOWED TALLY'S TRAIL through the woods. She couldn't walk well, and her injured leg made it easy to track her. Still, she'd gone a surprising distance. As the morning light grew brighter, he moved quietly through the trees. At length, he spotted her sitting on the ground, her back against a tree. His bow rested across her lap with an arrow nocked. She wasn't alone. A man he'd never seen before stood across a small clearing, facing her with a sword in his hand.

The man raised his weapon, smiling coldly as he approached her. "Found you. This time you're not getting away."

Icy fear for her settled in Flint's chest. He moved forward.

The girl showed no trace of fear as she faced the man. Her voice sounded even and sure. "If you come any closer, I'll shoot you."

The man stared at her and glanced down at the bow in her hands. His eyes flew to the bandage on her arm. He smirked. "I doubt it. If you could pull that bow, you'd already have done it." Making his decision, he charged toward her.

She lifted the bow and began to draw. A cry of pain escaped her lips. She released the bow string, only half-drawn, and the arrow flew harmlessly into the dirt between them.

Flint bolted toward them, tackling the man just before he reached her. Not giving him time to recover from the sudden attack, Flint seized a sturdy fallen branch and hit the man over the head. He collapsed, unmoving.

When Flint turned to the girl, he saw her fitting another arrow to the bowstring. He lunged toward her, seizing the weapon before she could try to pull it. "Don't!" he protested. "Last night, I thought your arm was broken. The last thing you should do is draw a bow."

She stared at him in disbelief.

"Was he alone?" Flint looked toward the unconscious outlaw.

"For now," she said.

He released his hold on the bow and stood. "We need to get out of here before more of them find us."

She appeared to agree and began pushing herself to her feet. A sturdy stick lay beside her.

His eyes widened. She wasn't seriously trying to walk, was she?

She slung the bow over her shoulder, leaned on the stick, and hobbled a few steps forward. Only able to grip her support with one hand, she lost her hold and sank to the ground. He knelt beside her. "We need to get out of sight before more outlaws find us. And you can't walk."

In stubbornness and pain, she narrowed her eyes. She obviously still wanted to object.

"Why run from me? I told you Thorvan sent me to help you," he said.

Her eyes widened. "I thought you were lying last night. It can't be true. You don't really know Thorvan!"

He stared at her. "Yes, I do. Thorvan told me you're the daughter of his old friend and sent me to find you."

Her eyes still looked wary. "That's *all* he told you about who I was?"

"That's all."

"I don't need you to help me," she said. "My friends can't be far away. I'll find them, and they can help."

He lowered his brows in frustration. "They aren't here now. What would you have me do, leave you here for your enemies to find?" When she had no answer to this, he pulled the quiver from her back, the bow from her shoulder, and thrust them into her hands. Without waiting for permission, he picked her up in his arms and stood up.

He wondered if she would struggle and refuse to allow him to carry her. For a while, he could feel the tension in her body, but as he walked, she gradually relaxed. He wasn't sure if she'd accepted his presence and help, or if she had drifted into unconsciousness. With no better hiding place in mind, he took her back to the nook where they had spent the previous night. When they reached the place, he set her gently on the ground and wrapped a blanket around her.

"Where are we?" she murmured without opening her eyes.

"Back in the same place as last night. I don't think anyone will find us here, and you're safe for now. Please don't run again. I swear, you do not need to run from me."

She blinked and looked up at him. "You saved my life today."

Her eyes were a deep, rich brown framed by thick lashes.

He stared back at her. "If you hadn't bolted into the forest, ignoring your injuries, I wouldn't have needed to save your life."

A slight smile lifted the corner of her mouth. "That's true," she admitted. "I won't try to run again."

"Good."

"Unless I have a reason."

He let out an exasperated sigh. "I won't be giving you any reason."

Her eyes had closed, and she didn't respond.

Slipping silently away from their camp, he listened for the sound of running water. He found a small rushing stream and followed it. The water soon led him to a thick growth of shrubs. Thorvan had shown him how to identify their small narrow leaves and smooth bark, which could serve as a pain reliever. With his knife, he cut several branches and slid them into his pack. Further up the stream, he found two herbs the old man had taught him to use and gathered large handfuls of their leaves.

Back in their hidden refuge, he rebuilt the tiny fire and opened his pack to pull out a small pot borrowed from the cottage. Now, he added water and placed it over the flames to heat. Settling down beside the fire, he took the branches from his pack and peeled off tiny shavings of bark, piling them carefully atop a flat rock.

Glancing up, he saw Tally's eyes open. She said nothing, just watched him cutting and piling the bark.

In the light of day, she looked younger than he'd guessed at first. Maybe the same age as Toban? Who else could he compare with? Flint rubbed his forehead. He didn't know how old *he* was. The skin on the backs of his hands was smooth, with no sign of age spots, and he had no wrinkles on his face. He'd seen no gray in his hair. How else could he tell?

She rested quietly now but still watched him warily, as if she expected him to attack at any moment. Someone had already attacked her. "Did the outlaws find you?" he asked, pointing toward her bandaged leg.

Tally nodded but didn't answer.

"You still don't want to talk to me." It was a statement, not a question. "I didn't have to come after you. I could have let the outlaws have you," he said. He met her eyes directly, and she stared back at him.

"You're right," she finally admitted, the tight set of her jaw relaxing a little. "Why did you?"

Somehow, he could tell that she hated to admit she was wrong. The beginning of a smile lifted one corner of his mouth. "I borrowed that bow." He gestured toward the weapon. "I needed it back so I could return it."

"What are you doing?" She glanced toward the little mound of bark shavings.

"I have been learning about the use of herbs from Thorvan. The bark of this shrub is a painkiller. I thought you might like to try it out."

One of her eyebrows raised.

"Don't worry. If you think it might be poison, I'll drink some first. Even though it tastes terrible." He gestured to the pile of leaves. "These are good to help with the healing of wounds. With your permission, I will apply them to your injuries."

"Thank you." Using her good arm, she pushed herself into a sitting position.

He didn't miss the way her lips thinned and her face paled as she moved. "How are you feeling? You must be sore."

"That's one word for it." Her words came out through clenched teeth.

The tiny pot of water was simmering now, and he dumped the bark shavings into it. "Just wait a little while, then you can drink it. It will help the pain. Do you need water?"

"I need... a moment of privacy." She attempted to get up. It took her a few moments to work her way up to her knees.

"Can I help?" He bent to one knee beside her.

"I can do it."

"I know. But it's not bad to accept help, sometimes." He had the feeling she knew that but didn't want to admit it. She put her good hand on his shoulder and pushed herself upright, balancing on her good leg. She stood still, breathing rapidly for a long moment. He took her elbow to steady her. "Are you all right?"

"Just a little dizzy."

"Even before your trip through the forest today, you hit your head hard and you've lost a lot of blood."

She took another breath. "It's passing. I'm all right." Stubbornly, she took a step forward onto her bad leg. It nearly buckled under her, and she lurched forward awkwardly. She would have fallen if he hadn't caught her waist.

She drew in a sharp breath at his touch, and he wondered briefly if he'd hurt her. No. He'd been careful to put his hands on an uninjured part of her body. "Steady now," he whispered.

"I..." Her voice trailed off, and she tried another step. This time her leg bore her weight, though her face had gone white and she was holding her breath.

"Will you please lean on me?" he asked. It was not taking long to learn that she was an exceptionally stubborn girl. He didn't wait for her permission. He put his arm around her waist and helped her forward. After several hobbling steps, they were out in the forest. "Where do you want to go?" He looked around.

"Those bushes there will be fine." She pointed to a heavy growth of green foliage.

He helped her over to them looking to make sure the area was safe before clearing his throat. "I'll just leave you alone. I'll be over there, if you'd care to tell me when you're finished."

Walking out of sight behind a stand of trees, he waited. Who was this girl? Thorvan had given him only a little information. When he found her, she'd been utterly alone and without help. The friends she mentioned were nowhere nearby, and she'd obviously been there a while. The wolf she had killed had time to grow cold, and some of the blood had dried around her wounds. Thorvan said she was traveling back to his valley. Why would she brave the dangers of the forest? Where were her friends? The outlaws could have killed them. The ruffian they met had recognized her. The outlaws wanted to find her. Who was she?

A grunt of pain distracted him. He peeked around the trees to see her trying painfully to climb back to her feet. Whoever else she was, she had to be the most stubborn girl in the world.

By midnight, Tally's skin burned with fever. Flint felt her forehead and shook his head. He'd done his best to clean the wounds, but they were deep, and now it seemed an infection had set in.

She needed more help than he could give her, here in the forest. There were towns at the bottom of the mountains, but he didn't know if the people were friends or foes of either one of them. The outlaws roaming the woods were obviously not her friends, and he couldn't let them find her, especially not in her weakened state. His best option for help was Thorvan. Flint could walk back up to the old man's cottage within a day, but it would take longer to transport Tally there.

In the fire's light, he cleaned her wounds again, applying more of the healing herbs. She stirred while he worked. "What happened?" she muttered. Her brown eyes appeared dazed.

"You're running a fever," he said.

She blinked. "Is that why I can't get up?"

He smiled at her. "That must be it. Will you take some water?" He helped her drink. "I'm going to take you to Thorvan. He can help us."

"Help?" she muttered. She blinked and peered up at him, her eyes unfocused.

"Yes. I'm trying to help."

Her eyes framed by long dark lashes gazed into his. "Did you change your mind, then? You're not going to hurt me anymore?"

Flint felt as if his insides had turned to ice. She knew who he was. She hadn't been afraid of him simply because she was injured and alone in the forest. There was a reason. What had he done to her? The truth was locked away in his past with his vanished memories. He clasped her hand in his. He had to answer her now. "Yes. I've changed my mind. I promise I mean you no harm."

"That's good," she murmured, her eyes closing.

He needed to get her to Thorvan as soon as he could. He attached the bow and quiver to the bottom of his pack. Lifting her as gently as he could, he settled her across his shoulders. She groaned as the motion disturbed her injuries.

Flint walked up the hill through the rest of the night. When the sun rose, the daylight made travel easier. He kept his pace slow enough that he wouldn't jostle her too much, but he made steady progress. Her fever only grew higher as the hours passed, and stopping to rest would only make it worse. Thorvan could help her.

He couldn't seem to get her words out of his mind. *You're not going to hurt me anymore?* What had he done to her? Maybe helping her now would convince her he hadn't meant to harm her before. He couldn't imagine intentionally injuring anyone.

Night fell, and the stars came out, glittering in a vast canopy between the branches. He passed through the last trees and entered the little mountain valley. A few moments later, the cottage came into view. Everything was silent, but a light burned in the window.

As he drew near, the cottage door opened. Thorvan appeared with a lantern in his hand. He strode quickly forward. "Flint! What happened?"

"I found her injured in the woods," he explained. "I used the herbs you taught me, but it wasn't enough. She's burning with fever."

"Bring her inside," Thorvan ordered. The cottage was silent and dark except for the light the old man carried. "Put her here." He pointed to the bed.

The old man helped lift her down from Flint's shoulders. Placing the light on a shelf beside the bed, he made a quick examination.

"She has a sword wound here," Flint pointed to her thigh, "and another smaller one on her back. Her arm is hurt here, and there's the cut on her head, bruising on her shin and ankle, and a wolf bit her." Flint looked up at Thorvan. "That's all I know of. Can you help her?"

The old man's eyes had gone very wide as Flint listed the injuries, but he spoke firmly. "Yes, I must."

Toban had woken and looked down at them from the loft where he slept. "What's wrong?"

"She's sick and injured." Thorvan gestured at the unconscious girl. "We have to help her. Can you please take Leya and stay with her in the stable until we finish?"

"Of course, Grandfather." Toban stared down at Tally with wide eyes. "Will she be all right?"

"I'll do everything I can," Thorvan promised.

Toban climbed down, picked up the sleeping Leya in her blanket, and carried her out.

"Good." Thorvan looked at Flint. "Are you prepared to help me?"

"Yes, of course," Flint answered. "I'll do anything I can."

"We'll need clean hot water and plenty of clean cloth. It's in the cupboard there." The old man pointed.

Flint went toward the cupboard while Thorvan grabbed a tray and began filling it with items. After a few moments, he brought a side table over next to the bed and set the tray on it. Flint had stoked the fire and set the kettle to heat. He brought the cloth and went to stand beside the old man, who was looking down at Tally.

"The leg wound is the worst," Flint said.

Thorvan carefully cut away the soiled bandages, widening the tear in her pants, pulling the fabric back to expose the wound. "Bring me the water and cloth."

Flint hurried to obey, watching as the old man cleaned the wound. In the lantern light, it looked much worse now than the last time he'd tended it. The surrounding skin was swollen and red, while the wound itself looked gray and puffy.

"We have to clean it out," Thorvan said. He took his knife and went to the fire to hold the blade in the flames for a moment. Then he returned to the bed. "It won't be pleasant," he looked up at Flint. "Can you hold her still? I'll be as quick as possible."

Flint positioned his shoulder against her ribs, and his hands gripped her leg, one above the wound, the other below it. He nodded at Thorvan. The old man made a deft slice to release the infection. At the feel of his blade, Tally screamed and jerked, but Flint held her tight. Her eyes flew open and locked on his face. "Please don't," she begged. "I can't give you what you ask! Please!"

Flint's stomach twisted at her plea.

Thorvan laid a reassuring hand on her shoulder. "It will be all right, Tally. You'll be better soon."

She calmed at the sound of his voice.

"One more," Thorvan said to Flint, focused on his work. Tally cried out again. "Keep holding her." For several moments, he worked over the wound. Then he cleaned it again and mixed several ingredients into a paste, spread it over the cut, and wrapped it. When that was done, he examined the gash on her head and the bruising on her arm. "I think those are all right. Help me turn her over."

When Thorvan had exposed the wound on her back, he cleaned it. "This one isn't so serious," he said, expelling a breath of relief. They rolled her carefully onto her back. "Now, her ankle."

Flint unlaced her boot and pulled it off as carefully as he could over her bandaged ankle. The long bruise down her shin looked worse than ever, and when he pulled back the wrappings, the puncture wounds around her ankle were swollen and oozing.

"That doesn't look good," Thorvan said.

Flint felt a pang of guilt. "I'm sorry. I found her as quickly as possible, and I did what I could for her out there. I didn't know what else to do."

Thorvan turned to look him in the eye and placed a comforting hand on his shoulder. "You did well. I'm sure you saved her life. She's going to be fine in time because of you."

Flint took a deep breath and tried to believe what the old man had told him. "I didn't hurt her," Flint said. He paused. "At least... not that I remember. Does she know who I was before?"

The old man's voice was quiet. "It would seem so."

Flint's stomach clenched into a tight knot. Who had he been before? What reason could he have had for wanting to harm Tally? It sounded like he had demanded something from her. Something she wasn't willing or able to give him. He couldn't imagine a good reason for him to have acted in such a way. Since he found her, he'd done nothing but try to help her. If only he could have protected her, so she hadn't gotten hurt.

He turned to Thorvan. "Who is she? You know, don't you?"

"We can talk about this later," Thorvan said. "Now, bring that basin and hot water and a chair. Put them here." He arranged the chair and basin beside the bed. He went back to his cupboard for a few more ingredients, which he added to the water. A strong smell wafted up, and Flint wrinkled his nose.

Thorvan knew more about Tally than he had said. Flint looked down at the unconscious girl on the bed. Taking care of her was more urgent than his search to discover his past. He could understand if Thorvan thought that too. When Tally was out of danger, Flint would ask again.

"Move her over a little, please," Thorvan said.

Flint lifted her so that Thorvan could soak her foot in the basin. "Hold her leg. It's going to sting." He gripped Tally's leg as the old man slipped her foot and ankle into the water. Though she didn't cry out again, her breathing quickened, and she attempted to pull her foot away. After a few moments, the sting must have eased, and she relaxed.

Thorvan removed the basin and dried and bandaged her ankle.

Flint tucked her feet back into the bed and covered her to keep her warm. "What now?" After so many hours of travelling without rest, his legs ached, and exhaustion dragged at him from all sides.

Thorvan pulled a chair near the bed and sat down. "Now, we wait. I suggest we save any difficult conversations for another time. You look like you need rest. Why don't you sleep? I will watch over her. You can go to the stable or up there, since Toban is gone." He pointed toward the loft.

As much as he didn't want to admit how tired he was, Flint agreed. Tally seemed to rest quietly now under Thorvan's watchful care. Too tired to think anymore, Flint climbed the ladder into the tiny loft and sank down on the pallet where Toban usually slept, unconscious as soon as he lay down.

Something tickled his nose. Without opening his eyes, Flint brushed at it. He heard a giggle, and opened his eyes to see Leya watching him, a blade of grass in her hand. From the light coming in the windows, the sun was high. "You fell asleep with your boots on," she observed gravely, "without even a blanket over you. And you're in Toban's place."

His voice sounded rough with sleep. "Toban took my place in the stable. What else could I do?" He closed his eyes again.

"You can't sleep now," she protested. "It's daytime."

With a sigh, he rubbed his eyes and sat up. When he looked down from the loft, he saw Tally lying in the bed, but the chair beside her was empty. Her color looked much better this morning.

"She's still sleeping," Leya said, peeking down beside him.

"Yes, but she is sick. You must not try to wake her up."

"No. Grandfather said I shouldn't." She looked up at him through her eyelashes. "He said I shouldn't wake you up either."

"I'm all right," he said. "But don't disturb her."

Leya looked down at the sleeping girl. "She's so pretty, just like a princess should be."

Last night, he'd asked Thorvan who Tally was. A princess? Flint took a second look at Tally's features, peaceful in sleep. Her long eyelashes were dark where they brushed against her pale skin. His eyes traced the graceful curve of her jaw and the delicate pink of her mouth. It wasn't hard to imagine her in a beautiful dress. Princess of what? He couldn't recall any kingdom or any city surrounding a palace where a princess might live.

Imagining her in a soft gown seemed at odds with her stubborn determination and the strength he'd already seen her display. If he'd known anyone with that rank before, he didn't know it. He couldn't remember any reason it would make a difference.

Leya smiled. "She told me she left her pretty dresses at home because she couldn't ride very well in them."

Flint returned her smile. Even after knowing Tally only a couple of days, that sounded like her.

Leya looked at him with wide eyes. "I can hear your stomach growling."

He grinned. "It's time for breakfast."

"Breakfast was a long time ago, but there's food." She led the way down the ladder, and he followed. When he reached the bottom, he brushed his hand across Tally's forehead. From the heat of her skin, he knew she remained feverish, but it was lower than before. Thorvan came back in and walked to Flint's side. "The fever hasn't broken yet, but I believe the worst is behind us. She's improving."

Gratitude washed over Flint at Thorvan's words. "Thank you for helping her."

Thorvan's eyebrows raised. "Of course. Now come, I kept food warm for you."

Flint's stomach gave another ferocious growl. The night and day before had passed in a blur. He hadn't taken the time to stop. It had been far too long since his last meal. Leya brought him a bowl, and he ladled thick porridge from the pot. She brought a pot of honey, holding it carefully in both hands, and he added a spoonful. "Thank you."

Leya smiled brightly at him, and he couldn't help but return the expression. Maybe everything was going to be all right. Tally was getting better. She would recover. There would be time later to discuss the questions that spun in circles through his mind.

CHAPTER 19

CROWN PRINCESS TAHLEA

T ALLY DID NOT KNOW where she was when she woke up. She no longer felt as if her body were burning, but jolts of pain shot through her when she moved, so she remained still, taking in her surroundings. She lay in a comfortable bed, warmly covered. Above her, rough ceiling beams held up the thatched roof of a cottage. In a chair beside the bed, a man sat, his arms folded across his chest, his head leaning back against the wall, asleep.

He had called himself Flint, but she could never forget his face: the finely sculpted features, the cold dark eyes. After all her searching, she'd found Andevaar. Only, his eyes hadn't looked cold at all the last time she'd seen him. The calculating look had been absent from his face, the arrogant sarcasm had left his voice.

His memory was gone. It had to be. There was no other explanation for the sudden change. He no longer remembered who she was. But *she* couldn't afford to forget who *he* was. Still, his behavior had been so different that it was easy to believe he was an entirely different person. The man who had patiently tended her wounds and supported her when she needed help was the complete opposite of the cold vicious criminal who planned to take everything from her and who had sent one of his men to attack her.

At the moment, he didn't look dangerous. He appeared to be sound asleep. His dark hair hung down around his face, a short beard covered his jaw.

Looking again around the cottage, Tally realized she'd been here before. This was the Mystic Thorvan's home. Had Flint brought her here? He said that Thorvan had sent him to find her. Did he know who the mystic was?

The soft patter of little feet drew her attention, and Tally looked to see Leya tiptoe into the room. She didn't look toward the bed; her focus was on the sleeping man in the chair. The child slipped nearer until she stood beside him.

Tally's first instinct was to cry out a warning to the child to stay away from him. He was dangerous. Maybe if Tally hadn't been injured, she would have jumped up and taken Leya away. Drawing in a breath, Tally focused on slowing her heart rate. Thorvan wouldn't have allowed him in his home if he were a danger to Leya. Releasing her hand from the fist it had tightened into, she watched.

Leya held a long green stock of grass in her small hand. With complete concentration, she held it out to tickle the end of Flint's nose.

With his eyes still closed, he brushed a hand across his face. He didn't appear to have woken, so the child tickled him again. He rubbed his nose again, and she giggled.

"What is it?" He sounded confused, but the hint of a smile lifted his mouth. "Is there a fly on my nose? Or maybe a buzzing bee?"

The girl laughed again, and he opened his eyes and grinned at her.

Tally bit back a gasp. In this moment, he appeared to sincerely enjoy the child. Tally would never have imagined he would play with Leya and smile at her. The expression appeared genuine.

"You fell asleep again!" Leya accused, facing him, her hands on her hips. "You said you could sit here all night and all day and never fall asleep!"

All night and all day? How long had he been there, watching over her?

"I wasn't asleep," he denied. "I was only pretending."

Leya laughed and crawled into his lap. She threw her arms around his neck, hugged him, and kissed his cheek. He smiled and held her. She settled more comfortably against him and rested her head on his shoulder.

What had happened to him when Tally took his memories? This man, who had obviously earned Leya's trust, seemed entirely different from the man she had met at Sathar. As she moved slightly, they both turned to look at Tally.

Relief and happiness lit Flint's expression. "You're awake. How do you feel?"

"The pain is less." Tally's voice sounded weak and scratchy.

"She needs a drink of water," he said to the little girl.

Leya jumped up at once. "I'll get it." She lifted a cup from beside the bed.

As Tally attempted to prop herself up on her good arm, pain flared from her back. Flint was already beside her, lifting and supporting her so she could drink. The water tasted wonderful and soothed her dry mouth. When she finished, he eased her back down. "Thank you," she said.

"Are you hungry?"

At his question, her belly woke up. "Yes."

He bent over her again. This time, he asked for permission. "May I help you?"

She nodded.

He carefully lifted her into a more upright position. "Leya?"

The little girl scampered forward and pulled two extra pillows into place behind Tally. Flint lowered her to rest against them. The child was already in motion again, taking a bowl from the shelf. Flint ladled something into it and brought it over, pulling his chair nearer to the bedside.

"I brought you back to Thorvan's house," Flint explained. "He prepared food for us."

With a bright smile, the little girl rushed to Tally's side and offered a spoon. With her good arm, Tally took it. She tried to raise her other arm. Instead, a gasp of pain escaped her lips, and she'd only lifted it a few inches. Allowing the arm to rest against the bed, she tried to slow her breathing.

"Don't move it yet." Flint's voice sounded concerned. "You're very lucky it's not broken. What happened?"

She met his eyes for a long moment. "I fell."

He appeared to accept that answer. At least, he didn't question her further, and he held the bowl for her so she could eat. She did not know when her last meal had been, and the food tasted wonderful. She emptied the bowl and lay back against the pillow.

They tended to Tally carefully. She had never needed so much help before, and she itched to be up and doing things for herself. By the next morning, she sat up, ignoring the pain in her back. As she made it into a sitting position, it eased. The sooner she was mobile again, the sooner she could be on her way. She didn't know where Arrick and the others were. With all her heart, she hoped they weren't dead or captured, but she had found Andevaar.

He knew where the stone was and she needed to return his memory, but not *here*. If she did that, Thorvan and his family might be in danger. Andevaar would probably try to attack her when she removed the spell. She needed Kylith and several of his most capable friends on hand before she attempted it. Even though her father and her people were still in danger, she needed to wait. Tally slid her feet to the floor.

Thorvan entered the cottage and smiled at her. "Well, my dear, you're feeling better this morning."

"Yes, thank you, Thorvan. I can't rest here for too long; I have to complete my errand." She looked around the room and saw no one else. "How did *he* get here?"

"He was alone after the spell. I let him in." Thorvan's tone was calm.

She raised her eyebrows. "Weren't you worried at all about him? He's a very dangerous man."

Thorvan shook his head. "He wouldn't hurt anyone."

Tally felt her mouth fall open a little. Thorvan didn't appear to have any problem accepting Flint as a different person than Andevaar had been. "Did you know he stole Namradill?"

"I realize that *now*," Thorvan said. "When we cast the spell... no."

She sighed. "Neither of us foresaw that, at the time. So, you know I have to find Namradill and get Her back before sand buries the entire land and my father dies without Her."

"Yes," the old man replied. "But for now, rest and heal. Your father will be all right for a time, and our people too. If you die along the way, you won't accomplish your goal."

Tally wanted to protest, but Flint came in at that moment, closely shadowed by Leya. The tiny girl appeared to adore him and took every opportunity to follow him wherever he went. Now she was dragging something behind her.

Flint turned to look behind him at the struggling child. "Would you like some help?" he asked Leya, his expression amused.

Tally couldn't help but be charmed by the way he treated her. How was she supposed to despise him when he was so sweet to the child?

"No!" the little girl insisted. "I can do it myself." She made her slow way to Tally and lifted her burden up. It was a crutch made of a sturdy branch with a cross piece set on top.

It was exactly what Tally needed right now, and the little girl presented it proudly. "Thank you," Tally said. Her eyes flew to Flint. "Did you make this?"

He looked embarrassed, as if he had hoped no one would discover his kind deed. "I did," he finally admitted.

As horrible as he had been before, now he deserved her gratitude. "I appreciate it." Tally took the crutch and pushed herself up, balancing on her good leg. She placed it under her good arm. She stood fully upright, and she couldn't help but smile.

"You should get some fresh air and sunshine today," Thorvan suggested. "It will help you regain your strength. I'm sure Flint will be happy to assist you."

Tally looked at Thorvan sharply. He could just as easily have helped her himself or asked Toban to help. The old man only gazed back at her with serene blue eyes. If there was guile behind his expression, she failed to spot it. What else could she do?

"All right," Tally agreed. "Where are my boots?" She resumed her seat on the edge of the bed, and Leya crawled around the floor until, with a delighted cry, she held them up. "Just one for today," Tally clarified. "Will you help me put it on?" As usual, the child appeared delighted to help. She slid Tally's sock onto her foot and then her boot into place. The child spent several moments trying to tie the lacings.

Finally confounded, Leya looked up at Flint with serious blue eyes. "I need help."

Trying to hide a smile, he knelt to take her place. Tally was suddenly aware of his nearness and the brush of his hands against her ankle. A flock of tiny birds took wing in her belly. What was she doing sitting here so close to him? She felt her face heat, and she looked down to hide it. Trying to breathe slowly and evenly, she worked to calm her emotions. She arranged her face into the practiced expression of serene calm that she used for public appearances.

"There." He finished the laces and stood, offering a hand to help her up.

His hand was warm and strong, but she tried not to notice that. On her feet again, she took her first few halting steps with the aid of the crutch. She wouldn't be going anywhere fast, but she could balance and move around with its aid.

Leya jumped up and down in excitement, clapping her hands before rushing to open the door for them.

Tally made her way slowly toward the door, concentrating on each step, trying to ignore the man hovering near in case she should slip or lose her balance. The thought of what it would feel like to have him catch her if she fell was very distracting.

No. How could she even think something like that? Even though he behaved differently now, he was still Andevaar, and she couldn't allow herself to forget that.

She made it over the threshold and out into the yard. Raising her face to the morning sun, she closed her eyes and smiled, taking a deep breath. There had been moments while the fever raged that she feared she would die. Now, in the morning light, hope returned. She only needed to regain her strength. Figuring out a way to get Namradill back didn't seem so impossible right now.

Tally crossed the yard to the edge of the trees, where cut sections of a large log created a flat surface. Pulling her crutch from beneath her arm, she sat down on one of them. She didn't want to admit how much effort it had taken to walk only this short distance or that she was already tired. Taking a deep breath of the mountain air, she enjoyed the sweet tang of pine trees. She hadn't taken enough time to notice how beautiful this valley was when she was here before.

"May I sit with you?" Flint asked.

She turned to meet his dark eyes. Did he want something from her? It seemed impossible that this man might simply want to spend time together.

No trace of deceit remained in his expression, no hint of the secrets he had formerly hidden deep. She had caused this change. She'd buried his secrets so deeply that he had no idea they even existed. Now, as he gazed at her, he smiled. The expression held nothing but honest happiness.

"Please, join me," she invited.

He slid another section of log to rest beside hers and sat down. Leya had followed them outside and was now playing in the grass, chasing butterflies. The child had boundless energy and zest for life. Tally smiled as she watched her.

"When the fever was so high, I was worried." His deep voice finally broke the silence. "I feared my primitive attempts to care for your wounds would fail, and you would die."

She took a deep breath. It was difficult to admit to herself how much he had helped her. She'd been completely alone and badly hurt, with the wolves circling closer. "I probably would have, without your help."

He spoke after a long moment of silence. "Are you ready to tell me?"

She looked back at him, questioning.

"The other night in the woods wasn't the first time we've met, was it?"

He would ask the most difficult question first, wouldn't he? She turned the words over in her mind for a long moment before she answered. "No. We met twice before," she confessed. She couldn't tell him everything. Not yet. "The last time, only for a few moments. We were together in a... political meeting. I'm afraid it didn't go very smoothly." A flash of the terror, anger, and pain she'd felt that day swept through her. He had threatened her and left her to be attacked by Saller, who struck her and cut her with his knife, and would have done more if he hadn't been interrupted.

Flint repeated the words, considering them. "A meeting... that didn't go well."

He met her eyes, and his gaze was penetrating. Could he tell she hadn't told him everything? Either way, he chose not to pursue it for now.

His next question was easier to answer. "What were you doing in the forest, alone and hurt?"

She smiled slightly. "Of course, it didn't start out that way."

He looked back, his face serious, waiting for her answer.

She took a long look at him. "I was looking for someone. I've lost something desperately important, and many people will die if I don't find it. I need to find the person who knows where it is."

"What is it?" he asked curiously.

A simple explanation would have to suffice for now. "A unique and priceless artifact. While we were searching, outlaws attacked my friends and me. We fought, and I held them off as long as I could, but they pushed me right to the edge of a ravine. A loose rock broke off, and I fell."

He sucked in a sharp breath of sympathy, and she could see the pain in his expression. "Well, that explains the sword wounds mixed with the results of a serious fall."

She nodded. "Thank you for finding me. Because of you, I'll be all right, and, soon, I'll be able to continue my task. Many others are depending on me. I can't fail."

He smiled slightly and met her eyes. His smile was nice. But how could she possibly be stupid enough to think that, after what he'd done? Jerking her mind away from that thought, she returned his gaze.

His eyebrows drew together in concern. "I'm not sure how much my efforts are worth, but I will do what I can to help you."

She heard the ring of sincerity in his voice, and moisture welled in her eyes at his promise. Blinking, she looked away. "Thank you." She turned to meet his eyes again. "Your help could mean the difference between success and failure and save many lives. Your offer of assistance is very valuable." Priceless.

He was the one person in the world who had the power to solve the difficult situation in which she found herself. Now, he had pledged his support. If only that were all that was needed. When he remembered his past, he would feel differently. He was a better person without his memory. She wanted him to stay like he was now.

His dark eyes were warm as he looked back at her. Under his gaze, the sunshine suddenly felt unseasonably hot. She looked away and took a long, slow breath, hoping he couldn't tell. They sat for a long time in silence, enjoying the view of the mountain peaks and the wildflowers blooming in the meadow.

CHAPTER 20

CROWN PRINCESS TAHLEA

T HE NEXT DAY, TALLY felt stronger and the pain a little less. She got up and used her crutch to hobble to the table and join the others for breakfast. As they all sat together, Thorvan observed her returning appetite with approval. "You'll have your strength back in no time."

She smiled. "Thanks to the care and help from all of you."

Leya grinned, while Flint focused on his food, not acknowledging his role.

The old man smiled. "All you need now is time and a little mountain air and sunshine. You should get more of them. Perhaps you'd like a short ride today?" He turned to Flint. "There's a spectacular waterfall not far away. It doesn't take long to walk there. You might lead one of the horses. If you're both careful, there's no reason it should cause Tally any harm."

Tally couldn't deny it sounded more fun than lying in bed, but Thorvan made it sound like she had come here on holiday instead of on a serious errand. He knew why she was here and what she needed to do. Still, he'd advised her to take time and continue to heal. She hoped he was right.

"Waterfall, waterfall, waterfall!" Leya exclaimed. The little girl turned to Tally with sparkling blue eyes. "I've gone there many times with grandfather." Her voice hushed suddenly. "It's so pretty."

Flint shook his head. "I don't think I can find it on my own," he said gravely. "It would make sense to take someone along who's been there before." He glanced over at Tally.

She resisted the urge to smile. "That sounds like a good idea." If Leya were with them, at least Tally wouldn't be alone with Flint. That idea still made her uncomfortable.

Leya's little face brightened. "I could do it! I could show you the way."

"As long as your grandfather gives his permission." Tally glanced at the old man.

Thorvan smiled down at the little girl. "You would have to promise to stay close to Flint and not go running through the woods alone."

"I promise." Leya nodded seriously.

Thorvan nodded. "Very well, then. Why don't you help Flint get the horse ready?"

She jumped up at his suggestion and a moment later was tugging Flint toward the barn.

When they had gone, Tally stared at the old man. "You know who he is. Are you sure you trust him with the child?"

Thorvan smiled gently. "I know who he was. I also know who he is now. If it wasn't safe, I wouldn't trust Leya with him, nor you. He will take care of you."

Tally met his deep blue eyes. He seemed so sure. She knew he loved the child, and Thorvan's confidence that Leya would be safe with Flint meant a lot. He had already proved himself a better man than Andevaar. They would all be happier if they could leave him as he was now, only, Flint didn't know where Namradill was.

Her mind flew back to her desperate errand. "What about Namradill?" Tally asked the old mystic. "Andevaar's the only one who would have stolen Her, and now he can't remember! I'll have to take the spell off, and as soon as I do, he will be just like he was before."

At that moment, Leya opened the door and came running back in. "We're ready! Let's go."

Pushing her doubts and questions to the back of her mind for now, Tally couldn't help but smile at Leya's enthusiasm. Tally levered herself up from her chair and picked up her crutch. As Leya held the door open for her, she hobbled outside. Flint waited in the yard, holding the reins of a brown horse. She made her way over to him and stopped beside the horse. She wasn't ready to put her full weight on the wounded leg to raise the other into the stirrup.

Flint had already considered this. "May I help you mount?"

She hadn't completely thought this part through. If she didn't accept his help, they wouldn't be going anywhere. How could she refuse with Leya looking up at her with obvious excitement? Tally lowered her crutch to the ground. As much as she hated being helped, she needed it. "Thank you." He came to stand behind her. She clenched her teeth to prevent a gasp as his firm hands grasped her waist. As he lifted her, she placed her uninjured left foot in the stirrup. With her weight supported there, he carefully lifted the injured leg across the saddle, and she settled into place. It was done. She'd mounted, and he'd stepped back enough that she could breathe again. It felt good to be on horseback again. Tally smiled.

"Now can we go?" Leya begged, dancing with excitement.

Flint surveyed Tally appraisingly. "Are you ready?"

"What about the crutch?" If she went anywhere without it, she would lose her only scrap of independence.

"If you're staying on the horse, it's probably all right to leave it here," he suggested.

She nodded, accepting that plan. They wouldn't be gone for very long. He took the reins and led the horse, so all she needed to do was keep herself in the saddle and enjoy the scenery.

The child gripped one of Flint's hands and pulled him forward. "Let's go. I'll show you the way."

"Not too fast," he cautioned. "We need to make sure the ride doesn't hurt her." He inclined his head toward Tally.

The little girl looked seriously back at Tally. "You're not hurting, are you?"

Their concern warmed Tally. "I'm all right. Thank you both for checking on me."

They moved along a path that led into the trees. A peaceful silence lay under the giant trees. The dappled sunlight peeked through here and there, and the delicious scent of warm pine filled the air. Flint tipped his head back, took a long breath of the fragrant air, and smiled down at the little girl.

"These are some of my favorite trees," Leya explained, leaving his side to throw her arms around the trunk of the nearest one.

Tally couldn't help but smile. After a moment, the girl came back to Flint and took his hand again. Their path wandered through the deep forest. Patches of ferns came up in the shadiest places, their stalks just beginning to unroll. Around them, the first of the flowers bloomed. Birds sang above them, and small animals rustled unseen in the underbrush.

They heard the waterfall long before they saw it. Tally felt the brush of damp air against her face, much cooler than the surrounding forest. The hint of water in the air reminded her of the palace in Namradan, built above the waterfalls. Home.

The trees opened, and they came out at the stony edge of the river. The rush and pounding of falling water filled the air as the river leapt from a rocky height to land in a wide pool. Tally gazed up at it in wonder.

Leya scampered forward and dangled her hand into the edge of the pool. She pulled it out after a moment, her eyes wide. "Why is it so cold?"

Flint pointed between the trees at one of the lofty peaks. "There's still a lot of snow up there. When it melts, the water is freezing."

Seeming to accept his explanation, she turned away and explored, climbing onto a large flat-topped rock. Flint came to stand beside the horse and met Tally's eye. "Has our ride caused you any pain?"

She shook her head.

"Would you like to sit on the rock for a while?" he asked, nodding toward it. Leya was now lying flat on her back against the stone, her arms and legs extended.

Tally admired the girl's wholehearted eagerness for life. "She lives with enthusiasm, doesn't she?"

Flint smiled. "That she does."

His smile made her feel warm inside. Tally wanted to sit on the rock beside them both and watch the endless flow of falling water. "I'd like to sit for a while."

His eyes focused on her and her stomach tightened as she realized she'd just agreed to allow him to help her get there. She almost spoke up, telling him she'd changed her mind. She could stay right where she was, thank you.

He was already walking nearer.

She took a deep breath. It would be fine. He would not harm her. She lifted herself in the stirrup on her good leg and slid the other across the saddle, but that was as far as she could go without lowering the injured leg to the ground. Instead of gripping her waist, Flint slid one arm under her knees and the other behind her shoulders, pulling her into his arms.

Now he was much too close, and his dark eyes held hers. For a long moment, neither of them said anything, and the feeling of his strong arms around her, the solid warmth of his body against hers, sent a shiver through her.

"Did I hurt you?" he murmured.

She shook her head.

He carried her through the rocks to the large flat one and set her down. He settled beside her, near enough that his leg just brushed against hers. They sat for a long while, silently enjoying the majestic scene. Even Leya was quiet. When she crept to Flint's other side, he put his arm around her and she snuggled closer, appearing content.

"You like waterfalls?" he asked Tally, finally breaking the comfortable silence.

"Very much." She smiled. "They remind me of my home. There are several large falls near the city. I've lived there all my life." She suddenly thought of her father. She shouldn't be sitting here enjoying the moment. "There's much to be done. I need to get on with my task soon."

Tally didn't think Leya had been listening, but she leaned around Flint to protest. "But you're still hurt. You can't go anywhere till you feel better." She wore a stern expression on her little face.

Tally couldn't help but smile. "You're right."

The child grinned back, but then turned to look at the pool. "Look, there's a fish over there! Can I go look at it?"

"Of course," Flint replied. "Just be careful on the wet rocks. They're slippery."

"I'll be careful!" The energetic child was already on her way, climbing through the stones surrounding the edge of the pool.

"It's tempting to just stay here in the mountains and let the rest of the world go on without us." He looked around at the trees and lovely moss and flowers around the falls.

Tally nodded in agreement, but it wasn't possible. If she didn't take action, sand would destroy this beautiful land. Even here, surrounded by living forest, she felt the hot sun burning down through the trees. This beautiful oasis of falling water wouldn't last unless she acted. She had to get the stone back. Now that she knew where Andevaar was, they could travel down the mountain until she found Kylith, and she could remove the spell.

She attempted to sneak a look at Flint but found him already watching her. He smiled as he caught her eye. How was it possible that someone's expressions could change the appearance of their face so much? Flint was nothing like the man she had met in the fortress at Sathar.

Tally slid to the edge of the rock and stood on her good leg, stretching. It felt wonderful to be upright. The wound on her thigh was healing, and she hoped to walk without a crutch soon.

A little way away, Leya climbed nimbly through the stones ringing the pool.

Flint looked up at Tally. "How are you feeling? We haven't tired you out?"

"No, it feels good to move around. I don't like to lie around so much."

He grinned. "I would guess you never like to sit still."

She felt her cheeks color a little. It was absolutely true, and others had teased her about it before. "I like to keep busy," she admitted, sitting down on the edge of the rock.

Flint interlaced his fingers behind his head and lay back against the stone. "Recently, I've learned the value of slowing down and taking plenty of time to think." His sharp eyes took in the sun sparkling on the falling water.

Tally raised her eyebrows. She was sure that the driven man he had been before wouldn't agree. "I will consider that," she said honestly. They shared another comfortable silence while they enjoyed the sunshine.

Finally, when she wondered if he'd fallen asleep, he stirred. "Are you ready to go?" he asked, sitting up.

She took a last long look at the beautiful cascade of water and the pool. "Yes."

He reached out tentatively and took her hand. His motion was slow, his fingers gentle, giving her every opportunity to pull away if she chose. His hand was rough and calloused and made hers feel small. She couldn't make herself want to pull away, it felt too good. The warmth of his fingers caused her pulse to speed up. Hopefully, he couldn't tell.

There was no pressure on him at the moment. He didn't have to reach for her hand. For now, he didn't remember who she was, her position or wealth or influence. Before, he'd known all of those things about her. No longer. Since the spell, he'd only seen her in the most utilitarian of clothing, trousers, armor, weapons. There was no formal gown, no crown, no jewelry, no palace. Could it be? Did he take her hand just because he wanted to? A young man who saw her for herself? It seemed impossible.

"May I help you back to the horse?" he asked.

She eyed the uneven rocks, wishing for the ability to walk as she usually could. This entire experience had taught her not to take good health for granted. "I would appreciate it."

Releasing her hand, he slid an arm beneath her knees and one around her, picking her up easily. She put her arms around his neck and held onto him. This close, she felt the hard muscles of his arms and chest. The wild scent of the forest clung to him, and his skin was warm where her arm rested against his neck. She felt his concern for her in the gentle way he held her. How could he possibly be the same man who had captured and humiliated her? The one who intended to take everything from her?

Glancing up, she found him looking at her. The heat in his gaze made her heart pound. For a long moment, they met each other's eyes. Tally tried, unsuccessfully, to guess what he was thinking. Finally, he broke eye contact and, lifting his gaze to the rocks, he carried her over the rough ground back to her mount. Supporting her injured leg, he slid her onto the saddle. Turning to look for the child, he spotted her tossing pebbles into the pool. "Are you ready, Leya?"

The little girl came at his call, jumping from stone to stone toward them. "I told you it was a beautiful waterfall, didn't I?"

"Yes." Tally smiled. "And you were a wonderful guide."

As she spoke, the wind rose sharply, and Tally looked up at the sky. The shadow of a storm hung over the trees. Flint saw it too. He ran through the rocks toward Leya. Before he reached her, a cloud of sand blasted through the forest hiding them from sight.

Beneath Tally, the horse pranced and snorted as the stinging sand struck. The animal neighed and reared, throwing her backward and forcing her to put weight on her injured leg to keep her seat. Pain seared through her as she fought to control the animal. At her soothing touch on its neck, the horse came down, prancing nervously.

Tally concentrated on breathing, fighting to push the pain into the background. Gradually, it eased. She gripped the reins, determined to keep the frightened horse under control. She couldn't see Flint. The storm had swallowed him. Had he found Leya? Tally pulled the collar of her tunic up over her nose and mouth to shut out the dust.

She could do nothing but wait where she was. The horse couldn't negotiate the rocks to follow Flint, and she couldn't go anywhere until she found them. Moments passed, and she saw nothing but flying sand. Her heart pounded. What if Flint couldn't find Leya? What if the little girl had wandered away in the storm? Tally fought the urge to get off the horse and look for them. It was impossible. She couldn't even walk on her own, and all she would accomplish was losing herself in the smothering dust.

It seemed hours before a dark shape appeared. Not until Flint stood right beside the horse, could she see the small body clutched against his chest. He'd found Leya. Relief flooded through Tally. They were still at the mercy of the storm, but at least they were together.

How could they get back to the cottage? The journey had been short when the weather was good, but, under these conditions, it was a long way. Flint took the reins and led the horse. The wind blasted at them, and the air was full of dust. How were they going to reach Thorvan's house?

Tally couldn't tell which way they were going, but the ground under the horse's hooves grew rockier. Tally was sure this wasn't the way they had come. Tall tree trunks loomed out of the murky air around them. What were they going to do? They couldn't make it like this. They needed shelter now.

As they fought their way through the storm, a dark wall of rock appeared before them. Flint followed it for some distance until a dark opening appeared. As he towed the horse inside, Tally realized it was a cave.

Inside, the air was blessedly still, and they all stood gasping, trying to catch their breath and brushing dust from their faces. Flint brushed sand from his eyes and looked at her. "Are you all right?"

For a moment, Tally coughed up dust before she could answer. "Yes."

He brushed loose strands of hair from Leya's face. "And you?"

"I was scared." Her tone was matter-of-fact. "I thought the wind would blow me away."

His arms tightened around her. "I won't let that happen."

She raised her eyebrows. "But how are we going to get home?"

He looked around the dimness of the cave and glanced back at the wild wind outside. "We'll wait until the storm passes. Thank you for guiding us here. We needed to get out of the wind."

"I knew where it was," she said. "Grandfather showed me."

Flint smiled at her. "You helped us find shelter. You saved us."

She returned his smile. "Tally said I was a good guide."

Flint exchanged a glance with Tally. "You are!"

Without some sort of protection from the wind, they would have been in serious trouble soon.

"We'll stay here until the wind dies down," Flint said. "We'll get back to Thorvan's as soon as we can."

The cave floor was uneven rock, sloping toward one side. It was dark and rough, not a comfortable place, but it seemed a cozy refuge after the storm outside. Flint set Leya down and lifted Tally from the saddle. With his arms around her she stood on her good leg. He supported her gently down to sit beside Leya. The child huddled against her side, and Tally put an arm around her.

Flint brushed the sand from the skittish horse's face, speaking to it in a low, soothing voice. He removed the saddle and left the animal to rest. He came to sit beside Tally. "You're lucky the horse didn't bolt when the storm hit."

"He tried," Tally admitted. "It was close."

"Did you hurt your leg?" His eyebrows drew together as his glance turned to the bandages on her thigh.

"Only a little," she admitted. "I think it's all right."

"Can I see it?" He pulled the bandages aside to check the injury. "I would ask Thorvan if he were here, but, to me, it looks the same."

The pain had eased back to the level it had been before. Hopefully, that meant no serious harm had been done. Still, it was kind of him to be concerned.

"What are we going to do now?" Leya asked, looking around the cavern.

"We're going to wait here," Flint replied.

The afternoon felt long. The light was dim and the cave uncomfortable, but none of them wanted to go back out into the storm. Tally was thirsty, her mouth dry from the dust. She was sure the others felt the same.

The light grew fainter with the approach of night, and the wind still shrieked outside. The warmth of the day faded quickly in the cave, and Tally shivered.

"It's c-cold," Leya said, her little arms wrapped around herself, "and I'm hungry."

Tally opened her arms, and the child snuggled close to her. "I'm sorry you're hungry. We didn't bring anything with us." They had only meant to be gone for a couple of hours.

"Will we make it home?" Leya asked.

"Yes," Tally said, confidently. "We'll go as soon as we can."

"I miss my pillow," the child murmured sleepily.

The cold stone beneath them was unyielding, and Tally agreed with her. Full dark fell, and Tally couldn't see anything.

"It's so cold," Leya said, still shivering.

"I'll keep you warm," Flint said. He slid closer, until Tally could feel his body against hers, the small soft weight of the child between them. He was so warm. She could feel his heat, welcome in the chilly black of the cave.

Leya immediately pulled herself closer to him. "Thank you," she murmured. Her breathing deepened.

Tally woke from an uneasy doze. There was no light, and she blinked, seeing nothing, sleepily trying to figure out if her eyes were open. The sound had changed. The howl of the wind had faded until it sounded almost quiet outside. She felt Flint stir beside her, and the soft sounds of him feeling his way toward the opening.

Gradually, a little light entered the cave. "The wind has died down," Flint observed, "at least for the moment. I can see a little." He stared out into the forest. "I think we should try to reach the cottage as quickly as we can."

"Has the storm passed?" Tally asked.

"I don't think it's finished." He shook his head. "But I think we have a temporary break. There's no food or water here. We need to go while we have the chance."

A quiver of fear twisted her belly. If they left this shelter and failed to make it back to Thorvan before the weather worsened, they might find themselves in a much worse position. They needed help. They had no supplies, and the storm might last for days yet. Thorvan would be worried.

"Do you think we can make it safely?" Tally asked.

"I hope so."

"All right," Tally agreed.

He swiftly saddled the horse and came to Tally, who held the sleeping child in her arms.

"Just keep her there, if you can." He knelt beside her and picked Tally up, gently holding them both. He slid her into the saddle, and Leya stirred.

"What's happening?" she murmured.

"We're just going to take a little ride," Tally assured her.

The forest was silent except for the remaining wind, much less than it had been. Sand had drifted against the tree trunks. Many of the trees and shrubs, which had looked lush, now looked ragged and wilted.

"Do you know where we are?" Tally asked, as Flint led the horse away from the cave.

"Yes. It won't take long to get back."

There was still enough sand on the wind to sting Tally's skin as they rode. She held Leya close. The little girl looked up at her with wide eyes. "Are you scared, Tally?"

"Yes," she admitted.

"Flint won't let anything happen to us."

The wind rose in gusts, increasing in frequency and intensity. They hurried through the woods as quickly as they could. Finding their way back the way they had come, Flint increased their pace until he jogged along the trail. They made good time, and it wasn't long before they emerged from the forest to see the edge of the wide meadow. Thorvan's cottage stood on the far side.

A towering wall of dust swirled above the trees, coming fast. Flint gave her the reins. "Go!" he shouted above the rising wind. "I'll be right behind you!"

He slapped the horse, and it surged forward into a gallop. Tally held on to Leya and bent low over her as the horse ran. The storm rushed forward to swallow them. She could see the house and two people at the door, watching the race.

The motion pulled at the cut on her leg with every stride, but Tally couldn't stop. The storm met them a few strides from the door with a harsh blast of wind and dust. She pulled the horse down into a walk, trying to settle the animal down as the sand drove into them.

A few more steps brought her in sight of the building. Two dark shapes came forward through the dust. Thorvan reached up to take the child from her arms and into the safety of the house. Toban lifted her from saddle and helped her inside. He went back out to care for the horse, leaving her leaning against the doorframe trying to catch her breath.

Leya was crying. "Flint, where is Flint?"

"He's coming. He was right behind you," Thorvan said.

They watched the door, not daring to relax, until a few moments later, Flint tumbled in on a gust of wind. He leaned against the door, coughing and gasping.

It took two more days for the storm to pass. Under Thorvan's care, Tally's wound was healing well, and with the aid of the crutch, Tally walked more each day. While the bad weather lasted, she could do little more than pace the cottage. She needed to go. The sandstorms were dangerous. How long could her people endure the weather before all their crops died?

As soon as the wind stopped, Tally took a walk into the woods near the cottage. It felt good to stretch her muscles and her leg grew stronger each day. It was also good to have a moment alone to think. So much had happened. Turning it all over in her mind, she moved slowly between the trees. By now, she could walk well enough. It was time to leave and return to her task.

The more time she spent with Flint, the more she dreaded what she had to do. She *had* to restore his past and convince him to return the stone. What would she do if he refused? If he wouldn't do it willingly? She had to get the stone back. The lives of her people depended on it, but the thought of Kylith or any of the soldiers harming Flint in order to force him to reveal the stone's location made her want to vomit. But what choice would she have?

She looked up. The soft sounds of late afternoon in the forest became silent. Where had all the birds gone? Tally turned back toward the cottage. In the quiet, she heard the distant roar of wind. A moment later, the tree branches around her were flailing in the gale. The light disappeared and a dark brown cloud of dust engulfed her. They wouldn't be traveling today.

The storm immediately veiled the forest around her. Tally squinted against the stinging dust and continued to make her way toward the shelter of the house. The howling wind and dust made finding her way difficult. She nearly ran into trees several times.

Planting the crutch in an uneven spot, she toppled to the ground. An unladylike curse escaped her lips only to be carried away by the wind. Leaning on the crutch, she pulled herself back to her feet. The wind struck her with even greater force and particles of sand stung her skin. Before the storm, she hadn't thought she'd walked very far from the cottage. Now, time seemed to stop as she made her slow way toward shelter and relief. It was difficult to know for sure that she was going in the right direction. If not for small familiar landmarks, the wind might have pushed her completely off course. She bumped into the wide section of log Toban used as a chopping block. Not long after that, one corner of the corral loomed out of the dust in front of her and she followed its edge, skirting a section of meadow, limping toward the house.

At the last section of the log fence, a tall black shadow appeared in the storm and hurried toward her. Flint.

"Are you all right?" he yelled above the wind.

It was difficult to speak through the flying sand. She nodded. He put his arm around her waist and helped her to the door of the cottage. They went in, a blast of wind and sand accompanying them. Flint pushed the door shut against the storm.

Tally bent over, coughing, trying to clear the dust from her lungs. Flint remained at her side and supported her.

"I was worried," he confessed. "You can't see anything in these storms. I was afraid we would lose you out there."

His concern warmed her. She coughed and cleared her throat. "Thank you for coming to find me." She scanned the room and was relieved to see the others safe sitting around the table. Thorvan sat with little Leya on his lap, and Toban was across from them.

"Thank the Divine that you reached shelter," Thorvan said.

Flint helped her to a chair.

"I'm very grateful for Her protection," she said. "But I don't have time for another storm. I need to go. My errand is urgent! My people need my help."

"Yes," Thorvan agreed. "You should be on your way as soon as the wind dies."

Chapter 21

Flint

THE STORM HOWLED FOR nearly three days, and though it was crowded, they all stayed in the little cottage together. Flint tried to come up with a way to ease Tally's worry. She paced the cottage with her crutch, unable to sit and relax. The situation must be more serious than he realized.

While the wind and sand scoured the walls of the cottage, travel was impossible. Tally grew increasingly restless. One night, as they shared a meal around the fire, Tally spoke. "I can't put it off any longer. Storm or no storm, I need to go down to the valley."

She'd told Flint she was searching for a lost artifact. What object could possibly be so important? Though he didn't understand, he could tell she believed it was.

The firelight reflected off her face, and her expression was determined. He had no doubt that she would do what she intended. She was the most stubborn person he knew. Even though his memory only extended to knowing four people, he was sure that applied to the time before he'd forgotten as well.

"Once you leave the protection of the valley, the way will be dangerous," Thorvan reminded her. "The outlaws are still there, and the weather is growing more dangerous. You need to hurry!"

Tally nodded, her face set in firm resolve.

Flint couldn't let this brave, stubborn girl face the danger alone. "I'll go with you." His eyes met hers when he said it, and he tried to convey his commitment to keep her safe.

"Good." Thorvan said. "You'll protect Tally on her journey. You can take the horses," the old man offered. "Though it's harder to hide that way, riding will be easier than walking."

Tally nodded, gratitude on her face. Every day, she'd worked hard to regain her strength, but Flint was willing to bet she hadn't admitted to anyone exactly how much it hurt to walk. It would be much less painful for her to travel on horseback.

During the darkness of the third night, the wind died. The silence sounded loud after they'd become so used to the wind wailing.

"We'll leave at dawn," she said quietly to Thorvan. She had already gathered everything they would need for the journey.

"As you wish," he replied. "Get some rest before then."

Flint could easily hear them from where he rested on the rug by the hearth. Peace settled over him in the storm's absence, and he drifted into slumber.

The boy jumped from his narrow bed at the sound of bells ringing. He ran to the window and looked out toward the palace. His view included a portion of the open market square and the other buildings crowding close. The few people out so early turned toward the sound.

As the boy watched, a messenger ran into the square. "It's the Princess's birthday! Long live the heir of the Seven Rivers!" Shouts and cheering echoed between the buildings.

The princess? All this fuss was because of her birthday? The little boy hugged his thin arms around his body to combat the chill. He looked around the dingy room and the other children, each as ragged, cold, and thin as he was. No one ever bestowed a bit of concern on any of them. No one ever remembered their birthdays. Why should one child cause an entire city to rejoice?

After a meager breakfast, the master gathered them into a group. "It's time for the celebration. Everyone is going," he explained. "Stay together."

The children obeyed, their small faces displaying a personal knowledge of what happened when things didn't go as the master wanted. Each of them wore bruises, mostly hidden under their clothes.

In a tight group, they followed the man into the streets. A few minutes' walk brought them into the wide plaza outside the palace gates. The boy looked up in wonder at the tall spires of the graceful stone building. This was the little princess's home. Everyone inside would take care of her. She would have warm water to wash in, clean beautiful clothes, and she would sleep wrapped in thick blankets.

Somehow, it all made the boy feel even more cold and alone.

The crowd thickened around the children until people packed every space. The entire city was here, along with anyone who lived near enough to have come for the special day. As a fanfare sounded, the crowd hushed. A tall man in a golden crown came forward. The king.

Beside him walked a tiny girl in a formal gown.

The princess.

How the boy wanted to have a talk with the king. He had promised to give his father fair wages, and that after his time in the king's army, his father would be back. Instead, they'd told him his father was dead. He'd never come back at all.

Now, he and the other orphans lived in the king's care. How often had the master reminded them of that? "Keep the king's house clean," or "The king paid for the food you're eating." All their provisions and clothes came from the palace. The master had told them that.

Why didn't the king send enough? Even if they were orphans, why didn't he help them when they were cold and hungry? Even from this great distance, the boy observed the care the king took with the child at his side, the protective way he stood over her, the gentleness of his hands.

The boy's father had treated him like that when he was alive, and the boy recognized caring when he saw it.

"My people," the king said. "Celebrate this day! My heir, Princess Tahlea, will grow up to protect and defend the Seven Rivers. She will follow in my footsteps to take care of this kingdom."

Everyone cheered, and the boy saw smiles on their faces. People dressed in palace livery carried baskets of sweets and passed them around through the crowds. Here in front of everyone, the master couldn't stop the children from enjoying them.

The boy took a strawberry tart in his hand. He'd never seen food so beautiful, and when he bit into it, he'd never tasted anything so sweet and delicious. His friends swallowed their treats just as quickly as he had. The princess would have everything she wanted. They would feed her treats every day. The sugar on his tongue dissolved, leaving bitterness behind it.

Anger burned Flint's belly. Why should one child have everything, while the others received nothing but deprivation and abuse? It wasn't fair. His breath came in a gasp, his eyes opening to see the thatched roof of the cottage. Outside the window, the last of the stars shone.

Had it been a dream? The images in his mind felt so real. Was he seeing his own past?

The cold, hungry boy would have no reason to feel loyalty to the royal family. Had he grown up to hate them? Flint searched his mind for memories. What had happened after that day?

He still remembered nothing before the day he met Toban.

Rubbing a hand across his face, he got up, quietly leaving the cottage. In the stable, he saddled the horses, leading them through the cool, clear, mountain dawn to the door of the cottage. He wrapped his cloak around himself against the chill air. A pack with provisions and gear sat outside the door.

Thorvan opened the door, and he and his grandson helped Tally outside. She was walking a little better every day, her wounds gradually healing. Flint went to Thorvan and embraced the old man. "Thank you for all your help." It was difficult to leave this place. Flint pulled back and looked into Thorvan's blue eyes. "And for your teaching."

Thorvan smiled serenely. "I am always here to give whatever service I can. You know everything you need to know, Flint. You have already done much for the benefit of others."

Flint nodded. He felt good about the service he'd given. Toban had been right about that. He turned to the young man and hugged him and slapped his back. "I hope we'll see you again soon."

Toban grinned. "I hope so too. Be safe on your journey."

A small figure bolted out the door and jumped at Flint. He caught Leya and lifted her. She threw her little arms around his neck and gripped him tightly. "I don't want you to go!"

He'd never felt anything like her unreserved affection. Her embrace was unbearably sweet, and he smiled. "I'll miss you too, but I have to keep Tally safe, don't I?"

Leya raised her head from his shoulder enough to look at Tally. "Yes. I guess you have to help her. She's a real princess. Make sure she's safe," she whispered in his ear.

A princess. Flickers of his dream came back to him. A princess in a tall castle. "*My heir, Princess Tahlea.*" Could the little girl in the dream have been Tally? He saw little in common with the girl from his dream and the ragged, stained and bandaged girl standing beside the little cottage.

"I'll take care of her," he promised, hugging Leya. "We'll come back to visit if we can." This child with her bright smile and large heart had given him so much. She trusted him. Her confidence made him want to be a better person.

"All right," Leya sighed. She drew back to eye him sternly. "Don't let her get hurt again."

"I won't." Flint gently lifted the child to the ground.

It was time to leave. They gathered their things, and he helped Tally onto the horse, tucking her crutch beneath the straps behind the saddle. "Thank you," she murmured. "And thank you, Thorvan, for everything."

The old man smiled at her. "You're welcome. May the blessings of Divine Namradill go with you both."

Flint heard the sincerity in the words of Thorvan's blessing. He slid into his own saddle, and they rode across the meadow, turning to wave at the old man and his grandchildren before the trees hid them from view.

They rode all day at a gentle but steady pace. The weather remained calm, and, by nightfall, they'd come a long way. Flint kept a sharp eye out for any sign of outlaws and made sure they were out of sight in the little hollow where they stopped. He helped Tally down from her horse, and she sank gratefully to the ground, where she sat with her back propped against a rock. She said nothing, but her eyes followed him. Something was on her mind; he could tell that much. He continued unsaddling the horses and rubbing them down. Whatever it was, she would tell him when she was ready.

They shared a meal from the food in their packs. The full day of travel had tired Tally. Her face was pale and drawn in weariness, and, from the lines of pain around her mouth, he would bet her injuries were aching. Pulling a blanket from his pack, he wrapped it around her.

"Thank you," she murmured.

He sat beside her, and she dozed off, her head resting on his shoulder. As the night deepened around them, the last colors of sunset fading into the distance, he looked down at the girl beside him. A lock of her hair fell across her face, and he reached up to smooth it back. She had a caring heart, and she was stubborn and strong. And so beautiful.

He could imagine her in a luxurious castle, but he had seen how determined she was to protect others. Neither pain nor fear had stopped her. Her commitment was more than a desire for power. She devoted her whole life to serving her people. She really cared. After getting to know her, he couldn't deny that.

She seemed so different from the image of the flawless, remote girl in the dream. What else could Flint do but help her finish her task? Were they headed for trouble? The thought of armed men attacking Tally bothered him more than he wanted to admit. He glanced toward the bandages still visible around her thigh. The thought of a keen blade piercing her flesh caused his stomach to clench. He would stay close to her, and he wouldn't allow anyone to hurt her again.

Flint startled awake, hearing a wolf howl. He hadn't encountered any of the creatures since the night he'd found Tally. Now wasn't a good time to meet them again. Already, the horses shifted fearfully.

At another howl, Tally gasped and straightened beside him. "Wolves."

"I'm going to check on the horses." Flint got to his feet. On instinct, he grabbed his pack and shouldered it. He slipped quietly through the dark woods to the patch of grass where he'd picketed the horses.

The animals were already jerking nervously against their tethers. He reached the nearest and ran his hand down its smooth neck. "It's all right," he murmured, soothingly. "I won't let them hurt you." Just as he turned to the second horse, a snarl and a chorus of howls caused the animals to squeal in panic and tear free of the picket lines. They fled into the woods.

Flint ran after them.

The terrified horses quickly left him behind, but if they reached a place where they felt safe to stop, maybe he could catch up and calm them down. Flint hadn't gone far when he saw a glimmer of light between the trees. He paused, staring toward it. Red torchlight advanced toward him. As he watched, several more flames came into view. Outlaws. If they continued on the same course, they would find Tally.

He turned around, trying to keep his footsteps quiet, and hurried back the way he had come. When he reached their camp, he found her, eyes scanning the dark trees, a dagger ready in her hand. She raised it as he approached.

"It's me." He stopped, breathing hard.

As she recognized his voice, she lowered the weapon, exhaling a breath of relief. "A few of the wolves came by." She put away her blade. "I wasn't sure if I would need to convince them to leave. A few moments ago, something startled them, and they all ran. Maybe they heard you coming."

"I'm not the only one who's coming." He offered his hand to pull her to her feet. "Outlaws. We have to get out of here."

"The horses?" she asked hopefully as she took his hand.

He pulled her up. "I'm sorry." He shook his head. "I couldn't get them back." He bent to retrieve her crutch from the ground and handed it to her. Moving as quickly as they could, they slipped away into the dark.

For some time, the outlaws gained on them. When he looked back over his shoulder, Flint saw flickering torchlight behind them. The increased pace had Tally gasping for breath. She never complained, though she had to be exhausted and in pain. Even in the dim light, he could see it in the way her lips pressed together in a hard line.

He wanted to suggest a rest, but, every time he thought about it, some sound or hint of motion from behind them informed him they had to keep going. Tally was far past exhaustion by now. Even so, she didn't like to accept aid. If given the choice, she would always choose to handle things on her own. She needed help now.

He put his arm around her waist to assist her along, taking the crutch and sliding it across his back to be held in place by his pack. She must have been more tired than he thought, because she didn't object. Her steps got slower and slower until he finally lifted her into his arms. She was so weary that he wasn't sure she was even aware of it. Her eyes closed; her head rested against his shoulder.

By the time all signs of pursuit had faded, the night was growing old. At last, the forest grew silent. Flint searched for a place to hide before dawn. When it got light, there might be even more patrols out. For now, hiding was best. They could rest and move on again under cover of darkness.

He found a tall, rocky ledge with a thick patch of brush growing up to it. Turning around to use his back to push through the branches, he knelt down in the small cavity between the trunks of the shrubs and the rock wall. There wasn't much room, but the foliage hid them well. He settled Tally on the ground and wrapped a blanket around her. "Rest," he whispered. She didn't respond.

Lying down alongside her, he pulled another blanket over himself. The space was narrow, and his back pressed against the chilly stone. He slid a little nearer and put his arm around her to offer added warmth. She sighed but didn't wake up or object. As the stars faded above them, he drifted into sleep.

Flint rested in a beautiful dream, the loneliness of his past gone. Warmth surrounded him. He wasn't alone. His cheek rested against the silken softness of her hair. His arms cradled her, her slender body soft against his.

He blinked. It wasn't a dream. The light of morning filtered down between the trees. They hid against the base of a tall rock. He could feel the chill of stone near his back. Tally lay in his arms, still asleep. She hadn't pulled away or run from him. Instead, her body moved slightly with each slow, even breath. He'd never held anyone like this. Or maybe he just didn't remember it. For the moment, she trusted him enough to stay beside him. He closed his eyes and drifted off again.

CHAPTER 22

CROWN PRINCESS TAHLEA

WHEN SHE OPENED HER eyes, Tally saw the gray cloth of Flint's shirt. They lay pressed together into a narrow space between branches and a tall rock wall. He lay with his back against the rock, but his arm was around her and her head against his chest. Under her cheek, his chest rose and fell in long, even breaths as he slept.

The details of last night seemed vague now. After yesterday's journey and the night spent fleeing from outlaws, she'd been so tired, her leg so sore she'd been on the brink of collapse. Maybe she had. She found a dim memory of him carrying her. She didn't know how long he'd gone on like that.

Now, the forest was quiet around them, except for birds twittering in the trees and the peaceful murmur of leaves. How had she let her guard down so far over the last few weeks? He wasn't just any man. This was Andevaar, the man who had abused and threatened her. He had been determined to conquer, with no consideration of anyone who might be in his way. Now, what was she going to do? Flint had offered to come with her because he wanted to help, to protect her. She was leading him toward her army and General Kylith. What would she do when they got there?

They would seize Flint, bind him, punish him for crimes he didn't remember committing. Tally took a deep breath. How could she do that to him?

If Tally removed the spell before they got there, Flint might do anything. When he became Andevaar again, he might attack her, hold her for ransom, or perhaps simply get rid of her and go on with his plans for conquest. She had to tell him the truth. How could she not? Tears welled in her eyes. When she took the spell away, Flint would be gone forever.

She curled herself even closer to him. It didn't seem to matter how many times she reminded herself that she was being a fool. She felt safe in his arms.

Four times during the morning, search parties moved past their hiding place. Tally sat beside Flint, concealed by the brush, staring at them and barely daring to breathe. Were they looking for her or still trying to find their missing leader? Flint closed a comforting hand around hers.

They were probably looking for him. If they recognized him and took him away, she wouldn't be able to remove the spell and her last hope of saving the land would be gone. She needed to stay with him, and she needed to tell him. Her heart and mind were torn between the man he had been and the man she had come to care for. Turning back, she met his eyes. "Thank you for all you've done to help me."

His dark gaze met hers. "Thorvan told me I should serve when I could, and Toban said it felt good to help others."

"And does it?"

The hint of a smile crept to his lips. Tally couldn't take her eyes off his face. He looked so different when he smiled that she would never have believed he was the same person. This expression was the exact opposite of the arrogant sneer she'd seen him wear before. His features had always been handsome, but he must not realize how people would respond if he turned a genuine smile on them. It made her feel as though her insides were melting. Her mouth responded of its own volition, turning up at the corners until she was smiling back.

"I find it feels good to help you." His voice was low and earnest. As they sat together side by side, he slid his arm around her and held her close. It felt good to be with him. Without his memories, he could simply live out his life as the good man he had become. Every moment she spent with him made the thought of losing him less bearable, but she couldn't put her own needs above those of her people. She couldn't sacrifice them to stay with him. She hated knowing that she had to make that decision, and she looked away, her heart breaking slightly as she did.

By afternoon, the woods were quiet again. At dark, the two of them ventured out. Tally began the journey leaning on her crutch to make her way along, determined to keep going. She lasted longer than she had before. For hours, she hobbled on, until they came to the bottom of a little rise in the land, and she sat down to rest on a rock, hanging her head in her hands. Going uphill hurt worse. She wasn't sure she could do it.

Flint knelt in front of her, putting one hand on her knee. "What is it?"

Furious with herself, Tally tried to deny the moisture welling in her eyes.

"Did something happen?"

She closed her eyes and felt the brush of his rough fingertip against her cheek, wiping away a tear that she was not prepared to admit was there.

"Tally?"

She looked down into his face. Even in the dark, his expression of concern shone through.

"I'm sorry," she muttered. "I can't make it up the hill."

"And why does that worry you so much? I will help you." His big hand cupped her cheek.

Their eyes locked, and for a long moment, neither of them moved. Her traitorous heart pounded, wondering what it might be like to feel his lips on hers, but he only took her hand, brought it gently to his lips, and kissed it. His mouth was warm and firm, and his short beard prickled her skin. Then, he pulled her to her feet, supporting and helping her up the hill.

Why did he care so much about her? All her life, she'd tried to prepare herself for suitors who only cared about power or money, never about *her*. Flint appeared to see her for herself. It was something she'd never experienced before, never expected to find.

It was nearly dawn when he paused. "I can see torches. We need to get out of sight."

He helped her to a clump of bushes, and they hid. It was not the best hiding place, but, hopefully, the leaves concealed them.

There wasn't much room, and Tally felt her shoulder against his chest and her legs against his.

"Are you all right?" he whispered.

She nodded wordlessly.

They remained still for a long time. Tally couldn't see much from her vantage point, but Flint turned his head and peered down the hill. "They're coming closer." He put his hand on the hilt of his dagger.

The men with torches combed the woods more carefully than before. That wasn't good. Maybe, since they hadn't yet found Andevaar, they were making a more detailed search. Tally's heart pounded and her breathing was rapid.

Flint put his arms around her and pulled her against him. "Don't worry. I won't let anything happen to you."

The men with torches grew closer still. Tally could see the first hints of dawn lighting the forest. A wind had come up, bending the trees overhead. Before the outlaws caught them, she had to tell Flint the truth. There might not be another chance. She *had* to.

She opened her mouth, but a sudden shout came from the opposite direction as another group of searchers spotted them. With any chance of hiding gone, Flint got to his feet and pulled her up as well. She gripped her crutch. Several outlaws fanned out, trapping them against the bushes. Flint drew his dagger and positioned his body to shield her.

"It's him!" a skinny man said. "Lord Andevaar, we thought we'd never find you! We'll make sure you get safely back to Sathar."

Flint stood motionless, staring at them. For a long moment, no one moved or spoke.

"Come with us," a burly man with a light brown beard said. "You'll be safe at the fortress."

"Your lady friend, too," the thin man added, surveying Tally appraisingly.

Flint's eyes never left them. "No." His voice sounded flat and hard. "I won't go with you. And you're not touching her."

His tone made him sound exactly like he had before the spell, but now, though his voice might sound the same, he was protecting her instead of attacking. Even without his memories, Flint understood that he could be killed in this uneven fight, and he took that risk. He was doing it for her.

"But, Lord Andevaar, you *have* to come with us. We've been searching for weeks. We can't leave you here."

"I'm not going," Flint growled, his dagger still pointed at them.

For a long moment, no one moved, until a few of them edged forward from one side. As Flint turned toward them, two outlaws lunged forward from the other side attempting to seize Tally.

"Stop!" Flint yelled.

Tally dodged their grasping hands, but her injured leg limited her movements. She needed a weapon. Even stiff and lame as she was, she could still wield a blade. Their hands closed around her arms.

Flint attacked. Tally had never seen him fight before, and she had to admit he was good at it. His motions were sure and deadly quick as he took on several of them at once.

When Tally wrenched herself free of her captors, the skinny outlaw raised his sword to attack her while Flint's attention focused the other way. She dodged the blow and seized his wrist in both hands. An elbow to his gut persuaded him to release his sword, and she grabbed it, shoving him to the side in order to block another blade.

With her weakened leg, her balance was terrible, and all her movements felt painfully slow. Still, her ability equaled that of any of these men. None of them had Gerran's skill with a blade, but even if she and Flint were holding their own for now, how could they get away? The outlaws had them pinned down, and the noise of fighting would only gather more enemies until Tally and Flint were so hopelessly outnumbered they wouldn't be able to fight anymore.

As the wind rose rapidly, Tally felt the sting of sand against her skin. The light darkened and had a brown tinge to it.

Sandstorm.

On a roaring gust of wind, a stinging cloud of dust enveloped them. Tally struck at her opponent, now only a vague shadow. Her blade struck something, whether his blade or the side of his armor, she couldn't be sure. A stronger gust pushed at her, and everyone else vanished behind the veil of dust. She held onto her crutch in one hand and her sword in the other, moving toward the clump of bushes where they had been hiding.

Where was Flint?

The dark form of a man loomed out of the storm. For a moment, she did nothing. She could barely see him. A blade slashed toward her, and she twisted to the side. It was definitely not Flint. Raising her sword, she blocked his next blow. Another dark shape barreled into him, and both figures disappeared from her limited view.

She turned to see another blurred form coming at her. The shape was too short to be Flint, so it did not surprise her when he attacked. She blocked his thrust. If not for her injury, she could have knocked him down, but, as it was, she had to wait where she was for his next attack. He appeared to realize she was off balance, and when their swords crossed again, he shoved her back. Unable to correct quickly enough with her injured leg, she went down.

She landed flat on her back on the hard ground with the added weight of her opponent on top of her. Her sword was still in her right hand, crossed with her adversary's blade. He jerked his weapon free and struck at her again. Bringing her own blade into position, she blocked.

Tally punched him with her left hand. As the blow connected, the jolt went all the way up her arm to her shoulder, pain flaring in the injured muscles. She'd intended to hit him much harder, but the blow was enough to knock him to the side. Tally searched the ground. Failing to find the crutch by feel, she crawled away from him, her weapon still clutched in her right hand.

By touch, she located the edge of the undergrowth. At least if she could get inside the thicket, it would grant a reprieve. A sudden stinging along her side alerted her to another enemy behind her. She turned to block his second blow, but she was in an awkward position to defend against someone standing over her. He drove their crossed blades down toward her throat. Another dark shape crashed into him from the side, knocking him away from her. For a moment, their blurry figures grappled. One of them knocked the other to the ground and came back toward her.

She raised her sword, waiting for him. Instead of a blade, his hand darted out to seize her wrist, firmly, but not painfully. He stepped closer until she could see that it was Flint. Relief flooded through her. She lowered the sword, and he pulled her to her feet. He put his arm around her waist and supported her as they slipped away into the swirling sand.

Flint was only a vague dark shape beside her. The howling wind made it impossible to hear if anyone pursued them. They trudged on, bent against the wind for a long time. It was impossible to tell whether they'd escaped the outlaws or if, when the wind died, they'd find them only a few yards away. They could barely breathe in the dust, let alone speak.

Flint pulled her closer, helping her forward. Time disappeared. Tally had no idea how long they'd been moving. The ground fell away sharply in front of them, and they made their way down into a rocky draw. When they finally reached the bottom, they followed the rocky terrain until they found an outcropping that provided a little shelter from the wind. They sank down to huddle behind it. Flint wrapped his cloak over them.

Tally sat with her back against the stone, coughing up dust and trying to catch her breath. She dropped her sword to the ground beside them. The light was dim beneath the cloak, but enough that they could both see his hand where it had touched her waist was red with blood.

"How bad is it?" he asked, setting aside his own blade.

She shook her head. "It's not deep. Are you hurt?"

"No."

"Thank you for protecting me. The storm—I couldn't see. How did you know it was me?"

He looked up from his pack, where he was pulling out a roll of cloth for a bandage and met her eyes. "I knew."

She couldn't look away. Her chest felt tight, and, for an instant, everything else in the world vanished except for him.

He looked down, breaking the moment. "Now, let me see the cut."

Trying to force her emotions into control, she drew in a long slow breath. She turned and pulled up the hem of her tunic to reveal a shallow slice along her waist.

His brows drew together in concern. "We'll need to clean it when we get a chance, but, for now, I'll wrap it to put a little pressure on it to stop the bleeding."

It stung, especially as he worked, but at least her clothing had kept the sand out of the cut. She closed her eyes, trying to ignore the brush of his fingers against her skin. The sensation sent shivers through her whole body.

"There," he whispered, trying a knot.

She felt his arm slip around her. It was time to tell him now. She had to, even if he hated her for it. She was sure he would.

"Flint," she turned to face him. "I need to tell you—"

His mouth found hers. Her eyes closed, and she couldn't stop herself from responding. His lips were warm and wonderful, and his strong arms pulled her closer. She tangled her fingers into his hair. It was the best thing she'd ever felt, and the sensation carried her to a place she'd never been before. She never wanted to stop. She didn't want him to stop.

At last, Flint pulled back. His features were indistinct in the dim light. "I've wanted to do that for a long time, but I was afraid that you didn't want me to." His arms tightened around her. "But you... kissed me back."

Tally's stomach clenched with guilt. She had. Whatever the consequences, she wanted to kiss him again. Her right hand slid along his jaw and through his hair to the back of his head. This time, she pulled him close and kissed him. Her mouth moved against his as if they belonged together, never to be separated.

The wind and sand still beat against the cloak that was sheltering them. If Tally didn't act, the Seven Rivers would be gone. The water would dry up into sand. One by one, the rivers would disappear, and the people would die or leave.

She tore her mouth away from his, her breathing ragged in the small space. "Flint," she gasped. "We can't... I can't... this is all my fault!"

He was breathing hard too. Gently, he held her close. "Tally," he murmured, his warm mouth near her ear, "you can tell me. Whatever it is, I'll listen."

She took a deep breath. "I didn't want to. I put it off because you'll hate me by the time I finish. But I can't go on until I do. I can't... kiss you without telling you the truth."

"I know we haven't known each other very long," he admitted, "but I know you. You're brave and determined and more stubborn than a stone, but I don't see how I could hate you."

Her eyes filled with tears, and she was glad he couldn't see. "You will."

He took a deep breath, and she felt the rise and fall of his chest beside her. "Tell me then. Tell me everything, and, I promise, I'll listen."

Her voice was low as she began. "It is my responsibility to take care of my people. There was a man who... caused many people to be killed or taken captive. He left others homeless and destitute. Can you understand why I had to stop him?"

"And were you sure that it was this one man who caused the trouble?"

"Yes, very sure. I had to act. I had to." Her voice sounded pleading.

He was silent for a long moment. "You're talking about me, aren't you? Those outlaws a little while ago recognized me and called me Andevaar. They were looking for me, weren't they?"

"Yes." She almost choked on the words and wondered if he would push her away, banish her from the shelter of his cloak and his arms. Would he throw her out into the storm to find her own way?

They were both silent for a long moment, and he did none of those things. Finally, she spoke again. "I know you don't remember doing anything like that. It's my fault that you lost your memories. I'm sorry that I did that to you."

He drew in a shocked breath. "How is that possible?"

"It was the only way I could think of to stop you... without killing you."

"You knew me, and that was why you were so frightened of me in the beginning?"

She didn't want to say it, but she had to. "I just... expected you to be like before, and I was injured... I felt vulnerable. I feared you would take advantage of my weakness."

His arms tightened around her. When he finally spoke, his voice was thick with emotion. "What kind of man was I before? I must have threatened you, and when I found you injured in the forest, you were afraid I might harm you?"

She nodded, her cheek against his shirt.

"I'm very sorry for what I did to you," she said, raising her hand to run it along his bearded cheek. "I was only trying to protect my people. Still, I'm not sure I had the right, but I had to do something. I chose this course hoping it would cause the least amount of bloodshed. When you remember everything, you'll think I betrayed you. Maybe I did..."

He tightened his arms around her, pulling her closer to him. "I don't remember you taking my past, and I'm all right now," he said. "For as far back as my memory goes, I have done nothing I'm ashamed of. I have worked hard, and I helped those I could. How could I have done anything other than help you when you needed it?"

"You've been wonderful." She reached up to run her hand along his jaw. "You saved my life."

"It was the only thing to do. If I had it to do over again, I would do the same. Will you tell me what I did to you?"

Tally stifled a sob. "I can't. Not now." She remembered how cold his eyes had been as he offered her those terrible choices. Then, he'd left her locked up, where his men could attack her.

"Is it that bad?" His rough fingertips brushed the tears from her cheeks. "Never mind. It must be; otherwise, you'd just say it. I'm sorry for what I did."

"I know."

They were silent for a long time, listening to the wild wind outside.

"Do you like me better now?" he finally asked.

"Yes!" Tally exclaimed. There was no comparison. She would never have kissed Andevaar, not in a thousand years.

"From what you're telling me, I think I like myself better now too. I fear I should be ashamed of the man I was, and I have no desire to go back. Why not leave things as they are?"

Another sob escaped her. "If only I could!" With all her heart, she wished it. Without his memory, they could have gone on as they were. She could have asked him to stay with her, and they could have been together. He would be the kind, brave, thoughtful man he was now. Andevaar would be gone forever.

But Andevaar knew where the stone was.

Tally touched his cheek. "I wish..."

Then he was kissing her again, and she felt as if her heart melded with his, their souls joined. But she couldn't have it both ways. Either she could keep him, or she could save her people.

CHAPTER 23

FLINT

H E WOKE TO HEAR the storm still raging. Despite the chaos outside, Flint had fallen asleep holding Tally in his arms, her head resting on his shoulder. He wished it were possible to stay here in this moment with her beside him. It was so good not to be alone. Her presence brought him a peace he didn't think he'd ever known.

Tally stirred and muttered, "Storm or no storm, I need to go out."

"Stay close," he warned. "I don't know whether we can find a more sheltered spot than this. At least the rock is blocking the worst of the wind."

They got up, facing the fury of the wind and the choking sand. He walked a short distance away to take care of his own needs and allow her a moment of privacy. A few moments later, he saw her returning through the wind, and he hurried to offer his arm. They ducked back into the shelter of the rock, and he wrapped his cloak around them. For a moment, they both coughed.

"Do you have any water?" she asked, her voice scratchy.

He dug the water skin out of his pack and they both had a drink.

"The storm is my fault," Tally said.

She took responsibility for the weather? "How could that be?"

"It's a long story," she warned, handing the water bottle back to him.

Revelations had already filled this day. She had stolen his past. She'd done what she had to do, but he wanted to know more about what had brought them both to that point. "Tell me." He settled himself more comfortably against the rock.

She moved closer to him. "Do you really want to know?"

"I do. I'm comfortable," he murmured, putting his arm around her. "Right now, I have plenty of time and no desire to move."

"Very well." She nestled against him, resting her head on his shoulder. "This began over a thousand years ago. Divine Namradill was the protector of this land. She had physical form then, much like us, as far as I know. She had a family, children, but She possessed power we can't even imagine. Her consciousness is still with us, though Her form is different, and Her desire to protect this land hasn't changed."

He found himself interested in her story. Had his parents once told him stories like this? He couldn't recall. "Her form is different? What do you mean? What does She look like now?"

"A blue stone. Namradill is a stone. But Her consciousness is still there. We named our capital city Namradan after Her, and the great river also bears Her name. Our people have placed their faith in her for centuries, and She is still very much with us. Someone stole the stone from the palace, and I don't know where She is. Namradill is not happy that She was removed from Her place. These strange storms are a sign of it. The weather is so dry. Not a single drop of rain has fallen since someone took the stone. If this goes on much longer, all our crops will die, and we will have to leave or starve. The desert will swallow our land. I used to think it was only a legend, but..." she gestured to the storm all around them.

"So, if you find this stone, it will rain again? And the sandstorms will stop?"

"Yes."

His gut tightened. "If you don't find it, we can look forward to the forest drying up, the valleys turning to sand, and all our crops dying?"

He could hear tears in her voice. "Yes."

It was a grim picture. The storm raging around them provided proof of her story. For a long time, he sat in silence, searching through his memory for a blue stone. He remembered nothing about it. "And you think I took it?"

A ragged sob ripped from her chest. "Yes."

He wrapped his arms around her and pulled her closer. "I'm sorry. I'm so sorry."

Before today, though he had seen a few tears, he hadn't really seen her cry. Despite her injuries, fear, and pain, she hadn't broken down. He knew her well enough to understand that she hated to show weakness. He was starting to realize that the disaster facing all of them was his fault. The thought settled like acid in his belly. "Did I know what would happen if I stole the stone? That it would destroy the land?"

Tally shook her head. "No. I don't think you did. You didn't believe it. To you, the stone was only a keepsake. You wanted power, and you took it, but you didn't know. Why would you have done it if you did? Who would want to be king of a desert?"

He choked on the words. "I wanted to be king? But isn't this *your* kingdom? Leya told me you were a princess. A *real* princess." A pool of dread grew inside him. "It was you. I wasn't trying to steal a kingdom from some faraway stranger. I tried to take it from *you*."

Tears leaked from beneath Tally's lashes. "I didn't want to tell you. There was nothing I could do about the position I was born into. I had no choice. Still, you hated me for the privilege of my rank. But I never thought I was better than anyone else."

He had never seen her behave as if she did. "I know." What had he been thinking? There was no reason for him to try to set himself above other people. He wasn't the kind of man who craved power over others. At least, he wasn't now.

His fingers stroked the silky strands of her hair. "I see only one solution to all of this. It's simple. You return my memory; I will find the stone and bring it to you. If I do that, will it make everything right?"

"Yes, it would."

For a moment, he heard a note of hope in her voice.

Then she bowed her head, and her words were quiet. "Only... once you remember, you won't want to return the stone. You are... Andevaar."

He searched his memory for any sign of the name. He found nothing. It was the name the outlaws had called him. It hadn't even sounded familiar. "And I'm an outlaw."

"Yes," she confessed. "The entire plan was yours. The outlaws would attack a village, then you would ride in and save them. Everyone loved you."

His chest tightened. "Only because I tricked them."

Her arms drew him closer. "I know you now, and you didn't have to deceive them. If you had only been yourself, the good man you are, the people would have loved you anyway. When you took the stone, you planned to use it to put yourself on the throne. When you have all your memories back, you'll remember."

How could he have been willing to sacrifice the well-being of others for his own glory? "Plans can change." He could alter them. "I promise that no matter what else I remember, I won't forget... this. I won't. I can't!"

When he pulled her closer and kissed her, he felt the tears on her face. He pulled back and brushed them away. "It will be all right. We can fix this." Thinking of her distress caused his stomach to twist. She wasn't worried for herself but for all the innocent people in her care. He had to help her. Whatever it took, he had to make this right.

Night fell, and Flint held Tally in his arms. Her head drooped in slumber. It felt so right to have her here beside him, the warmth of her body against his. He brushed his fingertips along the silken skin of her jaw. Feeling as though they were both charging toward some destiny neither of them had chosen, he fell into a restless slumber.

"Get up!"

The angry words startled the boy out of sleep. He got to his feet and faced the large man in the doorway. His ugly face wore a smirk, as if he could sense the boy's anger and invited a confrontation. The boy still had growing to do, still a half a head shorter than the man and much lighter. Every day, he grew bigger, and, sooner or later, the man would have the confrontation he craved.

"Farmer Jem stopped by. He needs ditches dug, and he's willing to pay good money for the work to be done."

The boy wanted to shout or start a fight, but he knew he wasn't ready. Not yet. Four other boys came to surround him. They went with the man into the predawn darkness. It was cold and their breath steamed in the air. The mud squelched into the holes in their shoes as they walked the path to the field. The man led them to the edge of a field and pointed to the ground. "Start here and connect to the main ditch over here." He tossed each of the boys a shovel. "I'll be back to check on your work."

There was a certain rhythm to the work, driving the shovel into the damp earth and lifting it and throwing it out, but it was hard to spend so much energy when they were hungry. No one brought them any relief until the job was done and the farmer came back with the master. They both inspected the completed work. "Nice job," the farmer said, looking up and down the completed ditch. He took out a pouch of money and handed it to the master, who grinned in appreciation.

"I'll divide it between them," he promised.

The boys watched him silently.

"My wife baked muffins for you," the farmer said, smiling at the boys. He opened a basket and passed them around. The boys each ate one immediately, desperately hungry.

"We'll save a few for later," the master said with a smile. He slapped the farmer on the back. "It's been a pleasure, Jem. Let me know if you need more work done."

"I'll do that. These boys are good workers." He smiled at the boys and went off toward his house, waving farewell.

On the way back to the orphanage, they passed the market. It took only a moment for the master to pocket a few more coins when he sold the rest of the delicious, freshly baked muffins. A few moments later, they reached their own back door. At the pump outside, the boys washed as well as they could in the icy water. Exhausted and chilled, they trooped into the kitchen and sat on the hard benches.

The younger children had been doing their best to prepare a thin soup. It wasn't good, but after the day's exertion, the boy ate every drop. Tired and defeated, he trudged up the stairs. The door to the master's office was slightly ajar, and a sliver of lamplight escaped. The boy saw a thin strip of the master's desk and his hands as he counted the money from their earnings. Anger seethed in the boy's belly. He found himself at the door. The master stood abruptly and faced him.

"We earned that money," the boy said, staring defiantly up at the man.

"Best to save it for a rainy day," the man said, closing the door of the safe and locking it.

"You give us nothing!" the boy protested. "It's not fair."

The man turned, a terrible rage darkening his face. "What did you say?"

"I said it's not fair!" the boy shouted at him. He ducked the large fist coming for his face and landed a couple of jabs to the man's beefy middle.

The master gasped but didn't stop for long. The boy ducked another blow from his right hand, only to have the left slam into the side of his head. Sinking to his knees, the boy covered his head as blows rained down on him, driving him to the floor. "Now get out of here!" the man screamed. "If you try anything like this again, I'll kill you!" He kicked the boy where he lay. "Get up! Get to bed!"

Slowly, the boy struggled to his feet and left the room, painfully climbing the stairs. He sank into his cold, narrow bed, wrapping his arms around himself, trying to ease the throbbing of his injuries.

Hunger woke him long before dawn. All was quiet. Ignoring the pain of bruises, he got up. On silent feet, he went to the window and slid it open. He slipped out onto the roof and closed it behind him. He went across the rooftop and climbed swiftly down to the street. No one had an honest reason to be abroad at this hour. He made his way to the prosperous part of town, slid open someone else's window, and slipped inside. A few moments later, he came back out, a loaf of bread and a wedge of cheese in his hands. He closed the window behind him.

Moving to an alley a safe distance away, he devoured the food. For a while, he sat where he was, savoring the sensation of nourishment in his belly. His injuries from the night before ached. His face was swollen and tender.

He spent the next several days on the streets. The orphanage had been so miserable that the boy noticed a distinct improvement in his circumstances. Sleeping outdoors was no colder than his bed had been. Stealing food at night was much better than the miserable fare he'd gotten before. As time passed, he noticed other boys who roamed the streets. There was a group of them, raggedly dressed and ready to steal anything they could, but they helped each other.

Every group had a leader, and it didn't take the boy long to spot him. He was the tallest of them, a couple of inches taller than the boy was, maybe a year or two older. The boy met him one day as he slipped through an alley. They stood facing each other, and the boy realized there were others closing in behind him. There was no way out of this without a fight.

"Who are you?" the tallest boy demanded.

"No one," the boy growled. "Who are you?"

The young leader grinned. "I'm in charge here in the streets. So, if you're going to stay here, you answer to me."

"I answer to no one," the boy said. "Never again."

"What about the king?" the tall boy asked.

The boy's memory flashed back to the master sneering at him. "Everything you have comes from the king." His jaws clenched. "He's not my king! He took everything from me and gave me nothing!" He punched the bigger boy.

His blow landed, but the tall boy turned his head so the fist aimed at his nose glanced off his jaw. "You're not afraid to fight." He looked impressed. "And you think you can take on the king." The other boys laughed behind him.

For a long moment, the two boys faced each other. "I like that you're not intimidated," the tall boy grinned and offered his hand. "It's a hard world, and a man can use a friend. My name's Drake."

His eyes never left Drake's. Slowly, the boy extended his hand, and Drake shook it.

The boy had never had friends before. Maybe they weren't good friends. They lied and stole, but they looked out for each other. They had a hideout in the back of an empty warehouse. It was nothing fancy, but it kept them warm and dry when the weather was bad. They stole food and money when they could get it. The boy was happier than he had been in years. While life on the streets was rough and he suffered the effects of frequent fights, there was no master to beat him, rob him, or humiliate him.

The boy and his friends grew quickly. They got taller, and, as the years passed, they learned they could flatter women and that girls watched them. As time passed, they grew more and more ambitious. They watched the merchants and the noblemen, and they made plans.

"We deserve to have everything," Drake said. "Watch the people with money. We can learn to act like them. They won't know who we really are."

"Money," the boy sneered. "We can get more. People listen to us. It's time we start planning to be in charge. When we have power, no one can ever hurt us again. I could be king. I'll be a hero. When everyone loves me, I can get anything I want."

Drake smiled. "Who are you then? A hero needs a name."

The boy had already been thinking about this for a long time. "Andevaar. My name is Andevaar."

"Good!" Drake slapped him on the back. "We have plans to make."

The moment felt like the beginning of everything. They shouted and cheered together. The future would be different. The boy lifted his fist into the air and shouted. "I am Andevaar!"

The sandstorm blew itself out during the middle of the second night. As the wind died, Flint lowered the cloak from their faces, and he slid down to lie flat. For a while they slept peacefully, enjoying the blessed stillness. Flint woke before dawn. Tally slept curled against him. He shook her gently. "We need to move," he murmured. "Once I know you're safe, then I'll go back for the stone. Do you have any idea where it might be?"

She sat up and looked at him. "I think the stone would be at the outlaw fortress at Sathar or somewhere nearby. You'll remember how to get there."

"Then I will find the stone and meet you there," he promised.

Tally shook her head, her eyes suddenly full. "I'm sure you won't want to see me again. Don't worry, I understand, and it's all right. I only plead that you forgive me when you remember." She looked down. "You'll remember *everything*."

He could see the pain of the memory as it crossed her face, and he bowed his head, unable to look at her. *Who* had he been before? "Tally, forgive me?" He didn't have the right to even ask it of her.

She reached out to take his hand in hers. "You changed."

Was it possible to change that much? They had been enemies before, and now...

Tally released him and got to her feet. "I will meet you at Sathar," she promised, "but I hope you understand why I can't go back there alone."

Silently, he nodded.

CHAPTER 24

CROWN PRINCESS TAHLEA

They traveled down through the hills, keeping out of sight under the trees. Having lost the crutch, Tally leaned heavily on a stick. Keeping a sharp watch all around them, they saw no outlaws. She would have been happy never to see any of those men again.

It was impossible to forget Saller and the pain he had caused her. He would have inflicted more if the others hadn't stopped him. Had Andevaar sent him? She shuddered and caught Flint's concerned gaze.

Tally's heart ached for him. He had become such a different person. Every moment he proved it more by the pain he felt. Maybe he hadn't known what Saller planned to do after all. Maybe he had no idea. Either way, she couldn't blame Flint. He would never have done it. She looked up at him. "I forgive you."

"I don't deserve your forgiveness." His jaw tightened.

"Yes, you do," she murmured. "If you truly wish to atone for what you did, bring me the stone."

He took a long deep breath and some of the pain faded from his eyes.

She smiled at him. "Are you ready to go on?"

"Yes." He offered her his arm.

As they descended and the woods thinned, they looked out into the foothills. The grass, which should have been green, looked brown and dead. They found only a tiny trickle of water falling between the rocks. They drank gratefully, and Flint filled his bottle.

Tally leaned on him, and he supported her as she walked. Their progress was slow, and, as night fell, it grew slower. Even with Flint's support, it was difficult to go on. Her whole body ached with exhaustion.

"You need rest," Flint said.

"But we're almost there," she protested. She was so tired. Maybe he was right. She paused, leaning against him in weariness.

"Rest here," he suggested, gesturing to a patch of grass beside a rock.

Tally was so tired she couldn't object. She nodded, and he helped her to sit down.

He lowered himself beside her. They were silent for a moment before he turned to look at her. "When you take the spell off... I'm afraid of what I'll remember," he admitted. "Do you have to do this so soon?"

Her heart twisted at the question. She would have given nearly anything for more time with him as he was now, but she couldn't offer the well-being of her people in exchange. How long before her land dried up and the sand buried it? How long before her father died? She could not ignore those things while she spent time with the man she loved.

Loved.

Her eyes filled with tears, and she leaned closer to him. It was true. There was no sense in lying to herself about how she felt. The thought of losing him forever was agonizing. If she asked him to go into that army camp with her tonight, he would go. And if she did that, when he recovered his memories, he would be her prisoner. No matter what happened afterward, she couldn't betray him like that.

When he fell asleep, she would reverse the spell, making sure she was far away from him before he remembered. At that point, there would be nothing more to do than hope he kept his word.

His fingers brushed tears from her cheeks. "Tally, I know you must do it. Please don't worry. I promise, I'll find the stone for you. Everything will be all right."

His earnest promise only made the tears come faster. If they got the stone back, her people would be safe and her father would live. When Flint recalled everything, the man he had been before would irrevocably change this beautiful thing that had grown between them. And how could she go on without him?

He pulled her close. "Please don't cry." His lips brushed against her forehead.

She drew him nearer and kissed him. The contact felt like an explosion. She wanted him, needed him, and held onto him with all her strength. This was her last chance to feel his touch. He returned her kiss, his warm mouth firm on hers. His hands held her waist.

"I love you, Tally," he murmured against her ear. "No matter what else happens, that will not change."

She wanted to believe him more than anything, but he couldn't know what it would feel like when he remembered. He couldn't feel the same, but none of that changed how she felt now. "I am Tahlea, daughter of King Allenthal, Crown Princess of the Seven Rivers, and I love you, Flint."

He kissed her again, and the heat of it flooded through her. His hands were in her hair, and she pulled him closer, never wanting to let him go.

Because she loved him, she risked everything to believe in him.

Tally lay in his arms with the cloak wrapped around them both, staring up at the stars. Though exhausted, she couldn't sleep. How could she waste her last moments with Flint in the unconsciousness of sleep? He had finally dozed off beside her. His breathing was deep, and he seemed completely unaware, though, even in his sleep, he pulled her closer.

She had waited as long as she could. It would take time for his memory to return. She had to remove the spell. Before he woke, she would be gone. Moving slowly, she eased herself away from him, terrified that he would wake when she couldn't bear to say goodbye. If she thought too long about what she was doing, maybe she wouldn't find the strength.

She was Crown Princess Tahlea, and her father's words came back to her now. "Always do what's best for your people." She knew what she had to do.

Tally knelt beside Flint as he slept, his strong features peaceful in the starlight. She reached out to touch his hand. "Memini."

In the first light of dawn, Tally limped toward the sentry guarding the army camp. "Soldier? Can you tell me where General Kylith is?"

The soldier, who had been staring at her in confusion, his hand on his weapon, suddenly realized who she was. He stood up straight. "The last message was that he was still with the army outside Edrithil."

"Thank you. Will you please find horses and gather an escort? I will ride to meet them."

He bowed. "Yes, Princess. At once. What else do you need? Food, rest?"

"Nothing, thank you," she said. "I need to go immediately."

It took only a few minutes to gather a mounted escort. The motion of swinging her injured leg across the saddle remained painful, but riding was a relief after walking so far. Her wounds were healing, though the process was slow and painful. Now, she'd added a sharp ache in her chest that might never heal.

By noon, Tally and her escort reached the army assembled outside the gates of Edrithil. She found General Kylith in the door of the command tent at the center of the encampment.

His grizzled face held a mixture of concern and relief when he saw her. She dismounted and hugged him. He held her at arm's length, taking in her torn and bloodstained clothes. "How badly are you hurt? From the messages I got, I feared the worst. We've been searching for weeks, but there are so many outlaws in the mountains, our soldiers couldn't find you. I couldn't risk a full assault on the fortress until I knew more."

She stood up a little taller. "I'm all right," she said firmly. "We are taking the entire army and riding for Sathar."

"Did you find him?" Kylith asked. "Where is the stone?"

"At Sathar. If Andevaar doesn't give it up willingly when we get there, we will attack. Are the troops ready?"

"Yes," Kylith replied.

Tally looked around the camp. "Where's Mariella?" She'd expected her friend to be here to greet her. She must have been just as worried as Kylith.

He rested his large hand on her shoulder. "She's not here. I'm sorry, Tally, but I don't know where she is."

Her whole body felt frozen with shock. He didn't *know* where her friend was? "W-what happened?"

Kylith shook his head. "I can't say for certain, but I suspect it was that young man."

Tally's mouth fell open a little. "Drake? He was here?"

"He returned briefly. A few of the guards saw him, and, then, he was just gone. Lady Mariella was at the governor's house in the city, and, suddenly, she disappeared. I had men searching everywhere for several days. We didn't find any sign of either of them."

"Several days ago?" Anything could have happened to her friend in that length of time, but if Mariella was anywhere, she was with Drake. Maybe he'd gone to Sathar, but why would he ever take her there? There was no logical reason. If he had harmed her... Tally's mind spun with fit punishments for the man if anything had happened to Mariella. "We're riding now."

CHAPTER 25

ANDEVAAR

His CHEST SWELLED WITH triumph, and he knew he had won. He had just obtained the final vital piece of his plan. Success was within his reach. All his hard work would be justified. The pain of his childhood would be avenged. He would pay the king back for taking his father away and leaving him alone. He felt a smile lift the corners of his mouth. It was time.

Entering the room, he saw her between the two guards. Their big hands stood out against the smooth pale skin of her arms as they held her in place. She was the only person who stood between him and his goals. Not for long. Crown Princess Tahlea. At his order, they had dressed her in rags, but the shapeless burlap failed to hide the confidence of her stance or the arrogant tilt of her chin. Her dark eyes met his directly. Despite the indignity he'd already ordered his men to inflict on her, she didn't look afraid.

Foolish girl. She should never have tried to thwart his plans.

She should be terrified now. Though she didn't know it, the jaws of his trap were already tight around her, and she couldn't escape. Soon enough, she would realize. Her brief reign was finished. King Allenthal too. Already deep in the stonesleep, he couldn't fight back. The Seven Rivers would belong to Andevaar. It already did, only

Tahlea didn't know. It was time to reveal to her exactly what her current position was.

By the time he'd finished, she'd never look confident again. He would crush her arrogance and take every bit of power from her. Let her enjoy one last gesture of respect. He bowed to her. "Your Highness." He almost choked on the title, and it left his lips drenched in sarcasm. "You look lovely. I must say, it's gratifying to see you dressed so... appropriately."

A flush she failed to hide crept over her translucent skin. She still looked angry and imperious. Not for long. He stepped nearer. It was time.

Flint woke, gasping for breath, the horrifying dream still with him. He had loathed her, and he still felt it, like a foul serpent twisting inside him. Tally! He'd looked at her familiar, lovely face in the dream, and he'd hated her, been determined to destroy her. Flint rolled to one side and vomited. Every muscle in his body clenched, and acid burned through his throat as he lost the contents of his stomach. It wasn't a dream. He remembered.

Instinctively, he reached for Tally. She'd been there, right beside him. He'd slept with her in his arms, the warmth of her body against his, the silken strands of her hair brushing his cheek. Now he was alone, and the chill of her absence seeped into his bones.

She was gone.

She'd probably gone right back to her army to get ready to attack him. That would be just like the spoiled, selfish, pampered princess she was. Princess Tahlea.

His hands tightened into fists, and anger flowed through his body.

No! She wasn't spoiled or selfish. Tally was brave. She'd endured great pain and hardship without complaining.

He put his hands on either side of his head, trying to ease the sharp ache of conflicting memories. "She knew who I was the entire time," Andevaar growled. "I'm such a fool! This whole thing was just an attempt to stop me in my plans. She listened to me baring my soul, claiming to *love* her."

His mind felt like it was coming apart. His hands tried to hold his skull together.

"No!" he protested. "I meant every word. I *do* love her."

It wasn't possible. There was no way to reconcile the stubborn, lovely girl with the fierce brown eyes and porcelain skin who had kissed him and trusted herself in his arms, with the arrogant, emotionless princess he desperately wished to depose.

They could not be the same person.

He hated her. Her family had ruled this land for a thousand years, and they thought they were so far above everyone else, that their bloodline entitled them to rule this land forever. They cared nothing for their subjects. The king had taken everything from him, left him to live in misery, lacking even the basic necessities of life. In contrast, the entire kingdom had celebrated and adored the princess.

He loved her. She had been brave, put her own safety at risk in order to save her people. He wanted nothing more than to protect her. His stomach had twisted when he'd seen her injuries. So much pain. He'd done all he could to help her.

She had done this to him. Crown Princess Tahlea had stolen his memories, his name, and identity. Everything.

Yes, and he'd brushed the tears from her face as she cried and told him how sorry she was. She'd been trying to protect her people.

Who was Andevaar trying to protect? Other than himself, who did he serve? Who did he love?

No one. He'd done it all for power. For years, he'd convinced himself that the royal family was doing nothing but living off the work of their people. He'd been determined to humble their arrogance. His mind flew back to the memory of Princess Tahlea, dressed in filthy rags, at *his* order. They'd taken everything, her clothes, her boots. He remembered that moment, how he'd wanted her to feel vulnerable.

His arrogance had nearly destroyed the kingdom. He'd intended to be the man with the blue stone in his hand, to become the king. He had never imagined that the office required the acceptance of the stone itself, never imagined that Namradill was real.

His mind was splitting. He had been Andevaar for many years, but how could he live with himself now? If the princess had never returned his memories, he could have lived happily, becoming Flint permanently.

She loved him. Now that he remembered his life, he knew no one had loved him in a long time, not since his father. Flint remembered his father. He had loved his son and tried to raise him to be a good man. His father had named him Flint.

Andevaar shook his head desperately. It wasn't him Tahlea loved. She loved Flint!

Sinking to his knees, he yelled in pain and frustration.

The choice lay before him.

Was he Andevaar? He had already conquered one province, and the others would soon follow. The throne of Seven Rivers would be his. He would never bow to anyone again; he would never be hungry, poor, abused, or powerless. He would control this kingdom, and he would have everything.

Or was he Flint? Was he content with the quiet of the forest? Did he enjoy the satisfaction of working hard and using his strength and efforts to help others? He was the man his father had hoped he would become. Flint was at peace with himself, and he'd never felt anything that compared with the sensation of holding Tally in his arms. She loved him. She had kissed him—wanted him.

The memory of her hands against his skin, her mouth against his, sent heat flooding through his body. Now that he remembered everything, he knew that he'd never experienced anything even close, not in his whole life. No one in the world had truly loved him since his father died. Different women had come and gone, but none of them had given him their hearts. None of them had loved him, not like Tally.

If Andevaar succeeded, he would become king of a lifeless land of sand and rock. He would never gain the throne while Princess Tahlea lived. Now, he had everything he needed to destroy her. She would keep fighting, even if she couldn't win. She'd never give up, never stop trying to protect her people. When he'd captured her and tried to force her to step aside, he'd had no idea how stubborn she really was or how much she loved her people.

Flint had the chance to help her, to help everyone. If he returned the stone, the Seven Rivers would regain Namradill's blessing. The land would be green and growing again. He could stop the fighting, save the lives of so many people. He'd promised Tahlea.

But how could he simply give Namradill back? Whoever had the stone had the edge in bargaining. He couldn't simply give it up now, could he? Drake would never agree to it. They had made their plans together so carefully. For years, they had dreamed together about achieving success, having everything they never had as boys. The stone was the key to their plan. And what about the others? Under his shirt, Andevaar felt the hard outline of the key he still wore around his neck.

He picked up his things and turned back up the hill, heading toward the fortress at Sathar, back to his army.

CHAPTER 26

CROWN PRINCESS TAHLEA

TALLY RODE INTO THE hills, leading her army toward the outlaw stronghold at Sathar. Kylith rode beside her, and the troops followed in a long column. The afternoon was clear and hot, the weather entirely dry. Even the air smelled dry and the vegetation burnt, as if it were the end of a summer that had lasted years. It got only a little cooler as they ascended into the forest.

When they stopped for the night, Kylith assigned large numbers of men to guard the perimeter of the camp. The outlaws made a few quick incursions, but the soldiers were alert, expecting attacks, and easily drove them off.

"Don't let them fool you," Tally warned. "These raids are only meant to test us. There are more of them than you think."

Kylith took a long look into the forest and nodded.

Tally slept in the exact center of the group, guarded heavily on all sides.

With so many men and horses, they moved slowly but inexorably up the hill. None of the smaller groups of outlaws dared to attack them. At noon on the fourth day, they drew up outside the outlaw's stronghold. Tally wasn't sure what they would encounter. Kylith had made preparations in case an army of outlaws held the fortress against them. Now, nothing moved. The whole place appeared deserted, and no one challenged them. The gates stood wide open.

Kylith stared at the heavy doors. "I don't like the look of this." He rubbed the short beard covering his jaw.

For several moments, they watched the open gates, and no one moved. Then, from the woods on both sides of them, shouts rang out, and Tally heard the pounding of horses' hooves. The sounds of battle erupted all around her. Kylith shouted beside her. A large force of outlaws on horseback charged toward them.

Amid the fight, Tally felt hands seize her arms. None of the enemy were that close to her. Twisting and struggling, she turned to see a man wearing the blue uniform of her own army. Several others suddenly surrounded her. She'd known there must be one traitor, but she'd never imagined there would be so many.

The one holding her arms dragged her from her own saddle onto his horse. He urged the animal toward the outlaws. Stuck at an awkward angle, Tally tried to strike him. When that failed, she struck the horse, causing it to break stride and shy to one side. Two more of the traitors seized her, pulling her away from the first. Their horses were already running, and the outlaw ambush surrounded them, their horses galloping toward the fortress.

In a flash, they passed the gates. Tally heard them shut with a boom, leaving her trapped with all her friends outside. The traitors, still dressed in Seven Rivers army uniforms, gripped her and took her into the courtyard toward a tall man armored for battle. He wore a black tunic emblazoned with a silver hawk and a piece of black cloth covering his face. His blue eyes were familiar.

She drew in a sharp breath. She'd feared for a long time that it would be him, but now she stared at him in shock. "Drake!"

Despite the army waiting outside, he didn't look afraid. Instead, he bowed. "Good afternoon, Princess Tahlea. Welcome back to Sathar."

"I should have realized from the very beginning that you were part of this." Andevaar was his business partner, after all. It only made sense that they would work together and that he would take charge in his friend's absence. "Where is Andevaar? And Mariella?"

Drake shook his head. "I haven't seen him for several weeks. I thought maybe you knew where he was. He's the man everyone wants to find. And Lady Mariella is staying at the governor's house in Edrithil."

"She's not there!" Tally protested. "She disappeared about the same time *you* did."

"What a strange coincidence." Drake came forward until he faced her. "Walk with me, Princess."

He seized her arm. At the moment, she had little choice but to yield to Drake's request. "What are you planning to do?" Tally eyed the large group of outlaws surrounding them, spotting an unpleasantly familiar face. She immediately recognized the bald head and thick form.

Saller.

By now, his face no longer looked swollen, but his nose appeared distinctly crooked, which did nothing to improve his looks or temperament.

Drake tightened his grip. "At the moment, I need you to prevent General Kylith from smashing through my gates and killing all of us. He has enough men to do it." He pulled her toward the wall.

With her sore leg, Tally struggled to keep up with his long strides. His assistance as they climbed the stairs felt more like being dragged along. Finally, they reached the top of the wall and looked out. From this vantage point, they saw that Kylith was indeed preparing to attack the gates. His efficient soldiers had already brought up a battering ram. A moment more, and they would use it. The ranks of his archers waited, ready to fire at anyone who shot down from the walls.

"General Kylith," Drake yelled, dragging Tally up onto the top of the wall beside him. "Put down your bows and stop your attack! Unless you want to see your princess dead."

General Kylith stared up at them. Slowly, he backed away from the gates, his men following him. Tally looked down into the abyss before her feet. Her stomach dropped as she saw the height of the wall, and below it, a sheer rocky ravine.

Feeling the stabbing pain of a blade point pricking her back just below her armor, Tally turned to see Saller wielding the weapon. He had followed them up and now stood just behind them.

Drake watched the furious, crooked-nosed man. "Saller is going to make sure you stay where you are. Try not to make him angry," Drake warned, "although, maybe he's forgiven you for breaking his nose the last time you were together?" Drake nodded over his shoulder at the big man.

Tally glanced back at Saller. Judging by his murderous expression, he had not forgotten. He stepped closer to Tally. With the point of his knife, he shoved her a few inches closer to the edge. She drew in a sharp breath.

"That's enough for now," Drake said to Saller. "Stay here. Don't let her move and don't do anything until I give the order."

"Yes, Commander," Saller replied.

From here, she could see Kylith and the rest of her troops. They all stared up at her, their hands on their weapons.

Drake yelled down at them. "Just stay where you are, General. If you attack, she falls." He stepped back onto the stairs.

Tally stood on the wall, the knife point digging into her back. Flint hadn't come. He wasn't here, and even if he was still trying to reach Sathar, he wouldn't be able to get through the besieging army. She had no way to get Namradill back. Drake said he hadn't seen Andevaar in weeks.

The moment lengthened. Drake descended the steps and disappeared, leaving her alone with Saller.

"I knew we'd be together again, sooner or later," he spat.

She felt his breath against her ear and fought the urge to drive her elbow into his belly. This wasn't a good place to start a fight. She glanced down. The unforgiving rocks were a long way below her.

A breath of wind touched her face, and she looked up. A thick brown cloud was advancing up the hill, swallowing trees and hills as it came.

Behind her, the outlaw let out a grim laugh. "Look at that, Princess."

She felt him step even closer behind her.

His voice was right in her ear. "It would be sad if you lost your balance in the wind and fell."

A thick, icy dread rose in her belly. She couldn't control a shiver that ran through her body. Saller crowded her even closer to the precipice. His rank scent and the feel of his body against hers made her sick.

His hand gripped her hip, and the point of his knife dug into her back as he bent his head close to her ear. "When the storm gets here, no one will be able to see what I do to you."

CHAPTER 27

ANDEVAAR

H E BARELY HAD TIME to speak to the guards and slip through the gates before the approaching army came into view behind him. Andevaar crossed the courtyard and headed toward the storage rooms while everyone else in the fortress ran back and forth, gathering armor and weapons. He could hear them talking and calling to each other. Word passed quickly. General Kylith and his army were outside the gates, ready to attack at any moment. Andevaar had little time.

Was Tally out there with them? He couldn't suppress the surge of anticipation at the thought of seeing her again, but he couldn't face her without the stone.

He needed to find Drake. They'd been close for years, never keeping secrets from each other. He had to tell his friend everything. The drought, the sandstorms, the truth behind the stone. They had been so wrong, and once he had a chance to explain, Drake would understand.

Andevaar slipped quietly down the stairs and through a doorway along the hall, making his way across the wide room filled with crates and boxes. In the far corner, he gripped one end of a heavy crate and slid it aside. Moving to the other end, he pulled it away from the wall, exposing the small hidden door. He took the key from the leather cord around his neck. It fit into the lock and turned with a click. The door opened, revealing the precious bundle wrapped in cloth, a leather bag beside it. He seized the stone and slipped it into the satchel, throwing the strap over his shoulder.

From behind him, the point of a sword pricked his neck. "This isn't what we planned," Drake hissed. "What deal are you trying to make behind my back?"

Andevaar dived forward out of the blade's reach and drew his own weapon, whirling around to face his friend. Drake slashed at him and Andevaar blocked. He had no desire to fight, but what choice did he have at this moment? If he didn't resolve things with Drake, he couldn't go forward.

"It's *her*, isn't it?" Drake snarled as he swung his blade. "I knew it! Somehow, the princess got to you. Two of our scouts reported they saw you with her last week. Not only did you refuse to bring her here yourself, but you attacked our own men when they tried to take her. We have the stone. All we needed was *her*, and we've won! Well, despite your interference, I captured her."

A thick combination of fear, anger, and worry surged through Andevaar, tightening his chest. "Where is she?"

"Somewhere she won't escape from," Drake said. "Now, we have everything we need to beat them. What about our plans? Why were you defending her?" He aimed another blow.

Andevaar remembered protecting Tally in the forest. He knocked Drake's oncoming blade to the side. "Did you think I would stand by and watch six armed men attack one injured girl?" Andevaar fervently hoped he would never have tolerated that, memory or no memory.

"You know they wouldn't have killed her," Drake protested. "Their orders were to bring her back here."

Andevaar shook his head. "She fights too hard to let them bring her in unharmed. I saw what they did the last time they cornered her. I found her, injured and alone, with the wolves closing in. She nearly died that night." And even then, she still fought, refusing to give up. It had been a moment he would never forget.

Drake stared at him, his mouth falling open a little. "Since when do you care what happens to *her*?" he snarled. "You and I have been friends for fourteen years. We planned to take her down together. Now, you're on *her* side?"

Andevaar saw the betrayal in his friend's eyes. He spoke slowly. "It's not like that. I never wanted to sell out, but I didn't know about the stone. I didn't know anything would happen when we stole it, besides it being a bargaining point and proof that I belonged on the throne. But it's not just a stone. Haven't you noticed it hasn't rained since we took it? And the sandstorms?"

Drake's eyes narrow in fury. "Your princess doesn't control the weather!"

Andevaar tried to keep his voice calm. "Not her. It's the stone. We have to return it to Namradan. I admit I was trying to take over, to place myself in power, but I never wanted to lay waste to the entire kingdom. No power is worth that. Please, Drake! You have to believe me!"

Drake's expression remained hard, and he slammed his sword into Andevaar's. "Why should I? We've hated the royals our whole lives! Now, one kind word from one, and you're ready to believe anything she says? Have you forgotten the hard times we went through?"

Andevaar's stomach tightened at the flood of memories. His mind had been so much quieter without them. Now, they would not allow him to push them aside. "I remember, Drake. Everything. We spent years together, with no one but each other to watch our backs, no one else to rely on when things went wrong. That time you broke your finger? We didn't have many options at that moment, so I set the bone."

Drake lowered his blade and took a step back.

Andevaar went on. "And you doctored me every time I got into a fight, which was often. And the winter I got sick? I would have died without you. We've done everything together all these years."

The muscles in Drake's jaw clenched. "So *why* would you change your mind now?" he demanded desperately. "I'm trying to understand, but I just can't figure it out."

Andevaar took a long breath. "I know more now. That's what I'm trying to tell you. When I took a hard look at myself and the mistakes I'd made, I saw things differently. We need to do the right thing for everyone, not just us."

Drake's eyes widened in disbelief. "But it's still about her, isn't it? You *want* her. What makes you think the princess would ever accept someone like you? The entire kingdom has adored her since the day she was born. They care nothing for us."

Shaking his head, Andevaar said, "It's not about her. This is my decision. I have to make the choice that will help everyone in the Seven Rivers."

Drake shook his head. "You've lost your mind."

"No," Andevaar felt completely sure. "I found it."

Drake stared at him for a long moment, his eyes hard. He raised his weapon. "You don't have to go through with our plans if you don't want to, but I'm taking the stone. Now."

Andevaar's heart sank. He hoped Drake would agree to do the right thing, but he couldn't allow his friend to steal the powerful stone. He brought his own weapon into position to block Drake's attack. They traded several blows. Neither of them could give up. He slipped past Drake's defenses and left a long cut across his side, just below his armor.

Andevaar saw the determination in his friend's blue eyes. Was he ready to kill Drake to end this? The man who had been his only friend for many difficult years? Drake would not back down. His thrust drove toward Andevaar, and he blocked just a little too late. A fiery burst of pain exploded through Andevaar's body as the blade pierced his shoulder.

Drake jerked the blade from Andevaar's flesh and struck his head with the hilt. The world vanished into light, and all sound faded into silence. He felt cold stone against his cheek and realized he was on the floor. He had to get up and stop Drake. Blinking in an attempt to clear his vision, Andevaar lifted his throbbing head.

It was already too late. Drake had the bag and strode toward the door. Andevaar struggled to his knees. "Stop!" he meant to shout, but his voice came out a strangled croak.

Drake froze in the doorway.

A moment later, Andevaar realized it had nothing to do with him. Two outlaws blocked the exit. One of them held a young woman. His arm was around her, pinning her against his body. He held a knife to her throat. It wasn't Tally. He'd never seen this girl before. She was beautiful, with long golden hair and delicate features. Her eyes were wide with terror, and her pleading gaze rested on Drake.

"Good morning, Commander," the man with the knife grinned. "It seems our plans have changed." His eyes flicked to the blood on Drake's side, and to Andevaar, still dragging himself to his feet.

"Let her go, Hargen," Drake ordered. "Now! I'll kill you if you harm her."

Hargen's grin widened. He glanced back at Andevaar. "It looks like you've decided to leave Andevaar behind. We have the princess, and we have your lady friend here. We can make this plan work without him."

"That's right," Drake said. "That's what we're going to do. Now. Let her go!"

Hargen didn't move. "We can make it work without either of you. Saller has the princess, and he'll do whatever I order him to. Now, hand over that bag, unless you want to watch me cut the lady's throat."

For a moment, they stared at each other, until the girl gave a desperate gasp of pain, and a trickle of blood ran down her neck. Drake held out the bag with the precious stone. "Don't hurt her!"

"Put down your weapon," Hargen demanded.

Moving slowly, Drake obeyed.

"Now, bring the bag to me."

Slowly, Drake moved closer to them, the satchel containing the stone in his hand. Did these men know what it was? They might. They seemed to know too much about Andevaar's plans.

Drake stopped, facing Hargen. In a sudden flash of movement, Drake seized Hargen's knife hand in both of his, forcing the blade away from the girl. Now in control of the weapon, he drove it into Hargen's throat. The outlaw's eyes widened in shock, and he collapsed.

Behind Drake, the second man raised his knife. Despite everything they disagreed over, Drake was Andevaar's best friend, the one person in the world he'd trusted. He grabbed his sword and bolted toward them.

The outlaw struck, and Drake grunted in pain. Andevaar arrived an instant later. The man with the knife didn't have time to turn and defend himself. Andevaar's sword slid between his ribs before he even knew what was happening. He slid to the floor with a groan, and Andevaar jerked his blade free.

The girl clung to Drake. He put his arms around her. "You're safe now," he promised. When she pulled her hand back, it was covered in blood, and she screamed. Drake sank to his knees.

Andevaar dropped his sword to kneel beside his friend, undoing the buckles on his armor. He removed the pieces, revealing blood spreading, rapidly soaking Drake's shirt. Andevaar put his hand over the wound and applied firm pressure, trying to stop the bleeding.

Drake's face had gone white with shock. Andevaar helped him lie down. The girl tore a piece from her skirt and handed Andevaar the cloth. He folded it into several layers and held it tightly over the wound.

She knelt, bending over Drake. "We'll take care of you. Just stay still. Hold on."

"My beautiful Mariella," he murmured, gazing up at her. "I couldn't let him hurt you."

She took his hand in both of hers. "You kept me safe. I love you, Drake."

His eyes widened. "You love me? Even after everything I've done? I thought if I won a crown, then maybe you would…"

Her eyes welled with tears, and they ran down her cheeks. "You didn't need a crown. I already loved you."

"Sorry to disappoint you," he said. "I shouldn't have forced you to come here. When you discovered the truth about me, I was afraid you would denounce me. I'm sorry, I wish I could be the man you deserve. I wanted to stay with you more than crowns or…" His voice trailed off.

She seized his shoulders and shook him. "Drake!"

His eyes closed. The little color that remained had drained from his face, and he lay utterly still. Andevaar felt frozen in place, still desperately trying to slow the bleeding, even though it was too late. He and Drake had shared their lives for so many years. Now, Drake was beyond help.

Slowly, Andevaar lowered the blood-soaked cloth. The bleeding had stopped because Drake's heart no longer beat.

Andevaar put his ear against his friend's chest, listening. Nothing. No breath, no heartbeat. Drake was gone. Mariella clung to him, sobbing.

None of this seemed real. A moment ago, Drake had been alive. But the outlaws had Tally, and Andevaar had to find her. He wiped his bloody hands on his pants. He knelt beside Drake and put his hand on his shoulder. "Goodbye Drake." His voice broke. He got to his feet, picked up the satchel, and slung it across his body. "I have to help Tally."

CHAPTER 28

ANDEVAAR

I GNORING THE PAIN FROM his injured shoulder and aching head, Andevaar raced up the stairs and out into the bright sunlight of the courtyard. He'd expected to have to search for Tally, but he spotted her immediately, standing high on the wall, right at the brink, where a single misstep would send her plunging to her death. An outlaw guard brandishing a knife stood close beside her. Her slender form looked small next to his bulk.

When a gust of wind whipped over him, Andevaar looked at the sky. High above the stone ramparts and the tallest trees, a wall of sand bore down on them. Already, the storm covered half the sky, and it advanced quickly. As the outlaws saw it, they broke and ran in all directions, searching for shelter.

He had to reach Tally. Andevaar sprinted across the flagstones toward the stairs, adrenaline coursing through him, providing a burst of energy despite his pain. Just before the curtain of sand covered them both, the outlaw on the wall seized Tally, raising his knife.

Sand blasted into Andevaar's face, hiding the struggling figures from view. He stumbled up the stairs, pushing his way past the last few men hurrying down out of the storm. He came out on the top of the wall so suddenly that he almost went off himself. Regaining his balance, he gazed in all directions but saw only driving sand and dust. Where were they? There was nowhere else to go up here. Had they both fallen?

Shielding his eyes from the stinging particles with his hand, he walked along the wall. "Tally!" the wind carried his voice away. A dim shape came into view, and he hurried toward it. A few more steps brought the shape into view. Curtained by sand, it appeared strange and grotesque. It couldn't possibly be a person. As he got closer, the mass resolved into the shape of a big man struggling with a girl. Andevaar felt his stomach freeze, as he realized the man held his knife point against Tally's chest, attempting to shove her off the edge.

She dropped to the ground suddenly, aiming a kick at the man's knee. He yelled in rage, stumbling forward over her. When he tried to use his bulk to pin her to the stones, she aimed her elbow at his jaw. The blow knocked his head back, but he still had the knife in one hand, and raised it to strike her.

As his blow fell, Tally jerked to one side and shoved the outlaw hard with her legs. He reached the edge of the wall and slipped out into space. He scrabbled frantically, trying to grip her boots. She wrenched her foot from his grasp. In a last effort to keep from falling, he gripped the edge of the stones.

Andevaar reached them just as the outlaw's fingers slipped from the brink, vanishing into the racing wind.

Tally was gripping her shoulder, but she was alive. He could barely see her in the storm, and he barely heard her words above the storm.

"Flint! You came!"

He didn't try to speak, instead he put his arms around her and pulled her close against him. It could have been her who fell. He closed his eyes hard against the vision of her body, crumpled and broken at the bottom of the slope. She was safe now. With her beside him, he was whole again. She was alive and here with him. A hard knot inside him loosened.

Over the shriek of the wind, a heavy boom shook the wall beneath their feet. From the sound, General Kylith wasn't waiting for an invitation to enter the fortress. Another blow followed the first.

"Are you all right?" Andevaar shouted.

Still holding Tally close, he felt her nod. They had to get off this wall. With his arm around her, they crept along the stones, feeling their way back toward the stairs. The wind blasted across the top of the wall with enough force to make it impossible to keep their balance. When they reached the stairs, Andevaar sank down onto one of the stone steps, his arm still around Tally. He placed his back to the driving wind, offering her what protection he could.

This storm was more powerful than the others had been. They were escalating. The wind grew more violent, as if the land itself had turned against the people. Now, instead of protecting, it seemed determined to scour every trace of them from its surface. How could any of the people survive like this? They had little time left.

Andevaar felt the weight of the stone inside the bag at his side. He pulled Tally closer and bent to speak in her ear. "I have the stone!"

Through the driving sand, he glimpsed dawning hope on her face.

He placed the satchel between them and unfastened the top. She reached inside, drawing out the cloth-wrapped bundle. Tearing aside the coverings, she placed her hand on the stone. Brilliant blue light flared, illuminating clouds of dust.

The wind calmed immediately around them, leaving them in the still center of a wild vortex of flying sand. Within the circle, the dust settled, particles no longer stinging their skin and eyes. Wrapped together in the unearthly blue glow, they stared at each other.

Tally coughed, drew in a breath, and raised her eyes to his. "You did it! You saved all of us."

Shame coursed through Andevaar, coalescing into a sharp ache in his chest. He shook his head. If not for him, none of this would have happened at all. "*You* saved us. I... remember everything."

Sand clung to her skin and eyelashes as she met his gaze. "Flint promised to meet me here. Is he with you?"

For a long moment, he looked down at her. Even now, with his memory restored, he couldn't see her the same way he had before. He remembered before the spell when he'd thought her cold and arrogant, but he also remembered everything that had passed between them since then. He recalled the way she'd held her knife ready, alone and injured, with a pack of wolves surrounding her but still refusing to accept defeat. His mind brought up the peace on her face as they watched the cascade of a mountain waterfall, her arms around his neck, her head resting on his shoulder. After the experiences they had shared, he couldn't help but see her as Flint had seen her. He noticed the warmth in her eyes and the enticing pink of her lips. And she'd been so brave. A smile crept across his face. "He's here."

Her beautiful eyes widened, and a flash of desperate hope crossed her face. "You won't forget him?"

The hope in her expression gripped his heart and twisted it, hard. How could he possibly forget any of it? "Never."

A smile lifted one corner of her mouth. "Even with everything you wanted within your reach, you still came to help me?"

An answering smile spread slowly over his face. "I had to keep my promise."

She laughed and threw her arms around him, the stone still clutched in one hand. The remains of the violent storm swirled around the small space of calm where they stood.

After a moment, Tally drew back and smiled at him. She held up the precious stone. The last gusts of the sandstorm were lit with blue all around them. Raising her hand high above her head, the blue light spread. The furious wind calmed. In the still air, the dust gradually settled.

With a resounding crash, the gates burst open, and General Kylith and his troops flooded into the fortress. Scattered by the storm, the outlaws weren't ready to fight. In small groups, they laid down their weapons, and the army quickly took control. The solid form of the general crossed the courtyard.

Sliding a helpful arm around Tally's waist, Andevaar assisted her down the stairs.

With a dozen soldiers behind him, General Kylith met them halfway. His eyes searched Tally up and down for any sign of harm. His eyes stopped on a blood-soaked tear in her sleeve. "How badly are you injured?"

She shook her head. "It's not bad, thank you, General."

Kylith's hand gripped the hilt of his weapon as his icy gaze fell on Andevaar. "Are we taking this outlaw into custody?"

Tally shook her head. "No," she said firmly. "He saved my life and returned Namradill. I have chosen to offer him my Royal Pardon."

Andevaar felt his jaw slacken, and moisture fill his eyes. She would pardon him? Now that she had removed the spell, he remembered what he'd done. No matter how badly he wished to forget, he remembered it all. Nausea swelled in his belly. He deserved any punishment she might choose to inflict on him. "Pardon?" his voice was tight with shock.

She drew herself to her full height and met his gaze, her brown eyes blazing. "I am Crown Princess of the Seven Rivers, and if that is my wish, you *will* obey."

One corner of his mouth rose. He bowed his head. "As you command, Princess."

Kylith's hard gaze remained fixed on Andevaar, his hand gripping his sword hilt, but then he turned to look at Tally and his eyes softened. It was easy to see that beneath his harsh exterior, and despite his reputation, the ruthless general really cared about her.

Kylith gazed at her from beneath thick brows. "You're *sure*, Princess?"

Tally nodded decisively. "I am."

The general took a step back. With obvious effort, and another long look at Andevaar, he removed his hand from his weapon.

When her eyes met his, Andevaar put his arms around Tally and pulled her against him. She was the center of his existence, the only thing left in the world that was important to him. He couldn't bring himself to step away from her. "You are breathtaking," he murmured, his lips against her neck.

He felt her gasp as she felt the touch of his mouth. He didn't have the will to leave her now. Against his lips, her skin felt like satin. His mouth moved, kissing just beneath her ear and down her neck. He felt her tremble in his arms. "Can you still care about me knowing I remember everything? I am Flint, but I'm still Andevaar."

"You've changed." She drew in another sharp breath.

He raised his head and brought his mouth to hers. It seemed impossible that she could forgive him, that she might... still want him. But her soft lips met his eagerly, and her hand tangled in his hair, drawing him even closer. For a few moments, they seemed isolated while the whole world faded away except for her. He never wanted the kiss to end, but they weren't alone. The men filling the courtyard began to cheer and applaud. With an effort, Flint drew back.

Crown Princess Tahlea raised the shining stone high above her head and shouted in triumph. An answering rumble of thunder came from the sky. The soldiers and the outlaws looked up in astonishment to see thick, gray clouds. With a deafening crack, a bolt of lightning struck a rock on the canyon wall above them. Thunder roared and shook the stones beneath their feet. Rain began to fall.

GET IN TOUCH WITH THE AUTHOR

aj@ajparkwriting.com

www.ajparkwriting.com

Subscribe to my email list and Get a FREE story:

https://dl.bookfunnel.com/hrkfkxjqam

Acknowledgements

Thank you for reading this book! Thank you family, friends and fans for supporting me during the creation process.

I cherish the opportunity to bring to life stories born in my imagination and share them. I hope you enjoy reading them and that we have many future adventures together.

About the Author

AJ Park is the author of several fantasy adventure books and has won multiple writing awards. She grew up reading everything she could get her hands on, and continues to cultivate her life-long love of stories.

When she's not working on the next book, she loves climbing mountains, being outdoors, and spending time with her family. She loves meeting new friends, being part of the local community, and works for a digital marketing firm that helps businesses grow.

RIVER IN THE SAND

SEVEN RIVERS BOOK TWO

Prologue – Crown Princess Tahlea

THE ROYAL STEWARD ARRIVED in Tally's sitting room, red-faced and breathing hard, interrupting what had been a quiet moment. She sat comfortably holding her baby, a small, warm weight, soft against her shoulder. Tally brushed her fingers against her infant daughter's downy hair. Despite his obvious haste, the man attempted to be quiet.

With a gesture, Tally invited him forward. "What is it?"

He hurried forward to kneel beside her chair. "Crown Princess, a messenger just arrived from Ondari province. Governor Gathan is dead."

Her muscles tightened in alarm. "What happened?"

"The messenger said he succumbed to a sudden illness."

Tally's eyes widened. "But he was no older than my father, and in perfect health the last time I saw him. Is there more information about what happened?"

"His son Conall is here. He brought the news to you personally. Perhaps you'd like to meet with him?"

Tally nodded. "I would. Immediately. Please have him wait for me in the council chamber. I'll join him there shortly."

"Yes, Crown Princess." The steward got to his feet, bowed, and departed.

As he closed the door behind him, Nita appeared from the next room. "Shall I help you dress, my lady?"

It was inevitable. Tally couldn't attend a meeting in the soft robe she wore here in her rooms. She stood, her baby cradled close against her. "Thank you, Nita, I would appreciate it. I'll just put her down."

Tally kissed her daughter and lowered her to rest in her cradle, covering her with a soft blanket. Her dark lashes brushed against her fair skin. A warm rose flushed her cheeks. "Sleep well, Kyjia."

Beside Tally, Nita looked down and smiled. "I'll watch over her while you're gone."

"Thank you."

A short while later, wearing a gray velvet gown appropriate for a princess and a silver crown on her head, Tally entered the council room. At her appearance, a stocky young man jumped to his feet and bowed. He wore the fine tunic of a nobleman, dusty from his ride. His shoulders slumped in weariness and grief.

Tally came forward and took his hand. "Conall, I'm so sorry about your father."

"Thank you, Princess." He closed his eyes, taking a deep breath as he attempted to master his emotion. He brushed a hand across his eyes. "I felt I had to come to Namradan myself."

"I'm glad you did." She gestured to a chair. "Please, sit and tell me what happened."

Conall sank into the chair. "My father has been governor for many years, and, lately, he began to think that it was time to turn leadership over to someone else. His good friend was the obvious choice; they'd worked together for a long time. But another man—Theron—has gained great power in Ondari during the last several months. Theron has positioned himself to take leadership. My father grew ill very suddenly, and his second in command suffered the same malady soon after. When they both died of it, Theron was named governor."

Tally's stomach tightened at the news, but she met Conall's gaze directly. "Do you believe it was an ordinary illness?"

Conall slowly shook his head. "How can I, Princess? The timing was too convenient, and I've never seen anything like it. They suffered a sudden high fever and were unable to see. They were both blind during the last few weeks of their illness."

"Was anyone else surrounding them affected?"

"No," Conall rubbed a hand across his face. "Only the two of them."

"Do you suspect it was some kind of poison?"

"Perhaps." Conall's voice was uncertain. "I've never heard of anything like it. My father had a strange injury, a cut on his arm. Perhaps the wound allowed the toxin into his body. We have a mystic in our household, but he was unable to identify the cause."

"We must investigate this further," Tally said. She looked up toward the door as the steward opened it.

His eyes were wide. "Princess, I wouldn't disturb your meeting, but I just received news that the delegation from Tyar is approaching the city."

"They're arriving now?" Her eyebrows shot up.

The Seven Rivers hadn't had official contact with their desert neighbor in many years. It had been a surprise when her guards had reported the group entering her lands. The two nations shared common roots, and had never been exactly at war, but Tyar had refused to set up trade or to maintain any sort of friendly relationship. They must have had some strong motivation that compelled them to break their silence now.

The steward nodded vigorously. "They are nearly at the gates. I had to tell you!"

Tally nodded. Her father remained in stonesleep. If he'd been awake, he would certainly have more information that would help to handle this situation, but she would have to do her best alone.

She kept her expression impassive and her voice calm. "Thank you. How many are there? I was told they appear peaceful. Is that still the case?" Tally needed to discover what this visit meant. It would be up to her to begin negotiations, and she wanted Tyar as an ally, not an enemy.

"There are a few dozen people, Princess, and, so far, they have made no attempt to harm anyone."

"As they arrive, please escort them to the throne room," Tally instructed. "Make sure our guards are in place and on the alert. Let General Kylith know they're here. Keep an eye on them." She didn't know what to expect.

Tally got to her feet, turning back to Conall. "I'm very sorry to cut our meeting short. I want to know more about this strange illness. Please, have something to eat, rest, and we will talk again soon. I will send someone back to Ondari with you to learn more."

Conall stood up, taking her hand and kissing it. "Thank you, Princess." He drew back, shaking his head. "I fear the news I brought means trouble for the Seven Rivers."

Tally agreed. She needed to learn more about Theron, the man now leading Ondari Province. Two guards took positions flanking her as she headed toward the throne room.

Outside the large, heavily carved doors, the familiar tall figure of her husband stood waiting. Flint wore a slightly dusty, blue military uniform and armor. His face lit up as he saw her, and he bowed, kissing her hand, his gaze meeting hers.

"You look stunning, my princess. And where is Kyjia?"

"Asleep." At least, Tally hoped she was. She returned Flint's smile, looking up into his dark eyes, savoring the warmth she saw there. "Where have you been?"

"Helping Gerran train a group of new soldiers, but, since we finished, now I am free and completely at your command." His mouth turned up in a slow smile.

Too bad she wasn't free to spend time alone with him at the moment. Ruling a kingdom reduced the amount of time she had to herself. Time with Flint would have to wait.

Instead, she nodded toward the door. "We have visitors from Tyar. If you would care to join me?"

"As you command, Princess." He offered his arm. She took it, and they entered the throne room together.

Several members of the court had arrived already. Another messenger hurried up to them to report that the delegation had arrived at the palace.

"Show them in," Tally instructed.

Flint escorted her to her chair at the front of the room beside her father's ancient throne.

Though Tally had ruled the Seven Rivers for nearly two years, she still refused to sit on the throne. It belonged to her father, and he would resume his rule soon. She occupied the smaller, plainer chair she'd always used, while Flint stood at her shoulder.

She wanted him to sit with her, but no matter how many times she asked, trying to convince him, he flatly refused to sit in the throne room beside her. "No one in your kingdom will ever question who rules the Seven Rivers," he'd said. "It's not me. You are Crown Princess, and someday you'll be queen."

Just as the doors at the far end of the hall opened to admit the visitors, General Kylith strode in through the side door and took his place standing on Tally's other side. His well-built form and stern face with its long scar looked intimidating, as always, but Tally appreciated his solid support.

At the doors, the delegation from Tyar appeared. With graceful steps, a tall, slender woman led the group across the hall. Her hair fell in soft, snowy white waves around her shoulders. A glittering gem hung on her forehead, and more sparkled around her throat. Her gown was of fine silk, deep blue, intricately embroidered at the neckline, hem, and cuffs.

As the woman drew nearer, Tally met her piercing, dark eyes. Though lined with age, her skin was as pale as Tally's own, her complexion contrasting sharply with the rest of her dark-haired, olive-skinned companions.

At the foot of the dais, the woman curtseyed, her movements graceful. "Crown Princess Tahlea, daughter of King Allenthal. I am Tillian."

Her words were spoken in the accent of Tyar, noticeably different from the speech Tally's people used, but still understandable.

"My son is King of Tyar," Tillian announced. "I'm your grandmother."

Only years of training to maintain her composure kept Tally's mouth from falling open. Her grandmother? She'd never known any of her mother's family, though she knew her father had attempted to reach out to them many times. Her father hadn't been very specific when he'd mentioned it, not explaining the reason. He'd certainly never told her anything that might have prepared her to meet a grandmother she'd never known.

No one else in the room moved or spoke as Tally got to her feet. She stepped down and stood facing Tillian. She was nearly as tall as Tally, and she wore an unreadable expression.

"Welcome to the Seven Rivers, Lady Tillian," Tally said.

Slowly, a smile spread across the old woman's face. With a start, Tally realized that tears welled in Tillian's eyes as she gazed at Tally.

"You look very like her. My Kyjia, my beautiful daughter. I'm so happy to see you. I came with urgent news and to see the new child who bears my daughter's name."

For a moment they looked at each other before Tally stepped forward to embrace her grandmother. With a sob, Tillian returned the hug.

"After all these years, I must beg your forgiveness, Granddaughter."

Tally drew back to look at her. "Why?"

Tillian wiped her eyes. "All this time, I have stayed away, when I might have been part of your life. I regret that very much, and I didn't have a good reason. Only that I was angry at Allenthal. The last time I came here was during Kyjia's final illness. When she died, I couldn't bear it. I'm afraid, in my grief, I blamed your father. It was never his fault. I see that so clearly now."

Her father had always told Tally that her mother had died of an illness. How could something like that have ever been his fault? "What happened?"

Tillian bowed her head. "There is so much to tell you."

"Then perhaps we need someplace to speak more comfortably? Your companions may wait here." She turned to take Flint's arm. "Lady Tillian, this is my husband, Flint. Will you join us?"

"Yes, thank you." Tillian turned toward her guards. "We will return shortly." Then she noticed Kylith, where he stood beside her chair. A sudden smile of recognition lit her face, and she hurried to embrace him. "Kylith! After all these years, it's so good to see you. You will join us, of course?" He nodded and offered her his arm as Tally led them from the room.

Soon, they were settled in a comfortable sitting room with food and drink spread before them. Tally had taken the sofa, Flint beside her, while Tillian and Kylith settled into chairs opposite them. For a long moment, no one spoke.

"It's been so long," Tillian said, breaking the silence. "For years, I thought I would never speak of those events again." Her eyes strayed to Kylith, glancing at the scar on his face. "But now, I feel I must." She reached into the small bag she carried over her shoulder and took out a slender shard of green crystal encased in clear glass.

At the sight of it, Kylith jumped to his feet. "Why would you bring that here?"

Tillian drew in a deep breath. "I had to. All those years ago, we tried everything in our power to destroy it. When we failed, we surrounded it in a protective coating to prevent its evil from harming anyone else."

"But the poison!" Kylith protested. "You shouldn't touch it."

Tillian looked up at him. "I have handled it like this many times. The toxin cannot penetrate the glass," she assured him.

Kylith stood stiffly for a moment, staring down at the crystal. "Forgive me. Even though it's been many years, I'll never forget that Allenthal nearly lost his life to its poison. And Kyjia..." His voice trailed off, and he slowly settled back into his chair.

Tillian turned back to Tally. "This is a rhan stone, containing powerful dark magic. It once belonged to a man who attempted to seize power in Tyar, a man who embraced evil and used his powers against our people. The poison of the stone causes illness, blindness, and death.

At the words, Tally's muscles tightened. "Blindness?"

Tillian nodded, her expression grave.

Sudden illness and blindness, exactly like the two deaths in Ondari province.

"I would never have brought such an evil thing here," Tillian said, with a quick glance at Kylith, "except that we have discovered that someone in Tyar is using a similar stone again. When we attempted to learn more, we discovered that this person is not acting alone. I fear another servant of dark magic has arisen here in your land."

A moment of silence fell.

Tendrils of unease wound through Tally's stomach. She needed to decide how best to combat this new threat to her kingdom. Reviewing the information in her mind, she nodded slowly. "News just reached me of two men in positions of power and influence, dead of a mysterious illness, blind in the last few weeks before they died."

Tillian's eyes widened. "So, it's true! Many years ago, when this evil showed itself in our land, it nearly gained power over our entire kingdom. We did everything in our power, but our people suffered battle and bloodshed before we could stop it. Once the evil sorcerer was dead, we searched for a cure for the poison but never found one. When your mother died, it broke my heart." She paused, wiping her eyes. "I'm sure, now that you are a mother yourself, you can understand how I felt. In my grief, I blamed Allenthal, thinking he should have found a solution. I know he tried..."

Shock flooded through Tally. "Are you saying this poison caused the illness that took my mother?"

Her lips tight, Tillian nodded.

Her father had never told Tally this. Flint's strong hand tightened around hers, and she held onto him. "Please. Tell me."

Chapter 1 – 22 Years Ago – Crown Prince Allenthal

Allenthal gripped the stone railing of his balcony as he looked out over the great river. Despite the lingering chill of night, sweat drenched his body. He took long, even breaths, attempting to slow the wild pounding of his heart. When he closed his eyes, he saw his brother's face, his eyes glazed in pain, his body broken and bleeding. The dream had felt so real. It had taken him back to that terrible night five years ago when he'd fought so desperately to save his brother's life.

Now all was quiet. The first hint of dawn glowed behind the mountains. Raising his eyes to the bright dome of stars, he drew in another deep breath, attempting to find peace. The quiet murmur of the river filled the air. Trying to regain a sense of calm, he paced the balcony.

At the soft sound of the door opening, he turned to see his father. Still dressed for sleep, King Valteron wore a loose tunic and pants, his feet bare. He came to stand beside Allenthal. For a moment, they watched the river in silence.

"You're up early," his father observed.

Allenthal nodded. "You too."

His father put a hand on Allenthal's shoulder. "Was it another dream?"

Allenthal drew in a deep breath, rubbing his forehead, as if that would wipe away the memory. "No matter how I try, I can't get the images out of my head."

Valteron nodded. "I understand. Sometimes, the most vivid memories are the ones we most want to forget. The events of that day have stayed with you. I want to help."

What could anyone possibly do to help? No one could change the past. Allenthal looked back silently at his father.

Valteron's gaze was kind. "I won't try to minimize your feelings by saying I know how you feel. I wish there was more help I could offer. In my own life, I have relied on the Goddess during my most difficult moments. I hope you will turn to Her. She understands our struggles and knows more than we do. Earlier this morning, I spoke to Divine Namradill. About you."

Allenthal's eyes widened. Since the day five years ago when his older brother had died, he'd suffered from nightmares, unable to move past what had happened. He was now heir of the Seven Rivers, but it would be many years before his time came to rule. What interest did the Goddess have in him now?

"Allenthal, you've been the best son anyone could ask for. You've always done whatever was needed." His father's words trailed into silence, and he took a slow breath. "Sometimes I worry that you're making an extra effort to serve because you're trying to make up for—"

"Please don't say it," Allenthal interrupted, holding up his hand. "Please. It's not because of Alvaren. You raised me to do my duty to our kingdom, and I respect you too much not to do whatever I can to help." He looked away, out across the river to the distant mountains. The morning light touched the peaks.

"What happened to Alvaren wasn't your fault," Valteron said, laying his hand on his son's shoulder. "I've never blamed you."

"You weren't there," Allenthal ground out through clenched jaws. His hands gripped the stone balustrade in front of him.

His father's voice was quiet, calming. "I didn't have to be there to know that you boys loved each other. You would never have done anything to harm each other. It was simply an accident."

All Allenthal's muscles were rigid. "An accident that took his life."

"Alvaren loved you," the king said. "He wouldn't have wanted you to spend your life grieving for him. I want you to know how proud I am of you. Our kingdom will be in excellent hands when your time comes to rule."

His father's words helped a little to soothe the ache inside Allenthal. His older brother, Alvaren, had spent his entire life preparing to be king. Allenthal hadn't been anyone's first choice...until he became the only choice.

Valteron's voice broke the stillness. "Divine Namradill requested that you go on a journey—to Tyar."

Allenthal's eyebrows shot up. "Tyar? No! I can't do that. Father, my place is here. You have no other heir. It's my responsibility to be here. I can't just leave our kingdom to travel."

"Our Goddess wouldn't have asked you to go if it wasn't the right thing to do, Son. Give it some thought." Valteron gripped his shoulder. "We'll talk about it more later."

He went back through the door, leaving Allenthal alone with his spinning thoughts.

At the end of the long day, when Allenthal finally went to bed, he lay tossing for hours, thinking about his conversation with his father. Why would he want to send Allenthal away? Maybe he was more disappointed in him than Allenthal had realized. But he was the only heir. His family and his nation needed him to maintain communication with Namradill. It made no sense for him to travel to another nation. Tyar was a desert land, a harsh and violent place.

Despite his worries, eventually Allenthal dozed.

A slender girl with dark eyes and long dark hair struggled to pull her arms free from two men gripping her from both sides. Though she twisted and fought, she couldn't escape. Fury was plain in her expression, and she lifted her chin defiantly. The light was dim, the rough stone walls of a cave surrounding them.

A man faced her, his expression dark with menace. "Tell me where the tablet is!" he demanded. "This is your last chance."

She struggled again, her eyes meeting his directly. "No!"

The guards dragged her around, turning her back to the man. As she fought against them, he tore her cloak away. With his knife, he cut through her tunic, ripping the fabric aside to expose the pale skin of her back.

He raised his hand, holding a sharp sliver of green stone. When he pressed the edge against her skin, blood flowed down her back. She screamed as he carved a symbol into her flesh.

Allenthal sat up gasping, his heart pounding. Another nightmare. By now, he expected the dreams of his brother, but this had been something entirely new. He was certain he'd never seen the girl before, but he wouldn't easily forget her.

He spent the rest of the night pacing his balcony, in his mind seeing the brave tilt to her chin and her determination to fight, despite the odds.

Eventually, morning came, and it grew late enough that his father might be awake. Allenthal dressed and went down the hall. He knocked quietly before slipping inside his father's chambers, hoping to have a quick word with him. Instead, he found the room quiet and empty. His father was usually here at this hour, but perhaps something had come up. He glanced inside the bedchamber and saw no one.

A bright blue light shone from an open chest in an alcove at the far end of the room. The pulsing glow intrigued him, and he moved nearer. Namradill. He had not touched the stone since the ceremony when he'd been a baby. Maybe he was never meant to. It had always been Alvaren who had planned and prepared to make a connection with the Goddess on behalf of all the Seven Rivers. The blue light drew Allenthal nearer.

He paused, entirely still, staring at the light. Would She speak to him?

Allenthal looked around. Still finding himself alone, he walked quickly toward the chest and looked inside to see the glowing stone. Reaching in, he put his hand against the cool, hard surface.

Allenthal, son of King Valteron. I greet you.

He gasped, pulling his hand away. She didn't sound angry, but should he even try to talk with her? Was he worthy to ask Her his questions? She must have far more important matters to attend to. He drew in a deep breath and replaced his hand. "May I speak with you, Divine Namradill?"

You may. Though it is not yet your duty to speak on behalf of all your people, speaking with me is the privilege of your bloodline. One day, we shall speak often. One day, you will be with me completely.

Was She referring to the stonesleep? Or did She mean he would be with Her at the end of his life? "Why do you want me to go to Tyar?"

Much good will be accomplished if you go. My brother Karineth was God of the land of Tyar. Once, He guarded and cared for His people. The royal family of Tyar was tightly connected to Him, just as your family is with me. But Karenith is lost. As He failed to care for His people, the rains fled and the land dried up into a harsh desert. His people are scattered, and the man possessing the sacred tablet of Karenith, who should be King of Tyar, is nothing more than a poor wanderer attempting to feed his family. I ask you to find him, to help him and his family.

"Why would they want my help?" Allenthal asked. "When I tried to help my brother, I failed."

Is one failure enough to prevent you from attempting the good you might do with the rest of your life?

Allenthal stood still, shocked. Maybe he had allowed himself to think that he had nothing to offer anyone. "Does the king of Tyar have a daughter?" The images from his dream were burned into his memory.

Yes. You have seen her already; the dream showed her to you clearly. She is Kyjia, daughter of Ashkan, and she needs your help.

"The tablet they spoke of," Allenthal said, "it's the symbol of the royal family? Their line of communication with Karenith?"

It's the most valuable thing in Tyar. A symbol of royalty. Everyone in Tyar would recognize it, though it isn't large, a small slab of gold engraved with the symbols of Karenith. The location of the tablet is a closely guarded secret. At the moment, it is kept by a man named Ashkan, uncrowned and unknown to his people, but by his lineage, King of Tyar. Will you find him and help him?

All his muscles tightened, but Allenthal couldn't refuse Namradill. He would have to trust that if She sent him on this errand, She would help him find a way to succeed. He would put himself in Her hands. "I will go, Divine Namradill."

Good. I will give you such guidance as I can. Karenith, God of Tyar, has slept for generations. If he is to care for his people again, he must be woken by an heir of the royal family. This prophecy speaks of his awakening: "While I sleep, my land is buried in sand.

The people of Tyar must rise again. Hold the tablet aloft and speak my name three times, and I shall hear and answer. A new ruler shall rise in the desert, and a light in the night sky from the ancient city of kings shall proclaim their coming. My power shall be in their hands and a river shall flow out of the sand."

In his mind, Allenthal repeated the prophecy, committing it to memory.

Allenthal found his father on his balcony, looking out over the great river. He came to stand beside him. "I'll go."

"Good," Valteron replied, "but not alone. You'll need someone you can trust along the road. Take Kylith with you. He'll guard you and watch your back."

Allenthal smiled in agreement. Kylith was a skilled fighter, his ability far surpassing any of the other soldiers. And he was already a good friend.

He found Kylith at the edge of the training field, gathering up his weapons after a practice session. "Am I late?" he called.

Kylith looked up and smiled, offering him a blade, hilt first. "Yes, but if you still want to practice, I'm ready."

"Today, it's something more serious than that," Allenthal admitted.

Kylith stood up and faced him, his arms folded across his chest, waiting for an explanation.

"My father asked me to do a little traveling. Will you come with me?"

Kylith's eyebrows rose. "Just me, or a whole troop of men? Don't tell me King Valteron is sending his only heir out of Namradan with *one* guard?"

Swiftly, Allenthal laid out the details of the journey to the desert. "Our errand is a secret. Divine Namradill asked me to go," he said. "I'm only a mortal, and I trust in my faith that She knows what She's doing. We plan to stay out of sight. No one outside our own lands will know who we are."

Kylith raised one eyebrow. "It's true you are mortal, don't forget that. Anonymity is no guarantee of safety."

"I know," Allenthal admitted. "But it will help."

"But... Tyar?" Kylith's eyes widened. "It's hot there. And from everything I've heard, it's a difficult place to survive."

"True enough." Allenthal grinned at his friend. "I understand. If the journey would be too *demanding* for you, I can see if one of the others—"

Kylith narrowed his eyes. "I didn't say I wouldn't go."

Allenthal smiled, clapping him on the shoulder. "Good. We'll leave in the morning."

With his plans made, Allenthal packed the few belongings he would take with him. He'd never been away from home for more than a few days before, but he trusted Namradill that some good would come of this. There was no way to know what would happen. With his packing finished, he went to bed. Pushing worry to the side, he closed his eyes.

Her body lay crumpled and still on the rough floor of the cave. The dim light illuminated her pale skin; the blood on her back was now dried and darkened. She was alone. With a groan of pain, she stirred.

She inched her way along the floor. With agonizing slowness, she crawled along the passageway toward a swift-flowing stream running along the cave floor. When she reached the water, she rolled over to immerse her injured back in the water. The lines of pain smoothed from her face.

For a time she rested, until her body jerked suddenly, and she cried out in pain and fear. When she pulled her arm close to her body, fresh blood ran down her skin. Something had attacked her, something out there invisible in the dark. Her eyes were wide in terror, her expression tight with pain. Dragging herself up, she struggled to her feet, leaning heavily against the wall. A hiss came out of the dark. Still leaning on the wall, she stumbled away. Hidden in the dark, something followed.

He was already out of bed, half standing, reaching out to help her. Allenthal had to do something to protect Kyjia. His hand searched for a weapon to defend her against the invisible danger lurking there in the dark. The dream had felt so real, as crystal clear as if he had watched the events with his own eyes. The Goddess said she was Ashkan's daughter and that she needed his aid. He had to find her. Was she even now lost in the dark? He prayed to Namradill that the events he saw hadn't happened yet and there was still time to help her.

At dawn, Allenthal met Kylith in the stables. They loaded their gear into saddlebags and strapped on their bedrolls. Allenthal met his friend's eyes. "Last chance to speak up if you don't want to go."

Kylith grinned. "It'll be more interesting than guard duty."

The spring sun shone clear and bright as they followed the road over the ancient stone bridge out of Namradan. For miles outside the city, the road wound between well-tended farms and little patches of woods. They took the path leading up the valley of the River Edri. Villages and fields gathered all along the river. It took them several days to reach the end of the valley. Beyond the city of Edrithil, the way wound northward, up into the mountains.

Allenthal had traveled this road before, but it had been five years. In the intervening time, he'd flatly refused to go anywhere near this place. Did Divine Namradill understand what it would cost him when she asked him to come this way again?

Riding cautiously through the rocky terrain, they came up over a rise into a narrow, rocky valley. Giant boulders stood at the feet of the cliffs above, standing guard over a slender path winding along one side. Below the narrow trail, the land fell sharply downward.

This was the place. Allenthal recognized it at once. Every landmark had been burned into his memory. This was where the accident had happened. A rockslide had come down the steep slope above and would have taken Allenthal off the edge, except that his brother had shoved him out of the way only to fall himself.

Allenthal sat frozen on his horse. All this time, he'd avoided this place. Now, he had to come this way. There was no other reasonable route to Tyar. His horse snorted and tossed its head uneasily, sensing its rider's discomfort.

Ahead of him, Kylith stopped and turned in the saddle. He knew a little about what had happened but not everything. "Are you all right?"

Allenthal nodded stiffly, his jaw clenched. "I need a moment."

Cold dread washed over him as he looked at the unforgiving rocks. He had to go on. There was no other choice, unless he wanted to go back and tell his father he couldn't continue the journey. Valteron would understand. Somehow, Allenthal knew that would be even worse.

"I can do this." He gritted his teeth and urged his horse forward.

He rode on, following Kylith at a steady pace. When Allenthal passed the place where Alvaren had fallen, he stopped, rigid in his saddle, beads of sweat forming on his forehead. If he dismounted and looked off the edge, he'd be able to see the exact place where his brother had landed. If he didn't look, he could pretend he was anywhere else in the world but here.

They'd rushed to Alvaren's aid, finding him badly injured but alive, wedged between the rocks. Today, the spring weather was soft as they rode, with no trace of the bitter chill of the day he remembered so well. Now, the sun warmed his back, and the breeze was pleasant, not the biting wind that had roared down the valley that night. It had been so cold. He'd done everything he could to keep his brother warm, but, by morning, Alvaren had been gone. With all his might, Allenthal tried not to remember.

Did the Goddess know how hard he had worked to avoid coming this way? Had part of Her reason for this journey been to encourage Allenthal to face what had happened? A wave of anger surged through him at the thought. His fury helped get him moving again.

He stared straight ahead, following Kylith until they traveled over another rise in the land and passed out of sight of the little valley. They crossed a small stream cutting through the path and paused to water their horses.

Kylith dismounted and turned to him. "I'm ready to rest a little."

Allenthal nodded, dismounting. He knelt beside the water, scooping up handfuls of the clear cold liquid. He splashed water onto his face and rubbed it through his hair.

Beside him, Kylith asked, "That was the place?" He motioned back down the trail.

Wordlessly, Allenthal nodded.

Kylith met his eyes. "Do you want to talk about it?"

Allenthal's stomach clenched. "No!"

Kylith shrugged. "Maybe a good fight would be better."

"Are you volunteering?" Allenthal growled, clenching his hand into a fist.

"Only if you're desperate," Kylith replied grinning. "If you think you're angry enough to take me."

Allenthal eyed his friend. Kylith was an inch or two shorter but broader and heavier in build. He could also defeat any man in the Seven Rivers. They had trained together enough during the last few years for Allenthal to know that he probably wouldn't win.

"I'll wait until we find a better fight," Allenthal said. One corner of his mouth lifted. "But thanks for offering."

They rode on. As they got further away from the narrow valley, Allenthal gradually relaxed, able to concentrate on where they were again. The icy dread in his limbs thawed. Hours later, with the terrible place far behind them, they made camp.

As they brought water and firewood and began to prepare a meal, Kylith didn't say a word, accepting Allenthal's silence and not pressing him.

Allenthal broke the quiet at last. He glanced over to find his friend watching him. "After it happened, we had to take him home," he said. "When we finally got back to Namradan, I couldn't do it. I couldn't face my father. I stopped outside the city and refused to go any further. Late that night, I was still there when he came to find me."

Kylith shook his head in sympathy. "I'm sorry. It must have been terrible."

Allenthal nodded. "Everyone in the kingdom loved Alvaren, my father especially. I couldn't stand to be there, watching them tell him the news, seeing his face when he looked at Alvaren's body."

Allenthal took in a long breath. "Back then, I expected him to be angry at me, to demand why I'd let this happen to my brother. I thought he'd wish for a way to tell me that I should have fallen instead. He needed Alvaren. All of the Seven Rivers needed him. He should be their king."

Kylith put his hand on his friend's shoulder. "He wasn't angry at you, was he?"

Allenthal shook his head slowly. "He never was. So many times, I wanted him to be. I was so angry at myself, it only made sense that he would feel the same."

"King Valteron is a good man. A good father. I know he loved both his sons," Kylith said. "He didn't really wish that you had died and Alvaren had lived. No one could ever make such an impossible choice."

Allenthal drew in a long breath, staring out into the gathering darkness. "Maybe that was me too. I'm the one who wished it had been me. I loved my brother. All my life, I thought that he would be a great leader. He should have been."

"Can't you live your life to be the kind of leader he would have been, in his memory?"

Allenthal's throat tightened. It was a good idea. Years had passed, and Alvaren was gone. Maybe attempting to honor his brother's memory would help him to move forward. He nodded.

"You took on this quest," Kylith pointed out. "You did it to serve the Goddess, your father, and people in a nation you've never even visited before. Maybe you can allow this act of service to make up a little for what happened to your brother?"

Was that the real reason he'd agreed to this journey? Allenthal couldn't be sure. It had felt like the right thing to do in the moment. Maybe his friend was right. He looked up to meet Kylith's steady, gray eyes and drew in another long breath. "Then let this be my way forward."

Continue the story in the full version of River in the Sand:

www.ingramcontent.com/pod-product-compliance
Lightning Source LLC
Chambersburg PA
CBHW022103310726
48972CB00007B/1863